# HOT
# CHOCOLATE

# HOT CHOCOLATE

## SENSUAL SHORT STORIES

### Edited by
### Vastiana Belfon

Kensington Publishing Corp.
http://www.kensingtonbooks.com

DAFINA BOOKS are published by

Kensington Publishing Corp.
119 West 40th Street
New York, NY 10018

# CONTENTS

# Brown Skin

## Jade Williams

No full sensual pout, no flowing raven locks, no swelling, heaving, or even pert breasts. Legs certainly not statuesque, more on the stumpy side. I stared at myself in the mirror, turning from side to side, craning my neck over my shoulder hoping to spy a voluptuous ass. To no avail. It just sat there looking slightly dumpy, cellulite threatening. Not big, not Beyoncé, not J-Lo, not Kylie. Just unremarkable. Like most of the rest of me really. So let's all get this straight from the start. I'm a middle-aged, middle-of-the-road, not-quite-frumpy housewife. Relatively happily married—couldn't really be otherwise with such an average lifestyle—with a husband who's kind, caring (if a little unimaginative) and two children who are, fortunately, old enough to spend much of their time away.

So you can see that I'm nothing special and by now you're probably gloating that you've got a lot more to offer the world than me. And you're probably right. So that's the reason I ask myself, "Why me?"

"Why don't you try it?" Sonya, my so-called best friend asked. "You're always on about sex, and this pays. It might just be worth it."

That's when the seeds were planted. They germinate as I tackle the piles of dishes, my rubber-gloved hands dangling listlessly in lukewarm, greasy water. They push their heads through the soil as I watch television with only half an eye. They seek the sun as I clean up the bathroom after three individuals who should know better. And, I'm almost ashamed to admit it, they burst into bloom as Dan and I make love. We're warm and cozy and relaxed after all these years together. Wrapped in a little bubble of domestic and sensual contentment. I love him. What can I say? So our love life might have had the excitement rubbed off the edges, but what can you expect when we seem to have lived through a century of sleepless nights—either feeding wailing babies or waiting for reluctant adolescents to return home. So these days, when we do get it on, it's likely to be slow, tender, still wondering at the affectionate passion that's survived all the domestic strife. So that's my life in a nutshell. Nothing too exciting, but not much to complain about either.

It makes you think, doesn't it? What kind of a woman does Sonya think I am? Although I might talk about sex all the time, that doesn't mean that I want to *think* about it, analyze it constantly. And that's what I've started doing since she came up with the idea. We had that conversation three weeks ago, and the subject has not been far from my mind ever since. They say that guys think about it around a million times a day, but I can tell you that I wouldn't recommend it. I don't know how they do it. It's exhausting! But maybe they think about it in a different way. I've found myself researching the subject, reading about it, watching videos, dissecting it, picking it apart. It should all come so naturally. For me, though, it doesn't seem to be working out that way. Maybe it's my age, but I find myself struggling.

It struck me that Sonya must think that I'm desperate to even suggest such a thing. What kind of vibes do I give off? I like to think of myself as a sensual, no, sexy, adult, open-minded woman, but even I would not have thought of this. I'd never have thought I was the type. After all, just look at my dull, suburban existence. Maybe I need to take a serious look at the image I present to the world.

As far as I remember, Sonya and I had just been chatting about the usual things: school exams, the new boutique that has opened down the road, and of course, men. I'm not sure what triggered the memory, but Sonya suddenly stopped midsentence, clapped her hand to her forehead, and fished in her handbag for a piece of newsprint raggedly torn out of a paper. She smoothed out the folds and handed it to me like a teacher presenting a certificate for good behavior in class.

"Girl, I been carrying this around with me for days. As soon as I saw it, I thought of you."

I didn't know whether to be flattered or offended as I struggled to make out the small print without my reading glasses. I don't know what kind of expression there was on my face, but Sonya laughed loud.

"Don't look so scared. It's made for you." And that's when she added those words: *You're always talking about sex, and this pays.*

Now, one thing I'd like to make clear is that I'm not "always talking about sex". I am not obsessed. I'm not sex-starved. I'm quite content with my married two-point-one times a month, thank you. It's just that if someone else brings up the subject, I'm not going to be one of those women who purses her lips and diverts the conversation to arranging the flowers for last Sunday's church service. That would just be plain rude. So, if my twice-divorced, longtime best friend feels the need to talk about her pathetic lack of a sex life, then it's only kind to try to accommodate her by sharing my thoughts on the subject. And if I tell a few tales about my own adventurous past (before Dan, of course), then it's just to make her feel better about her own celibate status. It's a kindness I'm doing, and then she has the nerve to say that I'm always talking about sex.

I think she expected me to be grateful or something because she kept staring at me with that "well . . ." kind of look on her face. I guess I was supposed to congratulate her for this unique opportunity that was being presented to me, but, well . . . always talking about sex, indeed!

I'm not even feeling oversensitive about it, but when she said those words, it was like every single sexual episode I'd told her about flashed before my eyes in glorious technicolor—not that my sex life is black-and-white or even gray these days; that's not what I'm saying. But, oh, there were some sweet, sweet guys in there, as well as some low-down dirty bastards. And I couldn't even tell you which ones were the most exciting. Look at me now: tailored pants and high-necked blouses for the neighborly coffee mornings, the obligatory velour tracksuits for lounging, hats and pearls for church on Sunday. Who would believe it of me, and what would they say if they knew?

No one would imagine, for example, that there was a Sean in my past. Now, thinking about it, maybe that's what made Sonya think I'd be up for it: what I'd told her about Sean.

We met, or rather glimpsed each other, on my first day at college in North London. He was a mature student, late thirties, I thought at first, but just as ill at ease, nervous, and unsure of himself as the rest of us. I guess that's one reason why I noticed him in the first place. That and the fact that, unlike every other guy in the place, he'd turned up in a suit and tie, so there was a huge empty circle developing around him as we all avoided his personal space, sniggering behind our hands as we went past. I was just as guilty as the others, secure in the little cabal of like-minded and similarly dressed students that was forming around me, eager to become part of whatever herd we could find. Except Sean.

I did look twice at him, though, and I suspect everyone else did, too, each with the same thought: how brave of this old white guy to put himself in this unenviable position. There he was, slightly nerdy-looking in his suit, surrounded by all these ultra-hip, super-confident, smoother-than-smooth black guys in the latest FUBU gear and designer sneakers ordered from the Internet, snaky wires dangling from their ears connected to the most expensive MP3 player on the market. Of course, we all knew that, underneath the bling, we were all equally scared and insecure, but none of us would admit it, especially in front of a white guy. So, like everyone else, I avoided Sean that day, going my own way, leaving him standing alone in the foyer, pretending to be absorbed in the notice boards.

He wasn't in my classes. He was doing something to do with computers, which only added to his geekiness. I only really paid attention to Sean because he'd be there when I arrived in the mornings and there when I left in the afternoons. He didn't hide the fact that he was waiting for me and it didn't take me long to get it. Within days, he'd ditched the suits in favor of black denim jeans and a black T-shirt, and I immediately noticed that under the middle-class businessman's camouflage gear, he had a good body with a well-defined six pack and the slightly baggy jeans couldn't hide the contours of his tight butt. But, of course, I still wasn't really looking.

And then he started leaving these little treats in my pigeonhole. I don't know how he found out my name. I only knew his because, those first few days, he was the talk, or rather the whisper, of most groups. It started with just a packet of Maltesers or a Galaxy hazelnut bar. Anonymous gifts, but I knew they were from him. That's when I began to be interested in those bluey green eyes fringed by long, long lashes in a face that was probably no older than twenty-eight or -nine. But when you're only eighteen, that seems positively prehistoric. Once, I got out early and skulked in the nearby bookshop to watch as he loitered, waiting for me. His hair was a little too long, but freshly washed, silky, reddish highlights glistening in the sun. I felt something drawing me toward him, making my nipples high and pointy through my summer dress as I sucked the chocolate off the malty honeycomb candy, and then crunched, greedily popping another into my mouth right after. He leaned against the wall, something about his languid, self-contained stance making me more than a little hot and bothered. And the heat wasn't coming from the sun glancing off the shop window. I watched as he stood and paced up and down taking long draws from the cigarette that he seemed so uncomfortable smoking. I wanted to rush out of the shop and run my fingers through his hair, but I waited until his back was turned and dashed out, running like a wild thing in the opposite direction.

The next morning he was there again. Waiting. His eyes lit up and seemed to change color and darken as I approached. There was an intensity that made some kind of unfamiliar, not altogether welcome emotion settle in my chest. He smiled. I smiled and walked straight past him. I spent the whole of the next hour's lecture thinking about Sean and wondering what made him turn up, waiting for me, hoping for something, each and every day come sun and heat and more sun and heat. What did he expect to happen? Some sort of romantic *Grease*-type shit where he turns into the college stud and we walk off into the distance daning and singing? Not likely. While there was a hint of John Travolta around the jawline and the hips and, okay, the butt, there wasn't one molecule of Olivia Newton-John in me. So he might as well give up with whatever nasty business he was thinking. Even though that dimple in his chin was kinda cute and I'd never been with a white guy before and was curious and it had been so long since I'd even had any nasty thoughts or feelings myself.

By the afternoon, I was wriggling in my seat, unable to concentrate on anything but the hungry look in his eyes whenever they met mine, his slightly pouty bottom lip, and that straight curtain of hair that he so often had to brush away from his forehead. I was aroused and wet, but was sure that had nothing to do with him, just the fact of how long it had been.

He wasn't there when I left. For the first time in what seemed like forever he wasn't there. And a little of the spring went out of my step as I trudged to the pigeonhole to check my mail. There was no little chocolate treat, just a single carnation. What was that supposed to be about? Didn't he know that I just didn't do flowers? Chocolate was far more my style, as witness the size of my hips. Still, I picked up the flower and brought it to my nose. Obviously genetically modified to be without the slightest hint of allergy-inducing aroma. I looked around for a wastebasket and was just about to discard it when I noticed him standing in the shadows like some supernatural Lord Byron–type figure. I jumped, completely taken aback and, for some reason, slightly guilty.

He walked toward me and I had to stop myself from laughing. His gait had taken on the John Travolta walk from *Saturday Night Fever*. I half expected him to grab his crotch next. What was he on? Any thought of laughter was strangled in my throat, though, when he took hold of my hand. In the heat of the summer afternoon, his palm was cool, contrasting with the glance that he threw in my direction. Something about him made me feel nervous now. Gone was any slightest, tiniest hint of reticence or shyness or doubt. I wanted to pull away and go screaming down the hall, but I also wanted to know what would happen next, if I let it. I looked around. The whole place had emptied. Not a soul. Not a sound. The flutter of nerves pit-a-patted in my solar plexus and snuck along my spine. He was walking faster, taking long strides, and my flip-flops skittered along the cool stone floor as I almost ran to keep up. He turned a corner and another that I'd never noticed before and twisted the brass knob of what might have been a concealed door.

Bright sunlight streamed in from a window somewhere high up and our movement scattered a cloud of dust that swirled in the gloom, outlining the stream of white. I glimpsed old, discarded school desks, legless chairs, shelves lined with yellowing stacks of files, cans of paint, the lids sealed with a congealed lava flow of color. Among all the clutter, he kissed me, his lips hard against mine, insistent, his tongue forcing my mouth open, searching, exploring, drilling a path to the point that lit a fuse, sending a shaft of heat down through my spine, rocking me back on my heels. He held me, and where his fingers touched, they left an imprint of fire, totally unexpected. Unexpected? Hell, I didn't even know this guy and there I was letting him touch me. He could be the reincarnation of Jack the Ripper, but Lord have mercy, what he was doing to me felt so good and he had such a wondering, expectant, adoring look on his face that, at that moment, I'd have taken a million-dollar bet on him being more Don Juan than Marquis de Sade. Okay, truth be told, I didn't even consider the possibilities, I just wanted to feel more of what he was doing and confirm to myself that I still had it in me to set a guy on fire.

One hand crept up the back of my blouse and the beads of sweat nestling against my skin turned to ice as I felt a shiver ripple through my body. His finger slid down my spine and I tilted my hips toward him in an involuntary movement that spelled T-a-k-e M-e in mile-high letters that he couldn't misunderstand. The fingertip braille down the curve of my buttocks was responding, "I'm gonna make you wait." I don't know why he felt the need, but there's no understanding men. They chase you desperately for months, and then when you offer it to them on a plate with ketchup and fries, they decide that they want to make you wait!

Still, I couldn't fault his tactics. Whatever he was doing was making me feel hot with a capital H. Capital O. Capital T. Plus three exclamation points. He pulled away leaving me with my mouth hanging open. He smiled that kind of sneaky man-type smile that tells you that they think they've got you in the palm of their hands. And I had to admit it: I was currently curled up in a little palm-sized, gift-wrapped package. I looked down at his long, white, curiously untanned fingers as they frantically fiddled with the buttons on my blouse and I hurried to help, slipping it off my shoulders, glad that I'd worn a sexy lace bra that morning. I reached behind to undo the fastening and the movement thrust my chest toward him. I hadn't meant to do it, but I smiled as he groaned and reached down to his crotch to shift his growing erection to one side, to shield, protect. I let the straps of my bra fall to my elbows and cupped my breasts, covering them, teasing them, keeping him from what he wanted. His eyes were transfixed by the swell of my bosom, the deep cleavage. I waited as I watched his fingers curl toward me, revealing the huge swelling. I was more than a little impressed, so in the spirit of give and take, I let my hands fall, the weight of my breasts making them sway slightly, the dark, blueberry nipples pointing directly at him.

His fingers stopped in midair as if they'd received some kind of electric shock and then dropped to his sides. I took a step toward him and he grabbed my arms, forcing me backward farther into the room. I felt a hint of panic wondering what he was doing, but I soon realized that he was positioning me so that the shaft of light from the elevated window fell straight onto my torso. He edged backward then, groping behind him until he touched a chair. He sat. In the gloom, I could only see the gleaming brightness of his eyes, the pallor of his cheeks, the ivory flesh as he unzipped himself, and the tight white of his knuckles as his hand folded around his cock. I watched, fascinated as his fingers moved slowly upward, caressing, loving, making love to the column of flesh that rose upward, bending toward his stomach. Grasping, rising, relaxing slightly on the down trajectory. Over and over, the reddened tip almost mocking me.

I felt more than a little self-conscious left alone in the

relative chill of the dark room, standing there like some life-drawing model while students took what they needed from my body. I might have walked away, but I was fascinated and, to tell the truth, more than a little turned on by the sight of his hardened cock, knowing that's what I'd done to him. His eyes didn't leave my breasts, and I could feel a telltale wetness in my panties. I reached down and lifted my skirt, meaning to slip a finger into the moist depths of my pussy, just to take the edge off the excitement that was building. But as soon as I did that, he stopped as if distracted, annoyed that his intense concentration had been broken. Without thinking, and as if I'd been given a silent command or rapped over the knuckles, I let my skirt fall. But I was so horny that I couldn't just stand there, watching him take his pleasure while I did nothing. The tension was building in my stomach, the muscles quivering in my vagina, and my nipples felt as if they might spontaneously explode.

I lifted my breasts, took my nipples between my fingers, and squeezed gently; his hand returned to his cock in approval. I rubbed, pulled, scratched at the hard tips of my breasts, anything I could think off to abate the itch that was growing stronger with every thrust of his cock into the tight circle of his fingers and thumb. I pushed my breasts together, lifting them toward him, jealous of the caresses he devoted to his own organ. I walked toward him and a look of panic invaded his eyes as the motion of his hand accelerated. I was standing no more than six inches away from him and still, he didn't look past my heavy tits. I could feel my pussy lips swelling, demanding attention, the tightness growing in my clitoris, an unbearably empty clenching in my womb. I looked at his cock, the strength of it wasted. Not caring what effect I'd have, I slipped my finger into my gushing pussy and brought it out, glistening. Once again, he stopped all movement, just waited, silently praying that I'd let him get back to doing his own thing.

I circled my nipple with the juice and straddled his knees, just letting the head of his cock glance against the satin of my panties. His fingers moved again, his knuckles brushing against my clit, and I almost screamed but didn't want to frighten the horses. I bit my lip and continued to circle my nipple with one finger, more and more aroused by the excitement in his eyes. As I leaned toward him, cupping the undersides of my breasts, his mouth opened and his breathing became harsh and fast, his movements more and more rapid, hands brushing at my desperate clitoris over and over. I clenched my thighs and presented my bruised nipple to his lips; he circled it, swirling with his tongue. I looked down into his lap, the flash of the white of his hands now a blur as I felt the touch of his knuckles flicking against my pussy. I raised myself and might have straddled his cock but, at that moment, his breathing stopped, his body became rigid, and I felt the hot, viscous spurt of cum against my thighs. I was just a little too late, and he flopped forward, buried his face in my cleavage, closed his eyes, and sighed deeply, his shoulders heaving. I found myself holding his head tenderly, like I was comforting a child.

It wasn't until we slipped out of the storeroom that I realized that we hadn't spoken a word to each other. The situation was awkward. I looked down at the wilted carnation that I must have picked up, without thinking, on the way out. I looked up again. "Thanks for the flower," was all I could think of saying. Duh!

I guess I shouldn't have told Sonya about Sean. Maybe

that's why she thought of me when she read the advertisement. My sex life must seem exciting to her. But I don't know if I want to take this any further. I mean, it's one thing discussing this in the secure comfort of your kitchen over coffee or white wine, it's another to . . . well . . . you know. How much does she really expect me to reveal? I'm trawling through my memories trying to figure out what triggered all this.

Maybe it was the tale of Derek, sweet little Derek. Guys always seemed to have a thing about my breasts in those days. Okay, so they're one of my most erogenous zones, but that makes sense; they're connected to my body, my nerve endings, with a direct line to my pussy, but the way these guys act, you'd think there was a string with one end tied to my nipple and the other attached to their dicks. All I had to do was go out in a low-cut or tight-fitting outfit and you could count the number of stares and place a bet on how long before their cocks would be getting hard. My girlfriends and I used to laugh at how easy it was to arouse them and, many a time, I'd be asked to put my tits away before I brought about an outbreak of mass blue-ball-itis. And you know, in those days, there were a lot of superfine brothas around willing to make their sacrifice at the temple of my breasts.

So everyone was surprised when I got together with Derek. Not that he wasn't cute, but Derek was small. Not just a couple of inches shorter than average, really short. His eyes were on a level with my nipples, so you would have expected him to be impressed, along with all the others. But that's why Derek was different. Maybe in his twenty-six years he'd had more than an eyeful of mammary glands. No, Derek was remarkable. Perfectly formed, everything in proportion, well, *nearly* everything. He had the most gorgeous, soulful, deep brown eyes, like a Saint Bernard's puppy, skin like milk chocolate, and a thick mustache that framed full, sensuous lips and tickled just in the right places. But the *real* difference with Derek was that, although he appreciated my breasts, his big thing was my ass. What an enormous relief, a change from guys who just fantasized about rubbing themselves off between my boobs!

We met at a club in Clapham where he was the DJ. At first, I thought the reason he wasn't staring at chest level was that he had to concentrate on the discs he was spinning, but even in the early hours of the morning, as I sipped the drink that he offered me, I couldn't help reacting to the fact that he looked into my eyes as he spoke, a fairly rare occurrence. It's not surprising that I agreed to meet him for a drink the next night; he seemed like such a rare specimen, almost a national treasure. He took me to his home, a ground-floor apartment in Bolingbroke Road, backing onto Wandsworth Common, eerily quiet except for the boom of the stereo in the apartment above. I looked around. It was decorated in neutral shades that revealed nothing about his personality, but each room seemed to be overflowing with piles of CDs, vinyl, and the decks he used in one club or another each weekend. He had probably moved into the apartment and not changed one single thing about it. Still, it was curiously homely and warm.

The kitchen was the most lived-in room. He cooked up a surprisingly delicious, hot, spicy chicken curry, and I watched as he made roti. I immediately decided that, short or not, this might be the man I would marry.

We argued passionately for several hours about the relative merits of Prince and Michael, Teddy Riley and Soul II Soul, Public Enemy and NWA. We ate, we drank, we kissed, and just as I was getting into the mood to let him slip into something comfortable . . . he drove me home. For the first time in years, I spent a sleepless night wondering what was wrong with me. Had I lost my powers? Had my boobs shrunk overnight? Did I have bad breath? I just knew he wouldn't call. But he did. Surprised me once more. He took me to the movies and we ended up in his place again.

He put on Meli'sa Morgan's *Good Love* album (my choice) and we snuggled together on the oversized, battered sofa, him lying behind me, crooning along, his breath tingling against my earlobe. By the time we got to "Dirty Weekend," I was a hot, molten, seething pool of shimmering, sparkling mercury, molecules shooting off in every direction, stinging wherever they collided. His hands fluttered along the curve of my waist, down over my hips, making me wriggle with delight. I squirmed against him and couldn't ignore the protuberance that pressed against my bottom.

I turned my head toward him. "Derek, please don't tell me you goin' get up any minute and offer me a lift home."

"Babes, the way I'm feeling, I'm not sure I could even stand up straight."

"I did wonder why you didn't ask me to stay last night."

He nuzzled deeper into my neck, lips brushing against the curve of my shoulder. "I've spent the whole day in the Laundromat. I had no clean sheets."

I giggled, grateful for the frank admission that allayed my fears of inadequacy, and Derek joined in. I liked the fact that he could laugh at himself.

When we'd both calmed down a little, he reached across me to retrieve his glass. His forearm glanced across my breast and I immediately felt a resurgence of desire. I noticed that he remained unaffected, and that puzzled me and made me want to try even harder. He tilted the glass toward me and I sipped the warm brandy, the hot liquid seeping through my veins, creating little ripples wherever it touched. I sat up and swung my legs over the side of the sofa, suddenly uncomfortable with his body so close to mine. Something about the extra stimulus of alcohol threatened to tip me over the edge.

"Phew!" I wiped a hand across my brow.

But he wasn't going to let me go that easily. He shuffled along the sofa and, planting soft kisses from the nape of my neck downward, he slowly, millimeter by millimeter, unzipped the back of my top and ran his tongue down my spine, the hot wetness sending chills back up to my brain. I must have shivered because he wrapped his legs around me, straddling my hips, holding me with one hand, slipping the other down toward the swell of my buttocks.

"Cold?" he whispered.

"No, getting a little too hot." I stood, keeping the top from slipping down my shoulders. I bent down to pick up my glass, probably presenting him with more ass than I would have chosen if I'd thought about it. I heard his low moan and I turned back to him. He was almost doubled over, clutching at his genitals. I walked toward him, let my top fall to the ground, and held out my hand. He stood, slowly easing his body into a vertical position.

I led him in the direction of where I guessed his bedroom was, pushed the door open, and navigated by the light from the living room. I sat on the bed, noticing the fresh scent of crisp, white, cotton sheets. Derek joined me, his fingers reaching for my derriere again. I pushed his hand away and, feeling at a disadvantage, began to unbutton his shirt, pulling it out from his belt, pushing it down over his shoulders. I liked the feel of his chest, not too hairy, but not baby-soft either. I spent a few minutes playing with the coils of silky hair, noticing from the way his breathing stopped that, although he might ignore my breasts, his nipples were, if anything, more sensitive than mine. I teased, I feathered, I breathed hot air in a circle, avoiding the most eager points, and when I finally took his nipple into my mouth, swirling tiny circles around the hardened bead, he made as if to push me away, the groan sinking deeper and deeper into his chest. I pulled my lips away and sought for his, probing, inquisitive, wanting to gauge the level of his desire.

He was restless, groping my flesh, frenetic, his hands all over my body, pushing me back against the pillows. He was on top of me, pressing hard, his rock-hard erection digging into me. Time to come up for air. I eased my way out from under him and stood. I looked at him, hungry, eager, ready on the bed. I walked around the room, swaying my hips vamplike, sticking my bottom out whenever I wanted a reaction from him. The response was immediate, his tongue almost hanging down to his knees, or rather, down to the hard-on that was tenting his trousers. I smiled to myself. Now that I'd gotten his attention, I wanted him to beg. I walked to within a foot of him and, with a finger, lifted his jaw, forcing his mouth closed. I kissed him briefly on the lips and turned away, looking over my shoulder, letting a lock of hair fall over one eye, hoping to look a little like Jessica Rabbit even if I couldn't do the blond hair. I unhooked my bra and dropped it to the floor. I bent my knees and did a little wiggle as I slowly, infinitely slowly, slipped my pants over my buttocks, revealing the scarlet G-string, down over the curve, letting my fingers linger in the cleavage, stopping suddenly as he pleaded, "No, no, no! Don't stop. Pleeeeease, please don't stop. I couldn't bear it."

I waited until he looked into my eyes. I slowly licked my lips, feeling more than a little melodramatic. "You can bear it." I lowered my eyes to his groin and he made a move to cover himself. But before he could get there I was in front of him, undoing his belt as he leaned back on his elbows. I unzipped his pants and fumbled in his pants to uncover his masculinity. It was with a certain measure of satisfaction that I noted the size, the hardness of him.

I slid out of my G-string then, presenting him with my round, brown ass. I edged backward, closer to him, until I was hovering over his huge, dark cock. I wriggled my butt, circled it above him, letting his prick touch me every now and then, just to turn up the heat. And when it was all too much for him, he reached for me, his fingers stroking the underside of my buttocks, straying close to my pussy lips and the opening between. I was rampant. I wanted to just let go and sink down onto him, but he held my hips, positioning my body so that his stiff cock rubbed between the cheeks of my behind, his palms holding me close around him as he rubbed backward and forward, each stroke accompanied by a deep groan of pleasure or agony, it was hard to differentiate between the two. And the friction was making me hot and bothered. I was about to take charge and force his delicious prick inside, letting it fill me up. And then suddenly, before I could adjust my position, before I could impale my pussy on him . . . yes, you guessed it, he was shooting off, wasting all that suppressed energy.

You might well see a pattern emerging here. A succession of guys leaving me hot, horny, and unfulfilled. So, yes, Sonya had heard the many stories of arousal and frustration. As I've said, I wouldn't have told her, except that I was just trying to cheer her up, make her see how lucky she was. There followed Stephan, Chris, Michael, Pierre, Gregor, and Cuthbert—Can you believe it? Cuthbert!— and one or two whose names I can't quite recall, each encounter less successful than the last. I was painting a picture of a sex life in terminal decline.

Looking back, I suppose that Sonya's perception of me changed with the story of how Dan and I got together.

It was quite simple, really: a close friend's bachelorette party. Someone, I can't remember who, had done the research on the Internet and found a local group of strippers who would do birthdays, going away parties, bachelorette parties, and most lucrative they explained, stag nights. It took me a while to get my head around that one. Anyway, we ended up in a small, slightly seedy club, but by the time we'd gotten a few drinks down our necks, it was looking more like a chic Parisian *boîte!* The strippers ranged in age from about nineteen to what might just have been forty-nine with the greatest stretch of the imagination. I can't say that they were the most erotic combination that I could imagine, and I don't think they intended to be. Just a bit of fun. Nevertheless, the oiled, smooth, glistening flesh and vast quantities of alcohol did a little something for me in the groin area. And, no, Dan wasn't one of the strippers.

We'd all tucked our five-dollar bills into the satin pouches, some of the more brazen in our group sneaking a quick grope in the process. I even noticed one of the girls disappearing behind the stage curtains with a stripper. But none of them did too much for me. Something a little too manufactured, too . . . well, *oily* for my liking. So I settled myself at the bar, being chatted up in a desultory fashion by the young bartender. Dan took the next stool and ordered a lager. Out of the corner of my eyes, I noticed long legs clad in worn, navy, cotton Chinos and further up, a striped, open-necked shirt. Not too brazenly open. No gold chains around the neck. Just a soft tangle of chest hair. I approved. I turned my gaze full on and liked what I saw. A short beard, near enough designer stubble but a little less studied. Carefully trimmed mustache, dark skin with an almost blue sheen, sculpted nose with just a hint of broadness, and eyes that turned up at the corners, narrowing to a point. I stopped right there because the skeptical look he turned on me wasn't one that I came across too often. His eyes said something in the order of, yet another blond bimbo here to ogle the guys.

Now, he was right as far as the blonde was concerned, but only by virtue of a wig with tumbling curls bought for the occasion. And I know that guys don't understand too much about what we women do with our hair, but even he couldn't have believed that what was on my head actually belonged to me. As for the bimbo part, well, I guess I'd had quite a bit to drink, bachelorette party and all that, and wouldn't have found it too easy to explain Einstein's Theory of Relativity, but then I'd only been out for a good night's enjoyment and hadn't expected to meet anyone like him. If I had, then I might have brought along an *Encyclopaedia Britannica*, the complete works of William Shakespeare, as well as Derek Walcott's *Omeros* just for light reading to get me through the evening. As it was, the only thing I could think of doing was whipping off the wig when his head was turned toward the bartender and stuffing it into my handbag. The things women do when they're attracted to someone!

I shifted on the stool, crossing my legs and revealing a

little more thigh. When he finally turned back to me, there was something a little stunned and slightly disdainful in his look, but he still managed to mutter, as if under duress, "Drink?"

I should have refused, but was it likely that I'd be sensible? We'd just spent most of the evening downing cocktails, screaming mild abuse, and groping scantily clad men. Who would claim that 2:30 in the morning was the right time for rational behavior?

"White wine spritzer. Not too heavy on the soda, please." I gave him what might have been a smile, but it felt slightly lopsided, my cheek, where I had been resting my hand, having gone numb.

He held his hand out. "Dan."

I let my fingers linger in his. "Um . . . um . . . I can't quite . . . at this moment . . . remember what my name is. But it's something nice. Something memorable."

He hesitated before handing me the ice-cold glass. He watched in astonishment as I swallowed it in one gulp. What can I say? I was thirsty.

Dan stayed by my side, like an anesthetist waiting for the effects of the drugs to kick in. And when it did, he piled me into a taxi and took me home. He retrieved the keys from my unsteady hand, ushered me into my apartment, found my bed, and tucked me in before leaving.

I woke the next morning with an aching head and limbs that refused to obey my simplest command. I thought I must have had a great night to be feeling so bad. I tried to figure out how I'd gotten home and what I was doing in bed fully clothed, even down to my high-heeled stiletto party shoes, and then I remembered: Dan.

I recalled tall, slender, cool, collected where I'd been a complete and utter drunken wreck. A long time since I'd come across any eligible prospect, and I had to meet him when I was at my worst, okay, when I was completely legless. I groaned, staggered out of the bed, and searched in the bathroom cabinet for whatever form of hangover cure first came to hand.

It was midafternoon when the doorbell rang, waking me from the tiniest doze. I didn't know where I was, couldn't remember getting back into bed, loathed whoever it was who was torturing me by keeping a finger pressed to the bell when all I needed was blessed peace, quiet, solitude, and *sleep*.

So I wasn't surprised when he recoiled as I flung the door open. I must have been a scary sight. I didn't realize how scary until I looked into the mirror as I attempted to brush my teeth. I almost frightened myself with the crescent of black mascara that had lodged under my eyes, the red lipstick smeared across one cheek, and the tangle of black hair with strands of blond mixed in. I repaired as much of the damage as I could and crept sheepishly into the kitchen where he was expertly manipulating poached eggs in a frying pan while brewing coffee in the percolator. I sat at the kitchen table and held my head in both hands, the rumble of the wooden spoon scraping against the bottom of the pan a little too much for me at that time of day. As I looked up, intent on begging for mercy, Dan smiled a smug little smile and shook his head woefully. I was determined to beg for nothing, to take my punishment like a man.

"I came back to make sure that you survived. The way you looked this morning, I wasn't sure you'd make it through the day. What on earth were you on all evening?"

I groaned. "We started with champagne cocktails; then I remember one or two daiquiris, a Guinness challenge somewhere along the line, someone bought me a brandy, and I'll feel sick if I think of any more."

"So that explains your behavior in the taxi."

"Oh God, what the hell did I do?"

"You'd blush if I told you."

"Tell me anyway."

"Well, let's just say that it was enough to make me fantasize about what you might get up to when you're sober and the taxi driver wouldn't accept a tip."

I hid my face in my hands, determined never to look at his self-satisfied face again, even if it meant walking around blindfolded for the rest of my life. I had to open my eyes when I heard the clunk of a plate being plopped in front of me and smelled the aroma of eggs and fresh brown toast. There was more than a hint of amusement on his face and his expression made me smile, even if the motion did send a wave of pain and nausea crashing through my body.

Dan stayed for the rest of the day, propping pillows beneath my shoulders, tucking in the blanket as I lounged on the sofa trying to concentrate on the soaps on the television. He stayed the night, just watching over me, bringing me glasses of water at regular intervals throughout the night to stave off the effects of near-dehydration. And he was there in the morning to give me a lift to work, waving good-bye as he sped off in his black VW Golf.

When I got home, he was waiting on the doorstep, a bag of groceries in one hand and a change of clothing in an overnight bag.

"I just don't trust you to look after yourself."

He stayed for nearly a week and, by the end of it, I would have begged him not to leave. I was tired of the creak of the springs each time he turned over on the

lumpy mattress in the spare room; the outline of his body
in the sheets as I walked past on my way to the bathroom;
the tentative steps I took toward his bed each night, re-
treating at the last minute out of fear of humiliation. But
he didn't seem to want to stay any longer and I let him go,
knowing that he had become a good friend, but disappointed that he wasn't looking for anything more. Here
was this incredible rarity: a guy who seemed to want to
take care of me and ask for nothing more in return.

It took several weeks of erotic and then devious
thought and a little planning.

A few sniffles down the phone to set the scene. Pale
makeup, carefully applied shadows around the eyes. Sure
enough, Dan arrived with his usual array of pills and po-
tions, determined to cure whatever it was that was ailing
me. I was out to make sure that he did.

I waited until he'd brewed some concoction that involved lemon, honey, and a great deal of alcohol. I sipped
it gratefully, holding the duvet up to my chin, shivering
slightly, but not with cold. Dan sat by me, watching me
keenly, ensuring that I drank the last drop. He reached a
cool hand out and felt my forehead.

"I think you're running a temperature."

I took his hand and rested my cheek against it. I
don't, for a moment, think he foresaw what was coming next. I let the duvet fall, revealing an expanse of
bare flesh, my skin flushed, nipples already puckering.
I still held his fingers and drew them nearer until they
rested on my breast. For one scary second, I thought he
might pull away and reject me, but he didn't. Taking my
lead, he traced a path from my nipple, round and round
and then down, pushing the cover away until my whole
body was revealed in its total nudity.

"I thought you weren't feeling well?" he muttered.

"You look absolutely fine to me." And he leaned over and kissed me very gently, very briefly so I might have imagined that it had even happened.

"I'm feeling much better now, but not totally cured yet."

"So what exactly is it that you need?"

"A good doctor might be able to solve the problem."

He moved across until he was sitting beside me and calmly leaned back, watching me, unsmiling. I couldn't take my eyes away from the fullness of his lips. I wanted to feel them cushioned against my flesh, any part of it from the tip of my nose to the soles of my feet and any area in between would do. I hadn't realized it until then, but the weeks of enforced celibacy with Dan infiltrating my space had been torture and I couldn't take much more. I'd had enough of his controlled coolness. I wanted to take my revenge.

I crawled across him on all fours until my thighs straddled his waist. My fingers flew to my breasts and started to caress them gently, slowly stroking in circles, spiraling closer to my nipples until they contracted, hardening into rippled peaks. I pinched them, squeezing until they hurt, producing a short gasp. His eyes were widening, the pupils dilating until they looked almost black. I wanted to tease him, continuing to fondle myself until I felt him shift beneath me. His eyes didn't leave my body for a second; he was concentrating hard, his breathing shallow, coming in sharp gasps. His fingers reached for me, but I pushed them away, wanting to make him pay.

I smoothed both hands down, around my belly, trailing circles, then lingering over my satiny flesh, fingertips alive to the electric sensation. I played with my pussy hairs, twirling them around my forefinger, combing through them with my varnished, red nails.

His eyes followed every movement, his lips parted now, tongue protruding slightly as he licked his dry lips. I smiled, knowing that he wouldn't notice. I sat back on his lap, opening my knees wider, letting him glimpse the glistening opening.

"Oh, Lord," he moaned, "what are you doing?"

I had no reply. I would have thought it was obvious. I raised one finger and pointed it at him for a moment, and then slowly slipped it between my lips and sucked hard, finally letting it go, wet, ready. I touched it to my clitoris, gasping with the sudden intensity of the pleasure, and then I moved it slowly down, down until I circled the swollen opening of my pussy, and then slipped it inside.

I let his hand come within a millimeter of my vagina, and then I pushed it away, wanting him to believe I could do without him, that I didn't need his fingers to bring me pleasure. In and out I thrust my finger, my thumb enflaming my clitoris all the while, the other hand clutching at my breast as I rode up and down, my muscles clenched around my finger as I simulated riding a cock. I stopped for a moment and looked at him. The dark skin of his face was suffused with red. He looked as if he were going to burst. He shifted slightly as if he intended to grab hold of me and I speeded my movements, thrusting fast and hard, rubbing furiously, watching the red tip of his tongue as it slowly licked his lips again. His fingers groped for his zipper, releasing his engorged, painfully red prick. His fingers circled it and started to move rhythmically. Just the sight was too much for me and I let his lips touch my breasts, and as his mouth encircled my nipple and his teeth bit hard into my flesh, I felt a shaft of heat zip through me, down, down into my hot pussy and I came over and over, my body wracked with powerful convulsions that left me weak, clinging to his body, needing tenderness and peace.

It wasn't to be. Dan pinned me to the sofa and, before I could even moan in protest, his finger and thumb were inside my pussy, clearing a path, and he held on to his cock, readying it, caressing the flesh, "Making it as hard as I can for you, baby. Think you can take all of this? I want you so bad. God, your pussy's so tight."

Then he'd found the spot and, hesitating for only one, blissful second, thrust hard into my wet, demanding folds. I must have screamed with the pleasure. It was either him or me, I couldn't be sure, but every nerve in my body was clamoring for him, wanting to experience that moment again, needing to feel him plunging into the depths of my pussy. He pulled out and held himself there, getting his revenge, punishing me now, holding my hips down as I made to push upward. He waited, hovering until I was screaming with frustrated desire.

"Please, Dan, please."

"Please what? What you want?"

"Please fuck me. Now!"

And he did. Long and hard and sweet, holding himself back for most of the night until I came, over and over, until I fell into a weary, contented sleep. Even then, I could feel him easing his cock gently into me, rocking slowly back and forth round and round as I drifted . . . drifted . . .

I can guess what type of woman Sonya thinks I am, but the thing is . . . that not much of what I told Sonya is true. Well, actually, not one single detail. No Sean, no Derek, and certainly no Cuthbert. All of it a lie. Except for the story of Dan, of course. They weren't exactly fantasies, more tales that I made up to amuse Sonya when she was feeling low, to divert attention from whatever trouble she was going through at the time. I wanted to make her understand that there were people with less satisfying sex lives than hers. And I think she believed it all, right up until I told her about Dan. That's when she started to get the idea that I was inventing my entire sexual history. How ironic! And that's why she must have thought of me when she saw the ad.

I unfold the tattered piece of paper that I've hidden in my drawer for over a week now.

*Publishing company specializing in erotic fiction by black women is looking for . . . send a sample of your work to: Brown Skin Books.*

For about the thousandth time, I look at the words and look at myself in the mirror again. I'm tempted to just take out a sheet of paper or sit myself at the computer and start writing. But the truth is, and you're going to think I'm a bit of a wimp, I don't know if I could do it. It's one thing making up stories for friends like Sonya or even telling you, but having them published for the whole world to read? No, I don't think I could *ever* do that!

## About the Author

Born in England of Barbadian descent, Jade Williams is in her late 20s, "which really *doesn't* mean early thirties." A freelance journalist, she has worked in television and radio and has contributed numerous articles to newspapers and magazines. She is the author of *Body and Soul*, published by Brown Skin Books. She has asked the publishers to point out that "Brown Skin" is a work of pure fiction and that, despite what anyone might say, her bottom isn't dumpy.

# The Learning Game

## Sheree Mack

"Then I would tell them: we've just created a poem called a haiku."

"Yes, we get the idea, Ms. Turnbull."

That Head Teacher was bitchy. Dismissive. It wasn't going very well. This was the third interview for my first teaching job, so I felt like an old hand at this question-and-answer game, but that was before this Head got snippy. I'd obviously read the situation wrong. I had walked into the room with the long table of faces. I hooked on to the sista and inwardly gave a sigh of relief. I made the assumption of kinship, of a common bond based on our shared gender and darker skin tone. I thought she would be on my side. How wrong could I be!

"When I was at school, all we read was the Bible and Shakespeare. What is your opinion on this?"

*Obviously that was a very long time ago, you crusty old cow.*

"Yes, well, they are both important texts, for different reasons. But there's the argument that education should broaden the student's horizons and experiences . . ."

Somehow, I scrambled out of that little beauty but not before presenting myself as a total blundering idiot. Oh well, I'll get the *Times Educational Supplement* on the way home.

I was led back to the debrief room to await the verdict. Before I entered, I squared my shoulders to take full advantage of my considerable height. I wasn't going to let the enemy see weakness. The small room smelled of coffee and dust. There were orange cushy chairs pushed back against the cream walls and round tables squeezed into the space between. This had probably been a mini staff room in the past where harassed teachers came to let off steam. Today it held me and three other hopefuls. I stood near the door to give the impression that a decision was imminent and surreptitiously surveyed the competition. There was a guy in a brown suit near the window, constantly shuffling through a stack of notes as if he had forgotten something. Too late now, buddy! Closest to the door was a blonde woman with worn-down shoes who was fiddling with the hem of her skirt, succeeding in fraying the edges. I ruled out both of these two sapless wonders.

My confidence returned until my eyes scanned the third and final candidate who was staring straight at me. I don't really know how long he'd been looking at me, but a slow, easy smile started from the corners of his mouth and ended up at his honey eyes. God! I hope I didn't have one of my goofy expressions on. My velvety dark face had a tendency to take on a life of its own. I admit I had no control over it. Controlling the dimple in my left cheek, I gave up in grade school; my inky eyes rolled of their own accord; my full, vermilion-red lips suggested things my mind never thought. Put them all together, I was no classic beauty, but I was moving in the right direction.

I was mad at myself for being exposed but it was easier to direct that anger at him, the stranger with the sunshine smile. My irritation was rising at the smug look on his dark face. I took another quick glance and dismissed him. The job was mine. Lawrence Bailey School was looking for an English teacher not a PE-cum-rugby-prop-forward teacher. Otherwise, this man might have been in with a chance. He was all brawn and no brain. I had nothing against a bit of muscle, especially when it's against me. And this was a gorgeous specimen; long legs with well-defined muscles, slim waist leading to a broad, solid chest, and the smile with the strong, white teeth. Hot damn. But not at work. Too distracting. So I mentally struck all three interviewees off the list. The job was mine.

"Mi name Mike."

I can't remember the last time I was dwarfed by a man. At five ten in my bare feet, I was used to being at eye level with friends and men. So it was a bit disconcerting to have this tower of a man standing in front of me. His gaze took in everything about me in one sweeping glance. I wasn't concentrating on introductions but on the juicy, full lips they came out of.

*Get a grip, girl. You can't look at the dreadman with honey eyes as anything but the competition.* I knew what he was up to anyway. He was trying to soften me up to get the lowdown on how the interview had gone. I wasn't giving anything away.

"Good interview," averted eyes, but not before he started that smile again.

The door sprang open.

"We're not going to be able to make a decision until to-morrow. We must apologize for any inconvenience, but as you all must appreciate, it is a difficult decision."

*Shit,* under my breath. But it would be just my luck that I didn't get the job because they found out what a foul-mouthed hussy I am.

Brown suit man and blonde woman quickly followed the Head of Department out the door.

"Want a drink?" He must have read my mind.

"Why not!" Any barriers I might have put up against this guy were soon toppled when those eyes rested on me. What was I getting myself into? If not trouble! My mom always said, "Keep away from those rough, dry, low-down, good-for-nothing black dreadmen, they're only after one thing." I was hoping she was right.

"Let's gwan to de local." Mike placed his hand on the curve of my back to guide me out. The feeling was electric and it didn't confine itself to my back. Tingling shock-waves ran up my spine, prickling behind my ears and coming to rest in the roots of my cropped, black velvet hair.

As we stepped out of the school building, night was beginning to fall. I couldn't believe another day had passed and I was no closer to finding a job. I was feeling exhausted and disappointed. It was the end of May, a bit late in the day for trying to get a teaching job. As we walked toward the bar, we passed a supermarket on our right with some carts keeled over on their sides. Vandalism touched everywhere in inner-city London. On the left was the projects, some blocks boarded up with graffiti covering the railings and trash collecting on the streets. I had purposely chosen this area, this school, to try for a job. It was where I wanted to be. An area where the students were predominantly black and disillusioned. I didn't have any time for those white, middle-class, snotty-nosed kids who arrogantly obsessed about their rights. I wanted to give something back to the black community by broadening their opportunities. I didn't expect the job to be easy. But just *getting* a job was proving to be difficult.

The local bar, The Dog and Ship, was a little farther on. It was dark inside, small and intimate. The lighting was subtle, with candles stuck in wine bottles on each table. Hints of leather mingled with beer and incense. The place was filling up gradually with a pleasant hum of voices accompanying the midnight jazz. Mike was right, it was a good place to relax.

And a place he visited regularly, for no sooner were we through the door than there were greetings of, "Yo, Mike," "Hey, Mike," "Mikey!"

"You seem to be a popular guy."

"Like mi say, it mi local. Mi just live round corner. Lawrence Bailey was mi school."

"Really?" through gritted teeth. *Well, that's put the last nail in the coffin.* He was a shoo-in for the job. Ex-pupil come good through education, the school's bound to want to cash in on him as a positive role model for the youth of today.

"What ya drinkin'?"

"Southern Comfort and lemonade. Double." I needed to deaden the pain of disappointment and drink to his success.

The bartender was a big blue-black woman with bright fuchsia lipstick whose eyelashes quickened their pace at the sight of Mike. *Bitch.* My claws were out. *Now hold on, girl. He's not even your date.* I didn't have any right to be jealous. But as my eyes lingered on his firm backside as he leaned up against the bar, possessing him did cross my mind. Mike carried our drinks over to a dark corner table. He pulled out a chair, seating me before he sat himself. The candle on the table was lit, sending out a tantalizing glow. Mike had cheekbones you could sharpen knives on. He had reggae-star good looks, a mean dress sense, and long, long eyelashes. And irritatingly smooth and creamy mahogany skin. He took a swig of his beer and rubbed the froth from his top lip with hands the size of plates. This man had looks and the physique. He would be a lucky catch. Probably already caught.

"So, your girlfriend's not coming to meet you to-night?" I was frank.

"Wat girlfrien'?" Good answer.

"Sorry, I just assumed a nice guy like you would be attached."

"Flattery will get yu everywhere."

"You waiting for Miss Right?"

"Me could ask the same of yu."

"Mr. Right? I'm not going down that road again."

"Tell."

"There's nothing to tell. I'm just a sucker for a pretty face. And did he have one! But it seems other women felt the same way about him, at the same time. So I left him to them."

"Ya jokin'?"

"No, I learned my lesson there." Well, that's what I thought, but here I was again being drawn to the pretty boys. Did I say boys? I meant man, oh man.

"Well, he must hava been a fool to let a hot babe like yu fall tru his fingers." Sweet. Under the table, Mike's long legs brushed against mine. I could feel the heat through his pants. I wasn't sure if it was intentional or not, but his leg stayed there. I took a big gulp of my drink, clinking the ice against the glass. The warmth of the smooth amber liquid seemed to intensify the heat moving through my body. With a hand on my chest, I blew out my breath.

"Whoa!" I gasped, tears coming to my eyes.

Mike flashed a wicked grin, "Wat? Yu caant take ya drink?"

I glared at my drinking partner. "It went down the wrong way."

He reached for my glass. "Mi don't tink so. Mi get yu some warter."

I slapped at his hand, pulling my glass out of his reach. "Touch my glass if you dare."

There was that smile again. "Mi just lookin' out for yu."

"I can take care of myself, thank you very much." I recovered from the burning sensation, savoring the heat spreading through my body. A slow, easy smile played on my lips, probably accentuating the dimple in my cheek.

"What makes you tick, Nikki?"

"What do you mean?"

"What do you want out of life?"

"Well, that's a bit deep. Chill, man. I'm stressed as it is without having to think about it." He was making me feel uncomfortable. Not only was his image invading my body, but now he wanted to invade my mind.

"Why yu waant to teach?"

I sighed deeply. "It's something I've always wanted to do. I got such a buzz out of school. At first I thought it was because of friends, having a laugh. But then I realized, it was because of my English teacher, Mrs. Cousins. I handed in my essays, thinking I'd done a good job until I got them back with a large red *D* or *F* at the top. After a few of these marks, I stayed behind after one class and asked her what was wrong with my work. Mrs. Cousins said, "Nikki, this isn't *your* work you hand in, but what you've read somewhere else. You're not writing your own thoughts and feelings but simply regurgitating the words of others. You won't be getting any higher grades from me until you start to write what's in your own head.' Well, that rattled me. I was so full of myself that I thought she was wrong and I went all out to prove it. I rewrote my last essay, putting in my own ideas, and I got a B plus. She made me believe that I had something to say, that my thoughts counted. She taught me to believe in me, to be me. That's why I want to teach. I want to do just that for the kids who are afraid of their own thoughts and feelings. I want to create an environment where they are willing to be themselves. . . ."

I trailed off as I felt the heat rush up to my cheeks suddenly. I was annoyed with how much I had revealed about myself. I should have been on my guard. But I had relaxed in Mike's company. Relaxed because he seemed genuinely interested in what I was saying. He made the right noises, the right movement of his head. He seemed content to be listening to me rather than hogging the air space talking about *him*. Now, according to my understanding, this is a rarity among the brothas.

"My round?" I had to put some distance between us,

move my legs, and stop the connection, because this man was too much.

Four doubles later, I had forgotten about the mind invasion and just wanted him to invade my body, literally.

"It's getting late. Let mi take yu home."

"Nah, man. I can manage."

"Do mi good to get out of dis yard."

Mike led the way out, to a chorus of "Later, Mike!"

When I reached into the cold night air my legs went and Mike had to grab me under the arms to stop me from hitting the ground. The shame of it! He didn't let me go. I felt his biceps flex as he took my weight, and for the first time in my entire twenty-six years of life I felt as light as an ebony beauty queen. It was spitting rain as we walked along Lambeth Road toward Vauxhall subway station. A chill ran down my throat to lodge in my low-cut blouse, meeting the goosebumps developing on my large breasts. Mike protectively held on to me as we rushed on. Once inside the main station, he pushed me up into a corner and looked deep into my eyes. What he read there must have been what he wanted to see as his dark head moved down to catch my lips in his. He slowly kissed me with the taste of beer and the scent of lime on his jaw. My shoulders relaxed and my body responded as he slowly explored my mouth. His tongue delved between my lips and found mine. I savored the growing sensations and longed for more. I moaned softly. He pulled me around the waist to fit more closely to his firm body, feeling his warmth, all the time exploring my mouth. When at last we surfaced, he looked at me long and hard.

"Damn do yu look good in de moonlight."

When I only smiled in response, he ran his finger along my swollen lips. Back and forth. I had thought the feel of his lips had been erotic, but what he was doing with his finger was even more arousing.

Mike pulled me down to the trains. We only had a few minutes to wait, time enough for him to do a thumb dance along the skin of my wrist. The subway was packed with commuters returning from work in central London. We pushed in with the others and stood in the aisle between the brushed red-and-blue-checked seats. The train eased out of the station and I immediately banged into Mike. I giggled like a school kid playing hooky. Mike's voice, deep like liquid gravel shifting over velvet, caressed my ear as he tried to talk to me over the station announcement. The hairs on my neck stood on end. As our bodies continued to touch, my nipples became taut and erect. With each lunge of the train, I banged into Mike's extremely hard, extremely wide chest. My suffering nipples poked through the thin material of my red blouse. He must play some kind of sport to have a body like his. This thought was not voiced as he looked at me with hungry eyes that seemed to reach deep inside me and awaken needs and emotions I had tried so desperately to deny. In the finish, Mike grabbed me forcefully around the waist, pulled me against the full length of his body, and held me there. It was like a solid wall. A heated flush built up to my face and I eased back into his embrace. The train continued to swing and sway as I pressed hard against all his muscles and bulges. The temperature was rising with no means of escape. I was riding the rhythm and enjoying it.

"That was some ride."

"Yeah, man, but mi nat complainin'. Ya body up against mi, mi do it again, anytime."

I was glad it was dark so he wouldn't see the color rise to my face, but my breasts responded in kind to the compliment, as did my swaying ample hips. My full figure got little appreciation when compared with the stick insects of today. I took it all in my stride.

I lived between Brixton and Streatham Hill, an ex-council third-floor two-bedroom apartment. My baby. So what was I doing bringing this brotha here? I was just hoping I left it halfway decent when I flew out in the morning.

As I opened the door, we were met by the smell of vanilla and lemon. Thanks, Mom—that was her other piece of advice: "Now it don't cost much to have a dish of potpourri at the front door to greet you on return." Excellent. I rushed in clanking on the wooden floor toward the living room, surveying the situation, leaving the lights off.

"Come on in, don't mind the mess."

"Dis is smart," he said as he reached the living room and his feet sank into the deep red carpet. I put the open fire on to create heat and light. He gazed respectfully at the settee covered with a beige, black, and brown mudcloth pattern. A Ghanaian mask hung on one wall.

"Yu neva say yu hava African blood in yu."

"You never asked."

Several woven baskets were placed on a three-shelf bookcase filled with books, titled *The Bluest Eye*, *The Autobiography of Malcolm X*, and *The Lonely Londoners*. Mike went to take a closer look.

"Mi suppose dese cum wid de territory?"

"Books have always been my source of identity, especially since coming to London. After living up North in a predominantly white society, it was difficult to gain a sense of cultural identity."

"Wha bout ya parents?"

"My father died when I was young, and my mother was mixed race and only knew about life up North. I had to search for my ancestral links. It was worth it. . . ." The words were rushing out. I knew I was speaking too quickly but I didn't want to linger on talk about me, revealing too much about me to someone I hardly knew. "Come see my balcony."

I flung open the glass double doors and let the cold air in. The view was nothing special, other apartments, a few trees, but it was mine. I used to dream of having my own space, away from the many bodies and petty squabbles in our house. I smiled with pride at my achievement.

"It's much warmer inside, come."

"Mi warm enough out here." He was behind me, and I could feel his warm breath on my neck. He ran his hands up my side, over my hips, and stopped at my breast line. I could feel his warmth penetrating my back as he pressed into me.

"Yu should see ya face when dey say decision nat until tomorrow."

"I'm not a patient woman."

"But a beautiful wooman."

My blouse failed to conceal my full curves but Mike didn't seem to be disappointed. His hands spread out confidently under my breast. They extended out to meet his flattened hands and responded immediately. He continued to breathe on my ear and neck, sending shivers down my spine. And his hard cock grew against my high backside.

I reached behind and grabbed his firm buttocks to pull him closer into me to accentuate the growing heat in my pussy. Mike worked his fingers into my blouse undoing buttons, making enough room for him to tantalize my right breast as he ran his finger between my bra and hot flesh.

"Just as me thought. Yu feel even more delicious than yu look."

His voice was intoxicating and flattery did get him everywhere.

I was proud of my breasts, but men were wary of them as if they were some kind of bodyguard to the rest of my body. But Mike knew what he wanted. He cupped my right breast in one hand and pulled and rubbed and squeezed, increasing the pressure, producing feelings of pleasure and pain. My head fell back onto his shoulder, my hands slid over his ass. I was pushed hard against the iron bars as Mike caressed me, moaning softly into my neck. He pulled me through the doors and kicked them half shut. I was thrown onto the rug, and he straddled me. He released the rest of my buttons and my bra was thrown off. We stopped and stared at each other like lions before they devour their prey. His eyes glistened and there was that smile again. With his dreads hanging down, the flames' reflection stoking his face, he looked as proud and ready as an African king.

"What are you doing to me?" I gasped.

"Mi waanted to touch yu de moment mi first see yu."

I plucked at the buttons on his shirt, not satisfied until I had undone enough to slide my hands inside. Short, curly knots of hair like liquorice twirls dotted his powerful chest and teased my fingertips.

His mouth found mine, fierce, hot, and demanding. His tongue parted my lips to explore inside. He ran his

tongue along my teeth and finally found mine. He
sucked hard. He pressed his groin hard against my
pelvic bone. I felt my breath rush in my ears. His hands
were warm as he kneaded my breasts. He found my dark
nipples puckered and pinched them hard so that I
squealed out in excitement. He left my mouth open and
wet to take each nipple into his mouth in turn and suck
and lick, until I throbbed with burning desire. Then he
started to move down the rest of my body, flicking my
belly button as he went.

Did I want him to stop? *Nikki, stop fooling yourself,
you know you want it, raw hot sex with a stranger. And
you're not going to see him again, whoever gets the job.
So just go for it, girl. Just enjoy it.* He sure could kiss!
Here I was a grown woman with a string of degrees, trading kisses with a man I hardly knew and loving it. I should
have been angry with myself, with him even, yet all I
wanted was more.

Mike undid my skirt and slid it down with my panties
to my ankles. He then fumbled to get my skirt and my
shoes off. Finally, he threw them and my underwear across
the room. I reached for him, but he stopped me, placing
each hand loosely behind my head with one hand.

"Nat yet. Let mi look at yu."

I felt exposed and horny at the same time. Now I was
totally naked, my swollen breasts were responding to the
heat from the fire and the cold air coming through the balcony doors. But inwardly I felt I was going to explode
with wanton desire.

"Ya body stunning. Mi waited for dis. Mi want to
see yu."

That was the second, or third, I'd lost count of the number of times he had expressed his admiration of me. This
was appreciation long overdue and I was lapping it up.

I wriggled my hands free to rid him of his shirt, pushing it over his broad shoulders. While I was that close, I nuzzled into his collarbone and received delighted groans for my trouble. But before I could continue, I was back on my back and Mike's tongue was at the top of my buttery thighs. The tongue paused briefly, and I raised my hips to get more of it. My legs parted eagerly. His tongue began to move closer to my now very wet pussy. The tip played with my curls, and then it shot in to part my lips, diving into the dark slit between. I gave an involuntary shudder and arched my back to receive even more of his eager tongue. The stranger's tongue circled the sensitive skin surrounding my clit. Suddenly, his tongue tapped my bud and flames spread through my body. My hips tilted, jerking into his face, wanting more. His tongue started to lick back and forth across the burning flesh. Instinctively, I parted my legs wider to increase the sensation. He had hit the spot; the excitement gathering in my belly moved down through my groin to that point, the electric center of my clitoris. Waves of growing pleasure rippled outward. Blood pumped through me as the pleasure swelled. He showed no mercy as his tongue gathered momentum and his fingers rubbed my damp hair. Then one finger slipped inside my pussy next to the tongue. And then another. They thrust hard. That was enough. I flung my head back as the first wave cascaded over my body. A groan from my throat followed. The long, hot tongue lapped feverishly, the fingers screwed into me, and I came, flooding. Juice dripped down into my ass, into his mouth.

I lay there panting, shaking with the powerful sensation. Mike undid his belt buckle and slipped off his pants. I gave myself the enjoyment of watching his massive body come into full view. He fumbled in his pants pocket for a small foil package and turned away from me for a moment. A warm glow lodged in my chest, as I thought: he unquestioningly takes precautions. I had my own supply, but the gesture was noted. When he turned back I eyed his manhood. It was definitely in proportion to the rest of his body. I wondered briefly if it was possible to have too much of a good thing, but quickly dismissed all rational thought as he lowered himself down at my side. One leg nudged my legs apart and his hand was again buried in my wet heat.

"Just checkin' ya still wet." Joker.

I could explode all over again. He must have known as he removed his hand and positioned himself on top of me.

"I waant to feel yu all aroun mi."

Holding my head still, eyes focused on mine, he gently pushed himself into my welcoming warmth. It was amazing. His cock edged slowly in, with each thrust deeper and deeper. My senses were heightened. My pussy walls gripped his long, thick shaft crying out for more. He whispered to me. I strained to catch his every word as he drove deeper into me. His back was bathed in sweat. His honey eyes fixed on me, watching my every expression of pleasure. I had no control over it. Round and round his hips ground, I grabbed them from behind and pulled him deeper. I took what I needed from him as my orgasm started in my toes. It rushed over my skin, to my muscles that clenched around his cock as I let go squealing and panting like some wild animal. My tightness gripped him in rippling waves. He muffled a shout of satisfaction into my neck and released his load.

We lay gasping for breath and relishing the afterglow.

"Thank you."

"Mi pleasure."

Hours later, or at least so it seemed, I tried to rouse myself. I ran my fingers through his rough dreads. I wiggled trying to get into a comfortable position as Mike crushed me with his weight.

"Ah, ya ready to go again." There was that smile.

"Stop that right now, or I'll hold you to it."

"Just give me someting to eat to keep mi strength up."

And before I had registered what he meant, he had one of my nipples in his mouth. He began a slow, sweet suckling, with one hand cupping the mound up to his mouth for a deep draw. The hot wetness just started the sparks of electricity through my body all over again. Amazing. It was hours later when I was pulled on top, and probably got carpet burns the length of Heathrow's runway. And not until then did he fall asleep.

We awoke, in a morning haze, to the phone ringing. I picked up.

"Hello, Ms. Turnbull?"

"Yes?"

"This is the Head from Lawrence Bailey School. I'm calling to offer you the English position."

"Excellent."

"I take it that means you accept the offer?"

"Most definitely."

"Would you be able to come into school today to finalize the details?"

"Sure, this afternoon okay?"

Howling with joy, I hung up. I caught sight of the stranger's dark, striking body on my rug. Mike. The job.

"Congrats to yu." He rubbed sleep from his eyes and stretched both arms up to the ceiling.

"Thanks. I'm sorry."

"Wat ya sorry for?"

"Well, I know you wanted the job too. I'm sure there'll be others."

"Mi got a jab. Mi PE teacher der already. Suppose mi be seein' a lat more of yu in de future!"

## About the Author

Born in England to a Trinidadian father and mother of Ghanaian descent, Sheree Mack is in her early thirties, recently married with a five-year-old son. After teaching English for several years, she has decided to hang up her red pen and register and devote all her time to writing. She is the creator and coordinator of *identity on tyne*, the only group in the northeast of England providing space exclusively for African, Asian, Caribbean, and Chinese writers. She currently lives in Newcastle upon Tyne.

"The Learning Game" is the winner of Brown Skin Books' first erotic short-story competition.

# Address Book

## Wanda Games

Her thumb pressed the arrow button and she scanned the names in the address book inside her cell phone.

How could she know so many men and still be single? Was it them? Or was it her?

She glanced at herself in the mirror. A friend of a friend had just plaited her hair but it was for convenience rather than part of a look. With her hair tied back, her face was exposed: round and—if she was honest with herself—chubby. Her dressing table was full of creams that she hoped would make her dark skin look healthy and even but—who was she kidding?—it was blotchy and often spotty.

She looked down at her phone. Was it them? Or was it her?

Ashley. Short. Very short. Too short. Nice face, slim, churchgoing, but just too short.

Brian. Average. Average height, average face, average mind. Brian was so average that she sometimes had trouble recalling his face.

Standing up to straighten her skirt, she looked at her bottom and winced. Where had all that flesh come from? It certainly wasn't something she'd asked Santa for! If she was fat, she would expect it, but she'd always been sporty. Men had told her she was "fit." She didn't feel it.

Colin. Questionable sexuality. Far too pretty. He had an entire closet devoted to shoes. What was that about?

Derek. Well-endowed. Roving eye. Gift of the gab. A deadly combination. Not marrying material.

As a realist, she knew that her plain features gave her no "pulling power." Her major weapon was being forward. Making the first move. Taking the initiative. It was a characteristic that had scared off a few predators, but at least she'd never been the victim of a philanderer. True, she was twenty-four and very single, but at least she was in control.

Ewan. A bookworm. A science-fiction buff as well. Debbie didn't like conversing in Klingon.

Francis. Hmm, Francis. How come they weren't an item?

Debbie paused for a second and thought about the glorious nights she and Francis had spent together dancing and laughing until they were drenched with sweat and tears.

For a good two years, Francis had been the perfect accomplice. He loved his music and was up for any party or club. He was tall, clean-shaven, shoes polished, smelled nice, and always knew the latest moves.

They'd met at a bank. Their first jobs. She had been taken by his smart suit and shy smile. Same age, both born in Tottenham, same church. They even had some friends in common. So, yes, how come they weren't an item?

She thought about the Friday evenings they'd left work together, gone to a bar, and then on to a club. Debbie cherished those Fridays. They were the highlight of her week. She would always carry an extra top, pop it on in the rest room, and then head out into the West End with her best friend.

None of her girlfriends could understand it. "How can he be your best friend?" "If he's your best friend, why don't you go out with him?" "If you like him so much, how come you don't find him attractive?"

Oh, but she did. She found him very attractive. He had a sexy way of catching her eye and pouting his lips. It wasn't the pout of a kiss; it was just his way of saying, "Oh my God! Look at the tits on that girl!" or "Boy, something smells rank!"

But every time he pouted those lips, she wanted to grab his collar and pull him toward her.

And one day she did.

"Why did you do that?" he asked.

"Why not?" she said, unable to confess the real reason.

"You can't do things like that!"

"Why not?"

"'Cause it will lead to other stuff!"

"So?" she said, bravely.

One Friday, they decided to take in a movie as well. They had chosen the new Chris Rock film, because they knew it would get the evening off to the right start. At 5:00, as always, she dived into the bathroom, rolled some deodorant under her armpits, changed into another top, something revealing, and applied some Danger Red Alert lipstick.

As she emerged through the front door of the bank, he stepped back with alarm. Surely it was a lustful look.

"Something wrong?" she said, innocently.

"Erm . . . no . . ." he mumbled.

She took his arm, as if they were a couple. They both knew they weren't, but he didn't mind her holding on to him.

Opening the door of The Casket Wine Bar, he ushered her in.

"Why, thank you, kind sir," she teased. There was definitely a different look in his eye. Was it the cleavage? Was it the red of her lips? He seemed jittery and not his usual confident self.

Without asking, he went to the bar and got her vodka and Red Bull. She loved the fact that he knew her favorite drink and bought it without even asking.

She found a table and he soon arrived with her cocktail and a cold bottle of strong lager.

She smiled at him and exhaled with great pleasure. "Thank God it's Friday!"

"Yeah, thank God!"

"I thought that bitch was going to ask me to stay late," Debbie grumbled.

"She wouldn't dare!" he said, supportively.

She looked at him. As it was the end of the day, his suit was slightly crumpled, but, boy, didn't it still look good on him! He had nice, broad shoulders and a slim waistline. What only lay beneath that shirt! She wanted to press her nose against the smooth skin of his chest and smell his sweat.

That night, he wasn't smiling as usual. He looked nervous. His eyes were everywhere but on her.

"What's wrong?" she inquired, apprehensively. "You okay?"

He opened his mouth to speak but nothing came out.

"Francis!" she snapped, assertively.

He jumped. "Yeah, sorry, Debs. Miles away."

"Not feeling well?"

"I'm fine," he began. "Listen . . . the other night . . . you know . . . when you kissed me . . ."

"Yes?" she replied, excited. "What about it?"

"I said we shouldn't because it would lead to other stuff. And you said, 'So?' How can you say that?"

She was confused. "There's no law against gettin' jiggy!" She laughed. "Don't tell me you haven't thought about it!"

"I have, I have, but . . ."

"But what?"

"What about *this*? Our friendship. Our Friday nights. What about all of that?"

He was right where she wanted him: horny and vulnerable. This evening was now certain to result in a satisfying conclusion. And if he came back for more, then he was The One.

"There's no reason why anything should change," she added, dismissively.

But he was right. It had changed. After that night, everything changed, and here she was, flicking through her address book, looking for crumbs of comfort and finding nothing but loose ends.

"Okay," he said, decisively. "Let's put it to the test."

She knew exactly what he meant but she wanted him to spell it out in more detail. It would be exciting to hear him talk about sex. "What do you have in mind?"

"My parents are away. My brother's at his girlfriend's for the weekend."

A flutter of excitement spread down from her belly into her pussy. Her body knew what was about to happen and began to get ready.

"And?" she probed, mischievously, enjoying his discomfort.

"And," he continued, "I thought I would blow some money on some champagne and take you home."

She was moments from kissing his lips, moments from biting his neck, and moments from sinking her nails into the muscular cheeks of his behind. She began to smile. It was a smile that wouldn't leave her lips.

Still, she wanted to punish him further. "Take me home and do what, Francis?"

Shocked, he gave her a stern look and swigged swiftly from the green bottle.

"Christ, Debs, what do you want me to say?"

She looked at him coldly and deliberately. As the day had finally come, she was going to enjoy every minute, every aspect. She leaned toward him and whispered in his ear, ensuring that her breath sent darts of pleasure up the back of his neck. "Take me home and do what? Are you going to fuck me, Francis?"

He recoiled with outrage, terrified but very excited. She watched him move a hand to his crotch, trying desperately to cover an erection. She winked at him with satisfaction.

"I think Francis wants to fuck me." She slid her hand very deliberately up her thigh and, when she was sure she had his attention, she moved her fingers slowly up across her breast. His jaw began to drop. She watched his eyes follow every movement of her fingertips, as she gently grazed her nipples. He was completely hypnotized. Touching herself in public was delicious. Having Francis watch her was even more fun!

He sat upright and straightened his tie. "What are you doing?"

"I thought we could talk about anything," she protested.

"We can."

"Didn't I help you with that Maureen girl?"

"Yeah, you did."

"Even told you what to say!"

He now looked horny, vulnerable, and full of gratitude. She had him in the palm of her hand. Any part of him she wanted!

"Well, now I want to talk about self-gratification."

"What?"

"Pleasuring myself. You pleasuring yourself. Pleasuring each other."

"Debs, you're too bad!"

"Lucky for you then!" she spat, with a beam of accomplishment.

Gulping urgently, he finished his beer and she took this as a cue to get up and leave. The day had finally come. She was moments from running her tongue around the tip of his cock.

Having invested in a very good bottle of champagne, they arrived at his parents' house. The lights were all off. No sooner had he shut the front door than she found herself pinned up against it, his eager lips kissing hers, her face, her neck. His tongue began to push its way slowly into her mouth. He tasted not unpleasantly of beer, but she was more than distracted by his strong arms holding her tight and the feel of his growing erection pressing against her thigh.

Coming up for air, she managed to gasp, "Easy, tiger!" She took the plastic carrier bag from him. "Shall we put this in the fridge?"

"Of course!" he panted.

They both stood at the bottom of the stairs. She handed him her coat and bag. Silently, he hung them on the hallway hat stand. "After you," he indicated. She began to shimmy her way up the stairs, knowing full well that his eyes were staring daggers into her ass.

Pausing at the top of the stairs, he opened a door and

she entered his bedroom for the first time. Neat and tidy like him. Posters of soccer players and R&B stars on the wall. A desk unit containing a shiny PC. A metal wall unit full of alphabetized CDs.

Unsure of what to do, he closed the curtains and turned on a small bedside lamp. Just enough illumination. Unable to wait for his next move, Debbie stepped forward and put her arms around him, grabbing both cheeks of his bottom playfully. He gasped with shock and excitement.

"Scrunchy like juicy apples," she said.

He nodded, numbly.

Moving a hand round to the front of him, she rubbed her hand against the hard lump in his pants. Again, he gasped and she could feel his cock flinch. A grin of enjoyment swept across her face. Looking around her, she saw that his chair was right behind him, so she gently moved him backward and sat him down.

Touching herself was delicious. Having Francis watch her was even more fun! His eyes followed her every move. She kicked off her shoes and wriggled out of her underwear. His eyes were bulging and blood had begun to rise to his face. Blood had definitely found its way to his groin. He was forever fidgeting, trying to push his hard-on to a comfortable place in his pants.

She lay back on his bed and began to move her hand up her skirt and between her thighs. She looked at his face. He had stopped breathing and his tongue was searching for moisture in his mouth. His eyes were glued to her hand as she moved it up and up between her legs. Finally, she reached her lips and, as she casually rubbed a finger along the wet gap, she could hear him choking for breath.

Moaning, she began to push more fingers into her pussy and up over her clit. It felt good. Better than usual. Gently, she pressed against her mound and began to feel her excitement increase. Rubbing herself softly and rhythmically, she could feel juice oozing out.

Suddenly, Francis got up, as if he was ready to join in.

"Wait!" she barked, breaking her concentration.

"Why?"

"Don't ask 'Why?' boy! You should be asking me 'How?'"

"Christ, Debs, are we going to do this or what?"

"Sit! Wait!"

Obediently, he sat back in his chair and watched her. The other hand moved under her top and he could see her rubbing and pinching a nipple. Although she wanted to watch his face, these sensations were too good. She collapsed back with her eyes closed and rubbed her pussy with greater force and precision.

She knew that Francis was watching and she imagined him filming her. She imagined his best friend—a stupid boy called Steve—watching the video some days later and drooling over her. Within seconds, she came deeply and ripples of wonderful pleasure covered her body. She shivered and tried to catch her breath.

"Mmm . . ." she moaned. "Good." Pausing for a second, she then leaned up on one elbow and looked at him. Those pretty brown eyes had been replaced by the lustful gaze of a panting dog. "Okay," she began, "your turn."

"What?" he inquired. "Play with myself?"

"Yes, please," she replied, "but don't come."

"Is this how it always goes down?"

She thought back to Shaun and his big clammy hands covered in semen, she thought of kinky Kevin falling to his knees with exhaustion, she thought of Roger, eyes rolling to the back of his head as he prematurely squirted onto his new sneakers.

"Yes, Francis, this is my idea of fun."

Trying to regain his composure, he stood up. Now it was her turn to watch him. He reached down and took his shoes and socks off. He fumbled apologetically with the buttons on his pants. Enjoying his performance and casually rubbing her breasts, she watched him trying to edge his pants down, made difficult by a rock-hard dick getting in the way.

"Why are you making me do this?" he squealed.

How many times had she heard that question?

"Stop!" she said, as she had said many times before.

She had stood time still. At that precise junction, life itself was waiting for the next utterance from her lips.

Nonchalantly, she looked around his walls. There was a huge, tacky print of a Dancehall moment above his bed. It captured that sublime instant when a woman arches her back, sticks her butt out, and feels an excitable man trying to penetrate the fabric of her dress.

"Why am I making you do this?" she enquired, cupping a heavy breast. "So that it doesn't flash past in the blink of an eye. I like it to last."

He threw his shirt carelessly onto the floor and, although she wanted to squeeze those small brown nipples, she let him continue until he was totally naked. She looked deep into his eyes and then all the way down his slim, muscular body. He watched her looking at him, appreciating him, evaluating him. She motioned her head that he should continue and, gingerly, he began to rub his cock. Grasping the shaft, he began to jerk it upward, and she could see his plentiful balls bouncing beneath.

"Don't come," she repeated.

"Christ, Debs! This is torture."

"More!"

As he pulled at his cock, she could see clear fluid emerge at the tip. How she longed to taste it.

"Protection?"

"Yeah, yeah," he spluttered, "in here." He moved over to the bedside table drawer and extracted a condom from a box.

"Put it on," she coolly added.

Getting out of the way, she pushed him onto the bed. Again, he looked unnerved but out of his mind with passion.

Slowly, she lowered herself onto him and felt him deep inside her. The sounds coming out of him were as exciting as the cock pushing up inside her.

"Don't come," she repeated.

"Debs! How?"

"Think of that bitch at work. Think of working late. Think of your shitty salary."

Moving her hips back and forth, she rubbed her pussy against his groin and, to sweeten the sensation, she put her fingers between her legs.

She closed her eyes and thought again of stupid boy Steve. She imagined him watching a video of her and what his primitive commentary would be. She imagined Steve grunting and calling her a "freak."

"Don't come," she said, as the first waves of her climax rushed through her frame.

She pictured Francis saying that she had "fucked herself with her fingers" on his bed and stupid boy Steve snorting at the vivid imagery.

Rubbing herself frantically, she came over and over again. He could feel juice spurt out of her and down over his thighs.

Breathing quickly and licking her lips, she smiled. "Good boy."

Slowly raising herself off him, she bent down and carefully pulled the condom off his angry dick. Resting her tongue on the top of his penis, she grabbed his length and began rubbing it upward. As his breath quickened and his hips jolted upward, hot semen spurted out of him. She smiled and licked the cum.

She looked down at his sweaty face. His body contorted with the echoes of his orgasm.

"Nice?" she inquired.

"Nice?" he repeated. "Different."

"Different good?" she asked.

"Yeah, yeah, different good," he affirmed, but she was not convinced.

And maybe that's where the problem lay. It hadn't been "different good," it had been "different: that bitch is crazy."

So, there was her answer: That's why they weren't an item. He was just a memory. Just a name in her address book.

## *About the Author*

Born and bred in London to Jamaican parents, Wanda Games is married with one child. She is a voracious reader and has been writing short stories for many years, but has never before been published. "Address Book" is her first attempt at erotic fiction but, if her friends don't like it, it may be her last. Wanda Games now works as a personal trainer, helping older clients to arrest the march of time.

# Be Prepared

## Michaela Greenidge

Now, in my humble opinion, spontaneity is not a good invention. People should plan, plan, plan. That way, you don't get into too much trouble. Especially when trouble goin' be lurking round every corner, just waiting to grab you up. So when they decided, just the night before, to take their cars, get out of London, and head for a little place somebody did once hear 'bout from his friend at work, you knew there was going to be more than a few complications.

Esther only ended up at the small marina outside Southampton because the day trip had gone wrong when the car she was driving got separated from the others. It was never a great idea to go tearing down the M3 motorway from London in convoy, with not a map among them. Now, what have I been saying about planning, back up plans, taking precautions? . . . Luckily, the birthday girl was in Esther's group, in fact, sitting right behind her in the car, tipsily shouting directions to a location she'd never even been to before, giggling hysterically at each wrong turn and consequent U-turn. Well, mix a lack of forethought with more than a little bit of spirits, the men-tal kind and the alcoholic kind, and you're heading for . . . well, you know.

The day, I admit, was gloriously hot, the kind that makes you forget about any cares. The kind that makes you start believing in all that talk about global warming. The top was down on Esther's Peugeot convertible and the air had a Caribbean quality, as if it had never known a hint of English chill. Magic fairy dust must have been sprinkled from the cloudless, blue sky because, for just a little brief moment in time, everyone they stopped to ask for directions seemed to be infected by their good humor and smiled happily enough, stopping to chat and wish Marion a happy birthday. Most unnatural in this northern country. Of course, their instructions were a little less than accurate, but then "How do you get to the pub that's by a village green with a well in the middle and has the word *stag* or *deer* in its name?" wasn't the most precise question they could have asked. But the truth was, by the time they'd made the fifth or sixth detour—the only person counting was Doug, squashed between Marion and Julie in the back and needing a pint and a pee in equal measure—they'd stopped even listening to the responses.

So they stopped at the marina in desperation, and Esther watched with smug amusement as the rest of the party burst out of the car, running frantically in search of toilets. Her mother had always told her to go whenever you can because you never know when you goin' find another one, and she was always the kind of girl who was brought up to listen to her elders. She watched as Marion staggered along the planks, high-heeled stilettos catching in the gaps, purple flounced mini-skirt blowing up in the breeze. Esther smiled. Her friend was like some exotic tropical bird blown here by mistake on some freak thermal current. I, myself, would have called her brazen, overblown, a little bit of a hussy; but then you didn't ask my opinion.

Esther took off her sunglasses and looked around. Serious money was what she noticed first. She knew next to nothing about boats but immediately sensed the wealth as if it floated in the air, as if money gave off its own peculiar odor and instantly made you feel a bit smaller. And this was old money, too, the kind that wore gray pants, navy blazers with a badge, and a discreetly striped old-school tie. So you knew you were appearing in glorious technicolor when the situation demanded sepia. Esther found herself tugging at the tiny shorts that were riding up her backside, replacing the glasses on her nose, and retrieving the long cotton shirt that lay crumpled on the driver's seat.

There were only a few boats. As the warm salty breeze lifted her shirttails, Esther thought how incredible it must feel to be out on a boat on a day like this, the hot sun beating down, the cool sea breezes brushing against your skin, the fresh spray of saltwater invigorating. She breathed in deeply. Not that she'd ever ventured onto anything like one of these yachts that were, in fact, much bigger than they looked on the movie screens. The closest she'd come was the ferry across to France for a day's booze shopping, but she could let her imagination take her anywhere . . .

"Hey, you guys lost? Can I help?"

Esther looked around quickly, feeling like a complete idiot. She hadn't noticed him and there she was, standing on the jetty with her eyes closed, face tilted up to the sun, lost in her daydreams of blue seas, clear skies, white sand. She turned her head right and left and then understood why she hadn't seen him. She had to look down to where he stood off to her left, several feet below, paintbrush balanced across a can of white paint in one hand as he shielded his eyes from the glare of the sun with the other.

Well, you just don't expect to see a black guy messing around on boats. It just wasn't their style. Cars, definitely. Motorbikes, possibly. In fact, most black men don't mess around with any vehicle—they just send it to the mechanic. But this one, somehow, in spite of the dark complexion, looked totally at home here. His head was a mass of tiny, red-tinged locks, held away from his face by a black band. His skin was the color of frothy cappuccino with a little too much milk and a sprinkling of cocoa freckles around the cheekbones. He'd obviously spent time in the sun because there was a triangle of copper shading his slender chest—if I were his mother, I would have made him apply sunscreen and wear a T-shirt! Anyway, Esther couldn't see his eyes, and needed to since that's how she always decided on whom to trust, but his voice was low with an accent that must have been American with a dash of Latin warmth. Canadian, perhaps?

Esther smiled at him, intrigued. "We sure are lost, but I don't know if you can help since we don't even know where we're trying to get to."

He nodded and looked over to where a screech of laughter suddenly shattered the stillness like a seagull's cawing. Marion, Julie, and Doug had obviously found something new to amuse them, not a difficult task since they'd been verging on the edge of hysteria since early morning, high on the weekend's freedom and the sense of adventure that always hovered in the air when this particular group of friends managed to get together. And all that stirred with a few cans of lager on the way.

"Seems like you're having a good time, anyway." He turned away from her, picked up his brush, and went back to his painting; the broad, horizontal strokes of his hands made the muscles in his shoulders ripple. A shimmering, kinetic sculpture against the stark, white backdrop of the boat. He was tall and slender, his baggy khaki shorts resting precariously on his hip bones. You could almost count the vertebrae in his spine, but the well-defined muscles hinted at a strength that belied the vulnerability of his form.

As she heard the sound of hurried footsteps approaching, Esther, for some inexplicable reason, felt the need to reach out, to metaphorically touch him. It was as if she'd rejected him by not accepting his offer of help.

"Where are you from?" she asked, more for something to say than genuine curiosity.

"Southampton." He didn't interrupt his work and didn't turn toward her. They both knew that wasn't what she meant and Esther almost missed the wave of gentle laughter that shook his shoulders.

And then they were all piling back into the car and Tony was taking the keys from her hand, slipping an arm around her waist, and kissing her lightly on the shoulder. She knew that his eyes, too, were on the stranger. She let him pull her back to the safety of the group. She climbed into the passenger seat, letting Tony take his turn to drive. She clicked her seatbelt across her shoulder and, as Tony steered away, looked back at the small patch of gray that was yet to be covered by white paint.

They found *a* bar, not *the* bar, but a bar that had the word *stag* in its name and was nestled by a village green but, search as they might, there was no sign of any old-world well or the rest of their party. The afternoon was filled with raucous, alcohol-fueled laughter, fond reminiscences, and old-time jokes that should have been recycled with the timbers from the ark. The day, though not as planned, would hold a host of tiny, joyful memories that they'd reshape, mold, and transform over the years to come.

As they set off back toward the city, Esther turned to watch the golden rays of the sun changing the horizon from blue to red to purple. She took one last look at the calm stillness of the sea.

Six-thirty was too early for the layer of smog to have burned away, but already there was a shimmering of heat in the distance. This would be another unbearably hot day in this city, not like in the islands where the heat is dry and the sea breeze brings a welcome relief all through the day. This was no longer a joke. How many days had it been since the last drop of rain? Thirteen, and still counting. Six-thirty in the morning and already unbearably sticky. Day after day, the same thing. That's not how London is meant to be. This city is designed for fog and wintry gray, the kind of scene you see in them old engravings in Dickens's books. And, Lord, it was becoming difficult to find anything new to say about the weather. How many more times I goin' hear the same thing from my neighbor, "Hot, ain't it. Must take you back to your country." And all the time, the same reply, "This *is* my country!"

Esther had been working in a call center throughout the summer, earning a little extra money for a sabbatical and cruise around the Caribbean. It meant working nights—at least that paid a little more—and so she and Tony saw little of each other, just an hour or so each morning as she prepared for bed and he got ready for work. At least they had the weekends, when Tony didn't have to go into the office, but soon, they would have a whole three months spending every moment together, making up for the time apart, and in a glorious, tropical setting, too, away from this stifling heat. Yes, the night shifts would be worth it.

It had been Tony's idea. She'd been getting more and more frustrated with her job as a teacher in an inner-city school. Tony was stressed out most of the time, struggling to claw his way up the corporate ladder in an engineering firm. And they'd come home to a constant niggling that never quite broke out into a fight. They sat down one evening, eight months back, and talked. They worked out that their relationship was important enough for them to make the sacrifice. Their work was not. So they'd agreed on the plan. Three months in the Caribbean. Three months' worth of planning and organizing when they got back (at least they could muster some little semblance of good sense between them). Then a big wedding to satisfy both sets of parents. And then spend another three months, if not longer, looking for work, followed by a lifetime paying off their debts. But it would be worth it.

Esther could hear the drone of the radio as she turned the key in the lock. Tony must be upstairs in the bathroom, probably shaving. She could imagine him, chin upturned, long, elegant fingers holding the razor, tentatively touching the blade to his skin. She loved to watch him shave, the jutting of his jaw, the bulge of his Adam's apple, the quick strokes through the white foam revealing the dark bluish sheen of his skin, the quick, precise flicks above his sexy full lips, the fluffy white towel wrapped around his middle . . .

As she ran up the stairs, she called out, "Hi, honey, I'm

back," unnecessarily, since her footsteps echoed loudly on the wooden boards. She pushed open the bathroom door, disappointed to see that he was almost dressed and just wiping away the last flecks of foam from his chin. Just a glimpse of his face in the mirror still made her weak even though it had been three years since they'd first met. He smiled at her, but the distracted look in his eyes told her that work was already on his mind.

Tony turned toward her and held his arms wide and, just as every day, she let herself be enfolded in his bear-hug as he kissed her cheek, the side of her neck, her lips, his strong hands fondling the curve of her behind, pulling her close, his strength, his potential for power over her making her skin tingle. He made to pull away, but before he could turn, Esther reached inside his unbuttoned shirt, sliding her hands around his waist, stroking the ridges of his spine with the soft pads of her fingers.

"Honey, what are you doing?" he muttered, burying his nose into her hair. "You know I've got to go."

"Why?"

"Work, money, meeting, Caribbean cruise."

Normally, the last two words would have made her back off, but it had been a long night and the air was so hot and sticky and sultry and she might not see him again until the next morning and it was three whole days until the weekend.

"Don't want no cruise. Get seasick. You can be late." She nibbled at his chest and then let her tongue dance toward his nipples.

"Can't. Important. No money, no wedding."

She took the dark swelling between her lips and let her top teeth rake across it. He winced, but didn't try to move away.

"Don't want no wedding. Hate wedding cake. . . ." She

was unbuckling his belt ". . . and marzipan . . ." and his fingers were under her T-shirt ". . . and that stupid bride and groom sitting on the top . . ." molding the flesh around her waist.

"I'll get fired. No mortgage payments, no house." He'd reached as far as her bra, slipping his fingers inside, flicking his thumbs against her hard nipple.

"We'll buy a tent, babe. Tony, please, please, please."

"No."

She trailed the back of her hand against his growing erection.

"Okay, it'll have to be quick."

"Ten minutes."

"Five."

"I'll take thirty seconds. Just fuck me now," she raised her skirt, "or you ain't getting any of this good stuff for . . . oh, for a whole week."

Esther wriggled against him, lifting her thigh high, resting the bend of her knee against his hip bone. God, make him hard enough, she prayed. There was no need. She could feel his growing erection pressing against her as she fumbled with his zipper, desperate to free him.

He left her breasts and reached under her skirt, pushing the fabric of her panties to one side, thrusting a finger inside to gauge her wetness, sliding it backward and forward as his lips sought for hers, and he bruised her mouth in his frantic hunger to probe her mouth with his tongue.

As soon as she freed him, he picked her up, the muscles of his strong arms rocklike. As if she were a feather, he walked her over to the basin and rested her buttocks against the cool ceramic. In less than a second, the hot smoothness of his cock was against the opening of her pussy, and without any further ado, he held her hips and pulled her down onto him, impaling her, forcing the breath from her body.

"Aaiiieee!" she screamed. "Oh God, Tony. Feels like it's been so long. I think I'm going to come right away. Can't hold it in."

"Lord, honey. You so tight, so fucking tight. Squeeze me. That's it. Oooh, baby!"

Esther held on to the rim of the sink as he pounded into her. She laughed as she heard the toothpaste, mug, deodorants, and brushes tumbling to the floor as he pounded against her, rattling the shelves. (I wonder how long they goin' be searching for the cotton buds that have rolled behind the sink stand. These young girls don't often think about cleaning behind things these days.)

She ran her palms along the broad expanse of his chest, looking down to the mass of tight curls that formed a triangle leading to the thick glistening cock that disappeared inside her and reemerged, strong, hard, demanding. She reached down and held her pussy lips open, widening them for him to reach deeper. Her breath was coming in short gasps. "Can't hold on, just can't . . . oh, oh, oh!"

He roughly pushed her T-shirt up, forcing her bra over the mound of her breasts, over her hard, long nipples. Round and round he moved his cock, making circles around the soft, swollen spot deep inside her. Esther squealed as he took her nipple into his mouth, biting softly, squeezing the other between his fingers, rolling it around like a fine cigar. All the sexual tension of the past week was building, rising from the tip of her reddened clitoris, soaring up past her breasts, swirling around her head, and shooting down into the depths of her womb.

"Honey, I'm going to come. Can't wait. Come with me." He grasped her breast, squeezing hard as he pounded her against the wall. Over and over, fast and hard, sweat dripping from his forehead, glistening against his muscled chest, cum shooting into her pussy as he found his release and thrust violently against the oh-so-sensitive spot that made her tense every muscle and gasp for breath. Her body seemed to shatter into a million sparkling jewels of ecstasy that she'd never be able to put together again.

He pulled out of her and looked down at himself. He laughed. "That must have been a world record, babe. I guess I better get changed."

As she lay on their big double bed, listening to the sound of the shower, Esther smiled to herself. What a waste this king-sized mattress was. How often did they get to use it? Five minutes later, Tony was kissing her good night, or good morning, or whatever. She returned his slow, seductive kiss wondering if she might not get him to take a day off. "See you later, honey." His voice was deep and husky like he smoked a hundred full-strength Gauloises a day. And there was that undercurrent of humor that made you think he was keeping a sexy, naughty secret, the sleepy, hooded eyes. Maybe he could be sick, take the day off, make *slow* love, in the bed. Then she remembered the cruise and gave up on the thought. If only sex was like eating too much chocolate and made you feel sick in the end! As she heard the door close behind him, she reached between her legs, stroking languidly, recalling the passion that had only just been sated and that his voice had stoked again.

Esther and Tony never argued. They were like the perfect couple. If you ask me, I don't believe people who say they don't argue. They're usually the ones who are hiding some dark, shameful secret, but the fact is, there was no dirty laundry between Tony and Esther. They liked each other, had the same values, shared the same humor, and made each other horny as hell. And don't think I don't understand what all *that* is about. I might be getting on a little bit, but I, too, did have my day. If you look back on the old photographs, you can see me in those little hot pants, booty shorts you would call them now, but I was a skinny little thing, not flaunting any parts of myself like Esther's friend Marion . . . Anyway, I was talking about Esther and Tony. They really were good together, made for each other in a way that made you wonder how, with all the hundreds of millions of people in the world, they ever had the good fortune to meet each other.

So I can't really explain why it was that the next Saturday morning, Esther stormed out of the house, slamming the door behind her. She got into her car, started the engine, and turned the nose of the Peugeot southward with no clear idea of where she was headed. You'll soon see what I mean about setting off into the world with no forward thinking. Trouble is where I said it would lead. Maybe she was alone in her car, headed who knows where because Tony hadn't told her, hadn't consulted with her. Not that he'd had much chance when she'd been already at work for forty minutes by the time he got home. Maybe she was just getting a little tired of money taking precedence over everything else in their lives. Maybe she'd just been thinking too much about a long, cozy Saturday lie-in, tea and croissants in bed, and a few hot, sweaty cuddles to follow. Whatever the reason, when she stormed out of the house, she'd been annoyed with Tony. Angry at his decision to go into the office on both of the two days they could otherwise spend together. Now you're already thinking that she was being a tiny bit unfair since Tony was working hard for the cruise, the wedding, the house, the debts. And I'd be tempted to agree with you. And so, in the end, did Esther. But by that time, she had managed to navigate her way on automatic pilot past the Whitton Road roundabout into Hanworth, and she was just minutes away from the start of the M3 motorway.

Hell, they'd had such a good time the weekend before and there was no reason why she should mope around alone at home. She shouldn't have taken it so badly. She should turn a negative into a positive: Instead of two days of lonely shopping, cooking, cleaning, and ironing, she should think of it as two days of complete and absolute freedom. The day was looking to be "yet another scorcher," the sky bright blue, the air already filled with exhaust fumes. Esther pulled over, folded back the roof, put the new N*E*R*D album in the CD player, and drove toward the motorway with her foot down, keeping one eye out for yellow speed cameras along the way.

The journey was longer than she remembered, but probably a little safer with no distraction other than the gloriously green and yellow fields, the odd stretch of vivid crimson poppies bursting out from the chalk rubble strewn along the roadside, the BMW filled with guys trying to chat her up at seventy miles an hour. Esther laughed happily, her mood having lifted considerably in the two-and-a-half hours it took to reach the outskirts of South-ampton. The sun was high in the sky now, and as the car slowed for the inevitable roadworks, Esther was already feeling hot and sticky. She hadn't stopped to change out of the cotton dress she'd worn to work the night before. She'd have to stop somewhere to freshen up. Maybe she should just book herself into a hotel. There was nothing to rush back for. She could call Tony, tell him that she'd be back on Monday. Maybe, she thought guiltily, that might even make him think a little more carefully before deciding to desert her on one of their precious weekends.

It was still relatively early morning by the time she parked in Southampton and looked around. Most of the people rushing past were, she could tell, locals on their way to do the Saturday round of shopping, lunching, and more shopping. Now that she was here, she wasn't exactly sure what to do. She followed the signs to the city's art gallery, not that that was her usual thing, but she assumed it would be cooler than standing like a lemon in the center of a crossroad. Esther shot through the gallery, almost pointless with no one to share it with, strolled through the park, and even headed down to the front where she watched big ships heading out of the port. She checked out a few of the many restaurants, but didn't like sitting on her own. She was hungry, but not hungry enough to risk being shunted to the lone table right by the entrance to the rest room.

She got back into the car and, before she had a chance to change her mind, set off for the marina they'd chanced upon last weekend. Her sense of direction was eerily accurate and her memory acute. There were only a couple of wrong turns before she found herself parking a short distance from the line of masts that punctuated the skyline. Esther walked along the dusty boards, looking once again downward, to her left. There he was, same coffee-colored skin, same finely honed physique, same paint-spattered shorts, filling in the outline of the name of the boat *Island Queen*. He turned at the sound of her steps and stood, staring straight at her until she was no more than four feet away. This time he was at eye level in a cradle strung over the side.

"Hey, city girl. You got lost again?"

She laughed. "You remembered!"

"Don't get too many strangers around this way. What you doing here? Thinking of buying one of these here boats?"

"If only! No, I was at a loose end. On my own. Looking for someone, maybe, to share lunch with me."

Now I don't agree with girls being forward, but I can sometimes see that there is no alternative. The girl was alone in the big city. And hungry. What was she supposed to do? He was the only person she came close to knowing and the restaurants and cafés would stop serving lunch soon. She couldn't do anything else but to come straight out with it. Besides, he was American. Or Canadian. Used to that kind of forwardness.

He grinned at her, put down the can of paint, and wiped his hands on an oily rag. He cocked his head to one side for a moment, checking her out.

"Give me one minute. I'll be with you."

He climbed over the side of the boat and disappeared into its dark interior. It was more like ten minutes before he reemerged, and Esther almost wished that she'd fled. Close up, in black shorts and a white cotton shirt, he was strikingly handsome, a little more formidable than she had expected. He was taller, too, than she'd thought; the bulk of the ship must have diminished his frame. Once again, she couldn't see his eyes, since he wore shades, but his lips were full, reminding her of Jay-Z or P. Diddy. He towered over her and Esther suddenly felt shy.

"Do you know where we can go around here?"

He didn't reply, but took her hand and led her along the

walkway, around to the gangplank that led to the yacht. She followed, picking her steps carefully, not wanting to trip and fall over the side.

There were two deck chairs set up with a makeshift table in between, covered with a checked cloth. He pointed in the direction of one of the chairs and disappeared down a hatch to reemerge minutes later with a bottle of chilled, sparkling wine and a couple of glasses. He handed her a glass and filled it, the foam spilling over so that she had to lick it from her hands. One more trip inside the boat and he carried a tray filled with cheese, ham, a baguette, potato salad, and ripe, red plum tomatoes.

"Oh, I didn't mean . . . this is your lunch . . . I can't let you . . ."

"No problem. Can't think of a better way to have lunch than with a pretty lady. By the way, I'm Gervais. They call me Gerry and that's cool with me."

"I'm sorry. Esther." Now Esther had been brought up right by her mother, so she extended her hand, almost as if she intended to say "howdee do." He took it and shook it quite formally.

"Pleased to meet you, Esther." He sat opposite her and reached for a plate. "Help yourself. And before you ask again, I'm from Rochester, New York State, by way of Paris, France."

Esther realized that she was starving and, forgetting her manners now, she piled her plate high, tucking in to the delicious tastes. He ate more slowly, watching her every move.

"So where does Paris come in?"

"Took some time out." Esther looked at him. She would guess that he must be around thirty-two-ish. A hint of frown lines puckered his forehead, but there was a youthful tautness to the shape of his chin, the curve of his neck. "Been working my way round the world on boats."

"Paris isn't by the sea."

"Guess I found that out. No, I got sidetracked for a while." She definitely wished that she could see his eyes. She sensed that there was a tale to be told, maybe one to do with a short-lived, torrid romance with a chic Parisienne, nights of lust-filled passion, a broken heart or two . . . she knew she should stop reading those sensual romances. She waited, but there was no suggestion of any explanations to follow and she was too polite to ask.

"So how did you end up in Southampton?"

"Look across. You can almost see the French coast from here. I used to look across that patch of water from the other side and wonder what was over here. Mild curiosity, I guess."

"So now you've found out, are you likely to stay?"

"Depends on whether I find anything to keep me here." He was looking straight at her. Something about the smile that tugged at the corner of his lips made her look away. She sipped at her drink, relaxing in the sudden stillness, in no hurry to break it. They ate in silence and he brought out fat, juicy black cherries which she bit into, letting the dark liquid spill down her chin. He reached out and wiped it away with one finger, licking the juice. Esther inhaled sharply, his touch like a naked flame.

He stood and took her plate. "Gotta get back to work."

She made an attempt to stand, but he stopped her. "No, don't move. You look so comfortable there. You're welcome to stay. I'll be done in an hour or so."

That's what you might call an open-ended invitation. What did the ". . . done in an hour or so" mean? Did he have some kind of plan? Was he inviting her to go some-where with him once he was done? Did he want her to wait? Your guess would be as good as hers was, but Esther remembered that she'd had no sleep at all, that she'd drunk half a glass of wine, that she was in no fit state to drive, and that, well yes, she was having a good time. She turned and watched as he strode with an elegant grace across the deck and stripped down to his shorts. She was tempted to reach out and run one finger along the curve of his spine.

She watched as he disappeared over the side of the boat; then like a sunflower turned toward the sun, within mo-ments she was fast asleep.

Now what happened next might surprise you. It cer-tainly surprised Esther. Before I tell you, you need to understand what kind of girl Esther is. She was raised by parents who were fearful of what life held for a young black girl in an England that turned its face against the likes of her. So the routine was school, homework, piano practice, and more homework during the week; Saturday school; and church twice on Sunday. Tony was her first and only real love. She thanked God that she'd found him and certainly wasn't looking for anything more.

So when Gerry kissed her, rousing her from her sleep, it must have been all the tales of Sleeping Beauty that made her respond in the way she did. I'm not saying it's wrong to give your girl children fairy tales to read, but look at what happened. Feeling all relaxed and drowsy and warm and cozy, she reached for him, touching the newness of his locked hair, running her fingers through the wiry curls, drawing him nearer until he was almost lying across her, his tongue searching her mouth, wrestling with hers for superiority. As soon as he came up for air, she pulled him back for more. It wasn't that, in her sleepy stupor, she mistook him for Tony. Oh no, she knew full well and relished the newness, the unfamiliarity of his scent, the unique feel of his touch as he fumbled for the buttons of her dress. By now, Tony would have had her naked, he knew her so well. But Esther had to wriggle into the right position for Gerry to navigate the buttons, and impatient with his ineptitude, she pushed his hands aside and undid them herself. She lifted herself up, her lips still glued to his, not wanting to break the spell, and pushed the sleeves from her shoulders. She was glad that, today, she hadn't worn a bra. She couldn't see him trying to manipulate the clasp on that.

He pulled away from her then and looked down at the full globes of her breasts, her dark nipples blossoming in the heat. He shook his head slowly from side to side.

"Mmm, mmm, mmm," he crooned. "I been watching you, pretty lady. You sure are somethin' else."

Esther leaned back on her elbows, presenting her breasts to him like a sacrificial offering. He held himself back for a moment, his arms dangling by his side as if he didn't know what to do. He licked his lips. She could see that they were dry and slightly cracked. She reached up and touched his bottom lip with one finger, brushing backward and forward until he opened his mouth and sucked it in. He held on to her wrist then and kissed her palm, tickling the middle with his pointed tongue. A snakelike current wriggled straight from his tongue, down to her nipples. She gasped and he watched, smiling as her nipples hardened. He reached for her then, his long fingers tentatively lifted her breasts, cupping them as he brought his lips closer. Esther held her breath as he sucked one swollen, sensitive nipple into his mouth, nibbling at it with sharp teeth. He squeezed her breasts together so that he could lick from one nipple to the other, back and forth, and he hummed like he was eating some delicious, rare, tropical fruit.

He lifted his head and Esther pulled away from him for a moment. She looked around furtively, remembering for the first time that they were out in the open and even though the marina was almost empty, there was no knowing when someone might return.

He read her mind. "Ain't nobody round here, cupcake." He waved his hand in the general direction of the sea. "On a day like today, nobody goin' come back before nightfall."

Esther was still skeptical, but she couldn't stop herself from reaching toward him and lifting the dark glasses that he still wore. She nearly dropped them back in place. His pupils were dilated, his expression so intense that it was like the whole surface of her skin prickled with static electricity. She wiped the sweat from her brow with the back of her hand. Her hair was damp, clinging to her neck, and she lifted it away. He took that as his cue to stand, take her by the hand, and pull her toward the cool depths of the boat. The chill was sharp compared to the sweltering heat on deck and Esther felt goosepimples standing up all down her arm. It was hard to see anything in the gloom, but his steps were confident as he led her to a tiny cabin paneled in dark wood. She could make out a narrow bunk and little else in the confined quarters.

He pushed her back against the wood, his arms bent at the elbows, palms pressed against the door, body leaning into hers. He kissed her again and she wriggled against him, this time allowing herself the luxury of discovering his taste, the feel of him, running her tongue against his teeth, licking the swollen pillows that were his lips. Her body ached for him. She wondered at how he was content to wait, seeming to be aroused simply by the sensation of her body touching his.

"You sure taste good, sugarbabe." His fingers roamed to her breasts and he caressed and fondled, squeezed and probed, intermittently placing a kiss in the cleft between. Esther clenched her teeth, feeling the deep pleasure that tugged at her womb, knowing that if he didn't do something, anything soon, she might just erupt. That's when he picked her up in arms that were surprisingly strong, his muscles as hard as twisted cords of metal. He dropped her onto the bunk and climbed in beside her, the confined space meaning that there wasn't a hairbreadth of space separating them.

Gerry leaned up on one elbow, his other hand idly tracing circles around her abdomen.

"So, pretty Esther. Tell me what you want."

This was a new one to her. Was this some kind of game? Esther thought she'd made it pretty obvious what she wanted. Did he want a contract signed in blood? He was staring at her as if he was trying to pierce through the darkness. He traced a line from her top lip, down across her bottom lip, and then up along the line of her jaw, following each touch with a gentle kiss.

"Um, well . . . I . . . um . . ."

"If we're gonna do this, then I need to get it right. I'm gonna want you to come back for more. I don't know what you enjoy. Tell me."

"Well, nobody's ever . . ."

His tongue was on her lip as she spoke, the sensation making her thoughts unclear. She wanted to tell him that it was impossible to concentrate while he was doing that to her.

"You like it when I kiss you here?" The heat from his hand was intense as he guided her breast toward his lips. Esther shivered, not from cold.

"Ahhh, yesss. Oh, yes."

"Good. I love the taste of your skin. The way you wriggle when you feel my lips on you. God, that turns me on." It wasn't intentional, but she wriggled again.

"Oooeee, honeybabe. That's it. I'm so horny. Now how about if I touch you here." A breath of touch circled her navel, a part of her body that she'd never known could produce such sharp sensation. He bent his head lower and blew warm air into the indentation. Esther jumped as if he'd touched her with ice. She could hear the smile in his voice. "You don't need to answer that one." He returned to her breasts, allowing her the space to come back down to earth and then, as soon as she thought she might be able to breathe again, he bent and touched his tongue to her belly button. She shrank away from him, unable to deal with the strength of the feeling.

"You see, I'm finding out all about you. Bet you didn't know I could do that to you!" His fingers were playing a tune up and down her spine now, using both the black and white keys, some kind of major piano concerto in D. The sensitivity of every inch of her skin was so acute that she wanted to beg him to stop, but she was scared that he might. "What about your pussy? Is it getting wet? Do you like having your pussy sucked? Want me to eat you out?" Now, what kind of a question was that?

His fingers delved into her panties, teasing the wiry pubic hairs and, like an arrow, his middle one shot down, over, past her clitoris, straight to the opening of her vagina. Esther's head fell back and she screamed loud as he licked her neck and plunged two fingers inside her. Her hips danced a figure eight as she struggled to feel his touch deeper, higher inside her. His thumb flickered over her clitoris, and the sensation was so fiery that she wanted to weep, to cry out, to shout, to beg him to keep doing what he was doing forever and ever, never stopping, even if she might plead with him.

And all the time, he was watching her keenly. Her eyes were so used to the darkness now that she could see the glint as his gaze was transfixed to her face. He pushed her legs wider and pulled his finger out of her pussy. Oh God Almighty, he was leaning in, his chin tickling the mass of crinkly hair. Every nerve ending in her body was on hold as he moved in slow motion toward the focus of all her desire.

"Tell me if you want me to stop, Esther. You might not like what I'm going to do."

"Don't you dare stop. Oh Lord. I might just kill you if you stop."

"You liking this?"

"Oh, yes, yes!"

He knelt between her legs, cupping her ass as her knees flopped apart. He licked, sucked, stroked, drank, supped, teased, spreading his broad tongue, bathing her in his fiery heat as he licked from her opening, right up to her clitoris, over and over, endlessly hungry, lapping away until she bucked under him and clutched his head, forcing his lips and tongue against her pulsating clitoris. She sighed loud and long as she came, her clitoris on fire, spreading concentric circles of ecstasy throughout her body.

He waited for a few seconds. "Now I know what you like, babe. We're going to need a bit of practice to get it perfectly right."

"Oh god," Esther moaned. "How much more perfect do you think it can get?"

"Much, much more." He kissed her chin and lay back, waiting. For what, she wasn't sure. In the slightly awkward silence, Esther had time to wonder how on earth she'd got herself here. Gerry was a stranger. All he'd had to do was give her food, look at her, kiss her, touch her, and here she was, in his arms. She wanted to feel guilty, but each time she acknowledged the circles that his fingers traced on the satiny skin of her inner thigh, she just wanted to smile and sink into the softness of his embrace. She was drifting, hypnotized by his touch when he broke the spell.

"My turn."

"Huh?" She was sleepy, sated, unable to string more than one word together.

"My turn to tell you exactly what I like to do."

In an instant, Esther was wide awake, her eyes blinking fast. There was a determination in his tone that scared her. What the hell did she know about him, after all? He might be some kind of pervert. Instinctively, her eyes flittered to where she knew the door must be, trying to get her bearings.

He kneeled up, crotch level with her eyeline.

"I don't want you to be scared." Was he reading her mind? What he was doing was beginning to terrify her. "I want you to unzip me. I want you to look at me."

All of a sudden, Esther was happy to comply. She reached for the zip in his shorts and tugged downward. She could hardly see the expression on his face, but knew from the sudden twitch of his cock that he was excited. She reached in, down into his boxers, and pulled him free. His organ shot out, hard, forceful, and Esther wondered what monster she'd released from the cage.

"Ooh, babe. I want to feel those tits around me." He pushed her breasts together, hard, wrapping them around his rigid tool. She watched in tense astonishment as he thrust the rippling skin of his prick up, rubbing against her flesh. As the bulbous head emerged, she heard his gasp. Over and over, back and forth, the beads of cum lubricating her skin. She heard his long sigh "aaaahh" as he finally pulled away. The sight of him getting ever harder excited her, too, there was no denying it.

"I can't do everything I want," he gasped. "You got me too excited. Now I just want to feel that hot, tight pussy wrapped around my cock. You ready, sugar?"

He was groping for her opening, clutching her ass cheeks, spreading her wide like she was some sacred offering on the altar of his manhood. His prick halted at the entrance, teasing her, making her wetter and more desperate as she attempted to suck him into her welcoming folds. He held himself high, resisting the thrust of her hips, the pull of her hands clawing against his hips.

He took himself in hand, unconsciously rubbing at his hard-on, guiding it toward her like a missile.

"You sure you're ready? I'm sorry, honeybabe, but I've been told that I'm rather large. I might hurt you."

Why, oh why had he said that? He'd set all her juices flowing again. Esther could feel a flood gushing from her as the walls of her pussy relaxed, releasing the gate, opening for him.

"Oh, yes! I'm ready. Take me."

He held himself steady for a moment in which she thought she might come just from the thought of that massive cock. She wrapped her legs around his hips and lifted her bottom from the bunk, poised, ready. He reached behind her then, holding her still, and with one enormous effort he thrust into her, forcing himself beyond the point that she believed possible. He was right. She *couldn't believe* the size of him. He did hurt, but the pain was one that she wanted to relive, would give anything to feel again. She dug her fingernails into his buttocks and felt him wince, the movement reverberating inside her.

"This good enough for you, babe? You want more?"

"Ooh, yes. Give me more. More. More. God, you . . . are . . . so huge . . . Don't know if I can take it . . . but don't stop . . . Please don't stop."

Each word was punctuated by the rhythmic pounding of his prick into her vagina, each thrust rubbing against her clit, every motion bringing her to the edge of the abyss that she was about to tumble into at any moment . . . All it needed was just one more . . . one more . . .

He grabbed at her hair, tugging hard as he forced himself ever deeper, farther, until she knew that she would faint, maybe die, certain that this was the best, the only, the one and only fucking great big dick she ever wanted to feel inside her again. He was filling her up, satisfying every need, every sensation her hot, wet, gushing pussy had ever desired. He pulled out to the edge of her desire and, with one, long, delicious thrust, he buried himself to the hilt, pushing, pushing harder, farther until he braced himself against the wood of the bunk, determined to punish her, take every last bit of sweetness that she had to offer. He came, a flood gushing inside her, and Esther gave in to his every demand, a pool of honey melting inside her, enveloping him in its hot, liquid heat.

I'd like to tell you that it was the gentle drawl of his American accent that attracted her. Or the Gallic charm he'd learned during his sojourn in Paris. But that wasn't it. Sure, she was impressed by his worldliness, the tales of his adventures in exotic landmarks across the world, the near-misses, the illegal encounters, the brushes with debauchery. But in the end, that wasn't it. I know you've all heard the mantra about size not mattering. You know, all that shit about it's not the size of the oars, but how you row the boat, when all the time, we girls know that size is, in fact, all important. If they've only got tiny oars, then let them embark on a solo voyage. So, I know you're all wanting me to tell you that Esther had this one earth-shattering encounter that would last her a lifetime, and then she went back to the security of a loving relationship with the one-and-only Tony. Well, I'm sorry to disappoint you, but it wasn't like that at all. Sure, she went back to Tony, explaining that she'd needed to get away, had driven to Southampton, had spent a day sightseeing, and then drove back as the sun set. Sure, all of that was true, but she'd left out the earth-shattering, life-changing experience in the middle. And it was without a trace of guilt that she had cheated on Tony.

She knew that Gerry had a woman too. He'd left her behind in Paris, but that didn't mean he wasn't committed. He described her with a warmth that evoked a twinge of jealousy. From Senegal originally. Tall, nearly his match. Statuesque with a regal bearing. Esther found herself standing taller, pulling herself up until her eyes were level with his chin. He showed her a photograph. Hair braided in intricate patterns, complementing her sculptured profile. Esther touched her own relaxed locks then, pushing them back from her face. There was no chance that either of them would get *involved*. He had his woman. She had her man. Esther told him about the plans and he showed a lively interest in the cruise. "You never know. We might meet up. Who knows where the winds will blow me next?"

Incredible sex was what they shared as he told her what he wanted and showed her what she needed. Esther hungrily looked forward to each weekend that Tony would spend in the office, earning money for the cruise that was in the bush while she had a real, live, active lover in the hand.

Time after time, she sped along the motorway, wishing the dull B-roads away, no longer hesitating at each crossroad, each junction, knowing the route like the map was engraved in some primordial memory.

It might just have been coincidence that placed Esther there, on the boat, at the moment when the call came. I don't know. I'm more cynical than her, being several years older. Looking back, Esther would tell herself that it was the gods' retribution for that summer of sexual bliss. Whatever the reason, she was there, wrapped in his thick Aran sweater, loaned to take the edge off the chill that he'd expected but she, being a city girl, had overlooked. They'd been out on the water, not far enough to reach any point of land, but just enough to let her take the wheel and steer past the buoys. She'd now spent long enough with him for him to teach her the etiquette of the sea, and although she'd panicked the first time he'd swung below deck, leaving her at the helm, she was now experienced enough to relax her grip on the wheel.

So he'd just maneuvered them into the marina when the phone shrilled. He raised it to his ear with an easy nonchalance.

"Hey."

Esther turned away, wondering if it would be the woman in the Parisian flat, but he took her hand and pulled her toward him. He nuzzled the tender spot behind her ear, the motion of his lips arousing her as he spoke against her neck.

"Yeah, man." And then he pulled away, his eyes clouding over. "Shit! Not today. You know I'm busy. No, it's important; can't you make it tomorrow? I ain't got no cash guy. Well, if you can't wait, then I'm going to have to forget the deal. I'm sorry, too, man."

He ended the call and moved away from her, lost in thought, leaning over the rail. She watched the way he pulled at the dry skin on his lower lip. She walked over to him and put a hand on his shoulder. "What's wrong, honey?"

"Hey, nothing. Nothing at all."

She knew he was hiding something, protecting her from whatever was troubling him. But, suddenly, he looked so vulnerable, so childlike, that she had to know.

"Okay," he started after a great deal of encouragement from her. "I'd negotiated a great deal on some spare parts for the boat. The owner's been waiting for a while. The delivery was arranged for Monday and I'd agreed to pay cash. Now the guy's saying that he needs to deliver today. The banks aren't open. The cash is being transferred from my account in Paris. Nothing I can do about it."

Esther was no gullible fool. She wasn't going to be taken in by any kind of scam.

"So don't you have a credit card or a bank card? Can't you get money from a cash machine?"

"Honey, I'm an African-American with dreads who's been living in Paris. What do you think the chances are of me being able to open an account with the local high-street bank? Anyway, don't you worry your pretty little head about it. This ain't the end of the world, you know."

But Esther knew that thoughts of this once-in-a-lifetime deal shadowed every second of the rest of the afternoon. She figured that he was examining all the possibilities, exploring every avenue.

The answer had been obvious all along but she'd kept it in reserve. In the end she wanted so much for him to be preoccupied only by her that she suggested it.

"Look, Gerry. We can drive into Southampton. I can get money out from a cash machine. You can pay me back the next time we see each other." The warning bells rang even as she spoke, but she couldn't stop herself. She so wanted the carefree, passion-filled Gerry who'd awoken her to a million new pleasures in the dying weeks of that hot summer.

"No, sugar. I couldn't let you. Don't worry. I'll figure out a way."

Esther thought guiltily of the joint savings sitting in that musty old bank vault. It could be put to good use. She insisted. He protested. She insisted some more and he accepted. Gratefully.

They got into her car. Gerry had never learned to drive. What was the use when his long legs could carry him to the nearest train station or boatyard? Esther always felt powerful at the wheel, and he made her feel even more so. She was gracious in her generosity as she handed over the cash that he needed. He smiled and kissed her warmly, his features relaxing into their habitual, confident nonchalance.

"Thanks, babe. I'll give it back to you."

I bet you want me to tell you that Esther never saw Gerry or the money again. And, sure, I'd love to be able to say that because in Esther's place, I wouldn't have trusted no man, no matter how cute he might have been (or how big his dick!). But the fact is that, three days later, a registered envelope arrived at her office that she had to sign for. She opened it and there were thirty crisp, fresh-smelling twenty-dollar bills. Now even Esther wouldn't have been able to pretend that she hadn't had the odd moment of panic when she'd thought about how rashly she'd handed over Tony's and her hard-earned savings, not even knowing Gerry's last name or where to find him, other than the marina. She took an early lunch and paid the money into the bank as fast as she could.

So the next time Tony was away, spending a whole four days at a conference in Leeds, who's to say that I wouldn't have done the same thing that Esther did. To tell the truth, it's hard for me to know. I've never met anyone who has turned me on the way that Gerry did Esther. I'm even beginning to wonder if she didn't exaggerate more than a little. But whatever the truth of his size, Gerry had talked many a time about coming to London on business, to suss out what deals there were to be made. So, since Tony was going to be away and she'd be all alone in that rickety old house that creaked and wheezed all through the night, you couldn't blame Esther for getting on the phone, calling his cell phone, listening to the gulls screeching in the background of the marina, and inviting him to stay. She could almost hear the wheels turning in his brain, the gears shifting.

"Sure thing, honey. Can't wait to see you."

She arranged to pick him up at the station, her heart treacherously counting the hours until Tony picked up his bag and walked out of the house, kissing her a tender good-bye. Twenty minutes later—and I know you're going to be hoping that she'll be punished for this—she was in her car driving to Waterloo station. I'm a little shocked myself that, no sooner had she ushered one lover out the door than she was welcoming another one in. Well, we've explored the reasons why, and whether you approve or not, the fact is that the train was only delayed by twenty-five minutes, and within two hours, Esther and Gerry were stark naked, wrapped in each other's arms, his oversized cock nestling in the welcoming folds of Esther's eager pussy, not in the warmth of the duvet that covered the king-sized bed, but perched against the thankfully cooled rings of the gas cooker, and then crouched over the coffee table, almost drowning under the hot shower, groping their way across the wooden floorboards toward the bedroom. Gerry had reached about lesson thirty-seven in the sexual manual that he was developing just for her, and as they neared the edge of the bed, his cock still teasing her pussy lips, he covered her hands with his, forcing them against her breasts, making her rub her own nipples. She tried to turn her face toward him, but he held himself away.

"Your turn now, baby. You can do it. It's up to you."

He forced her fingers, against her will, down to her pussy and pushed her legs apart with his knees. He used his own rhythm to guide her hands, and as she took over, enflamed by the pleasure that radiated from her clitoris, he left her and moved away, settling himself to watch. Esther had come so many times, her flesh bruised and swollen, that she hardly cared where the last orgasm of the night came from. She knew he was watching and the idea excited her. She reached behind and inserted a finger into her pussy opening. And as she writhed against it, swallowing it up to the knuckle, she pushed another finger, and then another until they churned in the wetness, stirring, inciting, building the pleasure. This time, it was a slow burn, the sweetness rolling in gentle caressing waves until her movements accelerated, faster and faster, her breath catching in her throat when she turned and saw the fire in his eyes. As he reached for his cock, she subsided into a warm, relaxed, silky, satisfying orgasm.

They used the bed for sleeping, his body spooned around hers, his warm fingers caressing her breasts until she disappeared into a deep, soothing sleep.

So, reader, beware. Close these pages now if you don't want to hear what happened. Or if you're the type of person to say in that self-satisfied tone, "I knew it all along." At least I'm not that arrogant.

Well, by the time Esther awoke from the most contented sleep for weeks, sunlight was streaming through the open curtains. They hadn't had the time to think of closing them the night before. She squinted her eyes and looked at the bedside clock, convinced that it must be upside down. Ten-thirty? That just wasn't possible. She never slept that late. But she was contented. This was the first time that she and Gerry had had the opportunity to spend a whole night together. She stretched, the first stirrings of desire invading her body. She reached across the expanse of the big bed, searching for him. She smiled when he wasn't there, glancing toward the open door and the bathroom, wondering if she'd find him shaving.

Esther crawled out of the bed, retrieved her dressing gown from the tangle of clothes across the chair, and slipped into it, not bothering to tie the belt. As she walked out of the room, the silence was ominous, but she forced that thought to one side. She pushed open the bathroom door. No one there. She took the stairs slowly, imagining him standing at the bottom, glimpsing her naked flesh as she placed one foot in front of the other. Empty kitchen. Quiet study. Silent living room. Esther retraced her steps, taking each room a little faster now. No note, not a sign of him. And in the study, no trace of Tony's laptop. She prayed that he'd taken it with him, but was sure that he hadn't. She ran up the stairs. She hadn't allowed herself to see it before: the open jewelry box. Diamond studs, the pearls her parents had given as a twenty-first birthday present, Tony's gold cufflinks and Rolex watch saved for special occasions. She looked around for her bag, open by the bed. Check book and credit cards all gone. The cash she'd taken from the bank intending to take him to her favorite restaurant. Personal organizer. Cell phone. Everything that said who she was. He'd stolen her identity.

Esther sat on the side of the bed, unconsciously pulling up the duvet, obliterating the outline of his form embedded in the mattress. Her eyes were wide and staring. She imagined herself turning up at the marina, but knew that the berth would be empty. He had, after all, warned her that he didn't stay in any one place too long. She looked around. There was no physical sign of the devastation that he'd caused, but Esther looked at the photograph of Tony that she'd forgotten to put away the night before. How the hell was she going to explain to him?

Now, I told you that I wasn't going to turn all sanctimonious and say, "I told you so." But I just can't resist it. You remember what I told you at the beginning of this tale? If only that group had had a little foresight. If only they'd gone prepared!

## About the Author

Born in Manchester of Guyanese descent, Michaela Greenidge's previous writing "has stretched as far as class reports with which I've struggled to be creative." She has written a number of erotic stories under different names for publication on the Internet. Michaela now lives in Leeds and teaches in a secondary school. She is forty-six, married with three children, and fits her writing in "sometime between midnight and dawn."

# New Year

## Zamo Mkhwanazi

It was a horrible New Year's party, which was pretty disappointing considering that they were on a beautiful island, the alcohol was free, and almost everyone was young and attractive. But it's hard to have a good time when something as significant as a change of year happens and there is no one you love in the same room. Of course in the objective sense there was no reason to be bored. There was every reason to laugh and flirt and talk about intelligent, interesting things. These were not tourists with Danielle Steele holiday paperbacks. These were travelers, real ones whose idea of roughing it was not Turkey. They drank the local water and had survived countless malaria attacks between them. They had chosen to dedicate the past few months of their lives to Africa. The beast of continents. The clinging, cloying mother whose fever never breaks.

And these travelers were notoriously interesting people. Please understand they were not hippies gone overboard. They were not the kind of people who went to India and suddenly turned into saddhus, renouncing their families and worldly possessions for a fake identity. They did not listen exclusively to "world music,' but to intellectual hip-hop, complex electronic, evocative tribal, and everything else they considered worthy of their educated ears. To be drunk and bored at the same time is a sin too unbearable even to the sinner. To be stoned and bored is a far more acceptable journey to stagnation.

So he went outside, selfishly not inviting anyone else for a hash smoke. Hell, everybody had their own anyway. Besides, what's this supposedly companionable obligation that people feel about joints? This pretense that this most loved recreational activity bore any relevance or connection with the much-touted Rastafarian philosophy of oneness and sharing between I and I was quite outdated, he decided. Anyway, these travelers, for all the street children they had fed and salvation armies they had volunteered for, were the most individualistic people in the world. Good for them that most of them could admit that they took on these activities to give deeper meaning to their own lives at least.

He had just finished rolling the blunt when he heard the grainy, sloshing sound of footsteps on the beach. Childish resentment made him cup his hand around the white shaft of the joint. But the slosher kept walking by, and in the absolute darkness of shore he could hardly make out the figure even though it only passed a few feet from him. A local fisherman, he concluded and suddenly *did* want to share the joint with him. He took a faulting step toward the figure walking away and his sandaled feet met with painful rock. In the haze of his pain he was certain that only a fisherman could walk with such confidence in this darkness. Deciding that the fisherman probably wouldn't speak a word of English and thus would not be much company when it was too dark even for hand gestures, he lit the joint.

He settled himself on the soft sand and immediately

felt warm, salty moisture absorb into his pants. He was very pleased that he had stopped wearing underwear ages ago and that his pants were of thin summer fabric. He opened his knees a little wider, letting the soft cotton cup his cock over the melting sand of the Indian Ocean. Inhaling deeply, he exposed his neck to the cooler breeze of the moonless night. And a thousand mosquitoes, he chuckled, his mood brightening with a secret arrogance. He liked the fact that he'd just ditched a party of people of whom he thought quite a lot, as if they were just a bunch of losers in comparison to him.

A splash and sudden glow in the water turned his head left. A night swimmer as well, he was pleasantly surprised. Most of the locals seemed to think that night swimming was some form of demonic Western habit. He was growing more and more impressed with his anonymous companion. He watched the phosphorescent lights blink on and off under the increasingly illuminated body. First, the long, graceful strokes, then the smoothly curving body made him aware that his "fisherman" was no man of any sort whatsoever. He was equally sure that the swimmer had not seen him and the darkness of her shimmering skin told him that she was a local woman. Impressive indeed. The local women were even warier of the sea than the men and most never came out after a certain hour. A dark horse, as it were. And then he felt a stab of middle-class guilt at comparing a woman to a horse. Was there any hope for this evening?

Resolving not to be a peeping tom, he took one last look to make sure he hadn't been mistaken and was rewarded by uncurling pubes trailing a squatting, froglike stroke. In a self-defeating moment, his penis unfurled, hardening against his relatively cold stomach and slowly shriveled back in unpleasant shock. He picked up his free drink and still puffing on the joint, which he wanted to share more than ever, walked in the opposite direction. He had somehow managed to leave his sense of humor with the night swimmer.

"Come, on," he thought, "plenty of dudes get it easy enough with the local women. You don't like traveler romances anyway, what are you moping about." Reprimanding himself when he was feeling a bit down was an incurable habit, which had the unfailing effect of worsening his mood. It also had zero effect on tempering his curiosity about the night swimmer. He felt around for rocks and large stones. Finding none, he settled himself, finished the joint, and immediately rolled another, hoping to revive his mood. It was like his brother said, "Sometimes your brain is like a computer with a virus. This window keeps opening up no matter how often you close or delete it. So the best thing to do is to shut down the whole system for a while."

He was glad he'd gotten a large glass of whiskey and that it was still pretty full. Deciding it couldn't be all that sleazy, he tried to turn his thoughts to a fantasy about one of the local women he'd seen hanging about the hostel. She was more than a little attractive, the sort of island girl of his dreams. Mocha skin with a small face dominated by sensual African features. But the reality was that more than traveler romances, he hated European men who preyed on the simple sensibilities of exotic third-world girls, dazzled by the glamor of sleeping with a white man and the futile hope of perhaps marrying one and escaping their poverty-stricken lot.

He was often faced with the dilemma of celibacy while traveling. Sometimes he gave in if he really thought enough of a fellow traveler, or if he believed that a local woman completely understood that it was just a passing thing and he felt her sufficiently attracted to him, not just bored with the local meat.

The process of shutting down the computer was turning out to be a rather enjoyable one. He indulged in a fantasy where he had a beautiful, super-cool girlfriend with whom he could travel without getting annoyed. They would have hot, sweaty sex in tents, get rocked to orgasm by the rhythm of long-distance trains. They would occasionally splurge on a cheap motel instead of dorm beds, and they would definitely skinny-dip in phosphorous-bedded oceans.

"Mark?"

He nearly tipped his drink over, so completely had he disassociated his imagination from its muse.

"Julie?" he responded incredulously. This was the Brixton girl who occupied the bunk above his in the dorm. The first serious, black female traveler he had ever met.

"Were you just . . ." The girl was dripping. There could be no mistake. "Did you enjoy your swim then?"

"Yeah," she said uncomfortably. "I didn't see you there."

"I wasn't here, I was a bit closer to your spot but I moved when you . . . um . . . started swimming."

He couldn't help hearing guilt in his own voice. But Julie seemed to lose interest and settled herself next to him, nicking the joint straight out of his hand.

"Happy New Year," she chorused, and he realized that she was quite smashed. Without thinking he put his hand on her neck and pulled her toward him.

"You shouldn't swim when you're drunk," he said into her mouth before putting his over it. As he had expected, she tasted of booze and smoke. And of salt and sand and the night. He licked the inside of her mouth until she retaliated with her own tongue, firm and slippery.

"Everyone's at the party," she commented.

They discovered that she did actually have a flashlight but couldn't quite explain or remember why she had neglected to use it earlier, which made them both laugh.

They weren't actually too far from the thatched huts that served as their dormitory. They climbed into his bed and lay still. Neither of them spoke. They were sweating and they didn't mind.

"So when did you start liking me?" he asked by way of conversation.

"What makes you think I like you?"

He couldn't quite think of a response, never mind what on earth had possessed him to say such a stupid thing. He put his hand under her T-shirt and squeezed the excess flesh around her middle. She curved her knee behind his buttocks and pulled his pelvis closer. He liked kissing her, he thought, and she was so warm.

He couldn't feel her anymore. He did not know how long he had simply lain there before he remembered that he was in the process of getting laid. The last few sips of the whiskey had taken effect, and with the fuzziness of too much marijuana in his system, his head was spinning. He had to stand up, and that's when he noticed her nudity. He assumed that he had undressed her at some stage but had failed to notice the voluptuous sensuality of her curving body. But he couldn't make himself concentrate on it.

"You got condoms?" she murmured lazily.

"Um . . . ah . . . no," he replied, which was true.

"Nor do I," she said a bit more soberly. "Well?"

He knew what that "Well?" meant. It was his line. That "Well?" which was an orange light. It was a "You shouldn't really but go ahead," sort of "Well?" He hated condoms and had managed, in his ten-year sexual career, to use them very rarely, since he tended toward monogamy and long relationships. He leaned down to rub her beautifully rounded brown stomach and felt another wave of dizziness. He needed to walk the alcohol out of him.

"Well, wanna go for a walk?" he improvised.

"No, not really."

He could hear the disappointment in her voice and knew she hoped that he thought she was disappointed by the lack of condoms, not because he was unwilling to indulge in unsafe sex. Like all those who did, she did not want those who didn't to know about it. To think her irresponsible and somewhat sinister and dangerous to others. She was putting on her clothes and each part covered became a sweet, taunting memory. He kissed her deeply for as long as he could keep his head from swimming.

"I think I'll go back to the party," he said helplessly. Somehow he couldn't bring himself to tell her that whiskey was currently proving stronger than her charms.

On a turning stomach he took in deep draughts of insect-bitten air. He stopped paying attention to the rocks that again and again smacked his fragilely shod feet. Shuffling through sand and water, he did not want to go back to the party but found himself in the tiny restaurant. The drunkenness levels had climbed, inhibitions had tumbled, and boredom was sulking in the corner. He evaded a fluorescent cocktail, ducked a weaving joint, and landed smack in the middle of a line of coke. Powder shoved its way up his nostrils and bombarded his brain with welcome clarity. He backed himself into a corner sending a halfhearted nod in the direction of boredom whose mus-

cles seemed to have gone too flabby to grab hold of him
for a second round. The coke-defined pieces fell abruptly
into place and once more the sharp edge of horniness nee-
dled his loins. Sharper still was the addictive thistle of a
coke yearning. A drink occupied and distracted the craving for a few more minutes before reminding him that
alcohol was the original sin and had scant room for pris-
oners. The music was shocking Portuguese renditions
of terrible, sentimental, American pop. Nonetheless, he
geared his limbs up for relative synchrony and minimal
rhythm. Dorkily enough, he found himself pouring out
the English lyrics of detested love songs from a far-flung,
best-ignored window of his unintentional memory. In the
midst of it he contracted a band of sodden accomplices
and the cheesiness commenced.

His coked-up drunken head proved exceptionally
suited to Celine Dion, Mariah Carey, Backstreet Boys,
and a plethora of other monstrosities. With each line
(seemingly there was an endless supply heretofore un-
broken out) embarrassment slunk closer to boredom and
eventually resigned itself into a broken down seat next to
him. The pair was said to have been sighted crawling out,
paralytic without inebriation, tails between each other's
legs.

What he didn't quite manage to escape were the jaws
of exhaustion. The lines were having a shorter- and
shorter-term effect and once more the alcohol was taking
the throne. A grass joint did it finally and he found himself dancing asleep. Mechanical swaying threatened a
group of cocktails on a waiter's tray and the collective
panicked objections were the cue to make his excuses.

"Awright, I'm topped. Best be going before I do something life-threatening like sneezing on the coke, or something. Cheerio amigos. So long and a Happy New Year to you all . . ." he called out in sonorous tones. The secret arrogance came back with a dizzying rush. Now that is the way to leave a party, he thought, and then walked into a largish rock that he really shouldn't have missed since the darkness was abating. Which was another thing he noted with surprise. He had actually been having a goofy good time for nearly the entire evening. The fashionably boring New Year's celebration had shed its pretentious skin and come out as a beautiful song and dance.

The sight of fishermen on shore, already preparing the boats and lines, reminded him sharply of the last "fisherman" he'd seen. The question mark hung over his head. Sure Julie was pretty hot, and in spite of his exhaustion, he knew that if the room just kept still he would be more than able to finish what they had started earlier. God, the booze had really done him in this time. And in vein with the entertainment he had chosen for the night, he had a corny thought, *well, lots of other fishermen in the sea.* Needless to say, he was more amused by his own idiocy than by the lame joke, and he tried to keep it in his mind as a pathetic shield against the memories of what he had seen, of how his penis had leapt at the sight of her glowing body. How was he going to get over the fact that for all intents and purposes he had dissed her? How do you go back and say, "I'm not really into condoms either. So I don't think you're dodgy for liking it the natural way. It's risky, yes, but could we try that shag again?"

By the time he reached the room his cock was semi-hard and he was hoping to find Julie awake and chat for a bit before kissing her again. He moved toward the bed trying not to muffle his footsteps. Unfortunately, it was already light enough for him not to bump into the things, although he did purposely kick someone's backpack over and then made another commotion of getting it upright. There didn't seem to be anyone sleeping in any of the beds he passed and he felt mild panic at the thought that Julie might not even be there. And if she had not been at the party, where else could one go on this island before sunrise? But she was there. A chocolate half moon covered her eyes. Smoother and darker than the rest of her face, like the deep, deep center of a sunflower. Eyes closed, twitching slightly. Dreaming. He let himself stare at her for a moment. She had more beauty in her body than in her face, but it was still enough to bring on more swelling in his nether regions and he made himself sit on his own bed before she sensed him and the heat of his arousal.

He felt her turning over above him and wondered if that was some kind of subconscious reaction to being freed from his stare. He liked the thought of infiltrating her thoughts without her awareness. His cock practically sprang out of his pants and he took it in his hand imagining it moving inside her thoughts, her sleeping mind, which was a mystery even to her. The ultimate penetration. He felt the orgasm on its way and the thought of spilling himself out into her subconscious rushed it along in an upward surge and he shouted within his own head.

## *About the Author*

Zamo Mkhwanazi was born in Durban, South Africa. She has been writing since the age of twelve and completed her first children's story at fourteen. She has traveled extensively and lived in Prague for two years where her works appeared in various English publications and Web sites. Zamo currently works for an independent record label in Cape Town, South Africa, and is making a documentary about reggae music.

# Snatched

## Clare Ewell

"**R**eady, honey?"

"Now?"

"It's all arranged."

"I'll be there."

Corinna heard the click on the end of the line. He'd hung up. Excitement rippled through her stomach, tying itself into a knot. He'd be getting ready for her. From his curt tone, she could imagine how desperate he was. And she knew why.

It had been so long since they'd had the chance to be together like this, to spend a few hours, with luck, maybe a whole night with each other. Alone. But perhaps they'd only have just one stolen hour. Even that would be enough. Oh God, how long since . . .

She sat down and breathed deeply, forcing herself to contain the anticipation. Breathe from the diaphragm. Hold it. Slowly, out through the mouth. Again. In. Count to three. Out. Let your mind clear. The only trouble was that she could still remember the excitement of their most recent furtive encounter, interrupted as it was, leaving them breathless, guilty, unsatiated, and ridiculously horny.

Each time she'd looked at him across a room, she'd seen the unconcealed lust in his eyes and she'd guiltily wished that everyone else would disappear so that she could be as close as possible to his luscious flesh and they could finish what they had started. They took every possible opportunity to caress each other, hiding their gestures from prying eyes, but it wasn't enough. Lord, how she'd wanted to hold him, to touch his naked body, to caress his bare skin, feel the muscles in his strong arms, even run her fingers over the slight ripple of flesh that distended his once-flat, washboard stomach.

She knew his body so well, but that didn't stop her, day after day, night after night, longing for it, dreaming of it, imagining it next to hers each moment that circumstances prevented them making slow, sensuous love, or even fast, frantic sex if that's what they had to make do with.

Corinna looked up at the screen and reached for the mouse with slightly trembling hands. See how just the sound of his voice and the promise of the fulfillment to come affected her. She knew that she should back up her work, but to do so would only delay her in the office for minutes longer than she could bear. God would forgive her, this once. How could she be expected to concentrate when opportunities like this presented themselves so rarely? She clicked. Yes, she was damned well sure that she wanted to shut down. Why did she have to confirm it over and over? Did the damn machine think her mind had turned to jelly just because she'd been offered the rare chance of some good, old-fashioned, down-home, nasty loving? And how did the computer know, anyway?

Finally, the screen went black; Corinna gathered up her bag and coat and was just about to run out of the office when she remembered that this was no ordinary night.

What was she thinking? Baz deserved better than this. She dropped her coat on a chair, emptied her bag on her desk, and scrabbled around for mascara and lipstick. The best she could do at short notice. She walked to the bathroom, her legs surprisingly shaky, and stood for a few seconds looking into the mirror.

There was a hint of gray at her temples. When did that happen? Surely it was premature? In any event, Baz didn't mind. Only two nights ago, before they were interrupted, he'd run his fingers through that same hair, tightening his hold until her scalp tingled, pulling her head back, licking the length of her neck right up to her chin, then up, up, up, till his tongue found her lips. Then he'd lingered at those lips, tracing the outline. Corinna looked at her lips now. Full, the bottom one looking as if it was continually pouting. How often had her mother told her to stop sulking when that was just the result of how her features were configured. But Baz had always loved her lips, taking time to caress them with his fingers, his thumb, his lips, his tongue. Corinna reached a finger to touch her bottom lip, tracing the outline the special way that Baz did. She bit on it and shook her head, clearing the fog that seemed to have come over her, making every movement slow and sensuous as if she were wading through honey.

She looked at her eyes. When had they gotten so bright? When she'd last thought about it, she'd been feeling weary from countless sleepless nights. Don't say that just the thought of how they would be together had brought that glint into her expression? She wasn't complaining, though, she liked the way it made her look. Almost how they used to be together, when there hadn't been these complications.

Recently, she'd been thinking, probably too often,

about the first time. Seven, or was it eight years ago? They'd made love the first night. She'd wanted to. He'd wanted to. Neither of them disguised it. He wasn't conventionally handsome. Shorter than average. Stockier than average, but dark. Skin almost the color of ebony, black eyes, and full, enticing lips seeming to be outlined in kohl pencil. No blurred edges. Short, cropped, velvet skullcap, the hairline defined, etched. He obviously worked out, the hard, menacing muscles of his arms and chest visible beneath the soft, worn cotton of his shirt. He just wasn't her type, but there was something indefinable, threatening but alluring in his confidence, the invitation in his eye, his unconcealed lust for her that attracted Corinna to him and seduced her to his room. That night there had been no interruptions, and since then, she had never stopped longing for more of what he gave her. Unconsciously, her fingers reached to the opening of her tailored shirt. Corinna smiled for a moment and undid the top three buttons, folding back the collar to reveal an enticing amount of cleavage and a glimpse of black lace. For all she knew, there might not be enough time for subtlety.

Her breath caught in her throat at the recollection of all that had happened that first night: frenzy, desperation, hardness, softness, tightness, moist, hot passion, and the knowledge of the hold she had over him. And he over her. She reached for the mascara wand and, fingers jittery, applied a dark layer to her already-long, curled lashes.

Corinna took a step back and surveyed herself. She would have to do. She hadn't had much notice, but she hoped that the promise in her eye would be enough for him. Walking back into the office, she delved into the pile of detritus from her bag to find the atomizer. She sprayed a generous amount of scent against her cleavage, laughed gently, and swept the pile back into the bag. She retrieved her coat and walked to the door. She waited for a moment, her finger on the switch. Oh God, please let there be enough time, she prayed. She so desperately needed the release. She switched the light off and opened the door. She stood there, briefly lost in thought, and then reached under her skirt. She swiftly removed her panties and stuffed them into her handbag. No sense in wasting valuable time.

There was a determined set to Baz's features. There was no way that he was going to waste this chance. Everything had to be exactly right for her. He'd rushed around getting flowers, candles, her favorite Merlot wine; he'd prepared the food he knew she loved; he'd cleaned the house, hiding away any distracting reminders. He looked around, the eyes those of a detective surveying a murder scene. Living room: check. Kitchen: check. Bathroom: check. Most important . . . bedroom: ouch! Shit, the pain of a fucking Lego. That was the last thing he needed. How many million times had he screamed at Jason to clean up his Legos? He certainly didn't want to make the mistake of letting Corinna spot Legos or Barbies, or PlayStation games, or any evidence of the children at all. That would be no way to get her into the mood for what he had in store. Baz picked up the recalcitrant piece of yellow plastic and looked again at the room. Burgundy satin sheets. Corny, but her naked, butterscotch skin and dark hair would look so good against them. Especially in the light of the candles he'd arranged around the room. With one finger he traced a line along the sheets, leaving a clear indentation. The silky feel reminded him of her. He dug his nails into his palms, need-ing temporary diversion to stop the surge of blood to his groin. He looked out the window, searching for her even though he knew that she wouldn't be near yet. He drew the curtains that were not quite heavy enough to shut out the light. The stereo was set up with Maxwell and Teddy and Stevie. He looked down at the Lego piece in his hand and felt a momentary pang of guilt, but recalling the last time they'd been able to make love, it was soon stifled. He threw the object into Jason's room and closed the door firmly. He'd have to make sure that she didn't have the chance to wander as far as the children's rooms. But then he was sure that he would be able to distract her.

Baz looked down at his watch. Twenty minutes since he'd called her. He looked out of the landing window. It was still light, a bright, full-on, goddamn summer light, but he'd close every single blind. They might not have until dark, so they'd have to pretend. He walked to the bathroom and started to run a bath. He poured in fragrant sandalwood oil, knowing how she loved the scent. They would start their lovemaking here. Slowly, carefully, the way she liked it. He would hold back as long as he could, caress her, tease her, please her, make her come over and over. He longed to see the look of total surrender, ecstasy mixed with desperation and a hint of disbelief when she came. Just the thought made him stand stock-still for a moment. Even after all this time, he wanted her so badly that just the thought of her made his breathing shallow and a prickle of sweat appeared, beading his forehead. Each time he stopped to think of how she affected him, he wondered at how she could absorb his emotions so completely, how he could, for moments, min-utes at a time, shut out all thought of anything, anyone else.

He turned off the taps and sat on the edge of the bath,

his head turned toward the front door, his senses alive, each one on edge, anticipating her arrival. He knew exactly what he would do. He would make it like the first time again. He would seduce her, first with his words, then with his eyes, then his fingers, his tongue, and then— please God, let there be enough time—with his entire body. He felt a stiffening of his penis and gently rested his hand there as if to reassure a worried pet that its mistress would soon be back.

She felt ridiculously hesitant. She wanted to laugh at herself. This was a man she knew so well. Why, suddenly, be nervous and shy? Why the fluttering behind her ribs? Well, because this time alone together was so rare and needed to be so perfect, she didn't want to put a foot wrong. When would they have another opportunity like this? It would be criminal to waste it.

Corinna groped in the depths of her bag, too flustered to locate the reluctant key, so, feeling like a shy adolescent, she rang the doorbell.

He opened the door, looking impossibly young. He didn't know what to say and they stood there, separated by space and time and emotion and lust. He stood aside to let her in and she stepped into the well-known hallway that suddenly seemed unfamiliar. Could she be feeling guilty? She took off her coat and at the same moment he reached out and placed one finger on the exposed curve of her breast. They looked at each other. He took the coat from her. Silently. His eyes never left hers and they burned into her. The heat rose. She dropped her gaze and with one hand reached back to lift the weight of her hair from her neck as the sheen of sweat moistened her skin.

He closed the door behind her and she looked around, avoiding his gaze. It was as if she'd never been here before. Everything seemed different, even him, but that was a ridiculous thought. She looked down at her hands. She was holding her handbag with both hands, the straps wrapped around her entwined fingers. She looked at where he was hanging her coat on a hook in the hall. There was a sudden hint of panic as she looked at the muscles of those strong arms. She was here for one reason. One reason only. From the moment he'd made the call, they'd both known that reason and there was no disguising the purpose with talk of feelings, fondness, empathy, understanding, or love. Sex was what she wanted. The time for feminine coyness was past. Gripping her bag, staring at him, there was no question that what she wanted wasn't tenderness, subtlety, gentle caresses, endless foreplay. No, she wanted raw, hungry, frantic, bestial passion. That might be all there was time for. Lord, why was he being so slow about hanging up a damn coat? Had he never done it before? Didn't he understand that there wasn't time to waste?

Baz turned toward Corinna but couldn't move. Couldn't breach the distance that separated them. He was suddenly immobilized by his desire for her, by the heat that singed every nerve ending, paralyzing him.

For a moment, Corinna was uncertain, unsure of herself. But this was Baz. She took two steps toward him and cupped his beloved face in her hands. He knew that she was about to kiss him and prepared himself for the sensation that would surge through him, but the kiss didn't come. He felt his body tremble as she took hold of his hand and placed it under her skirt to a wet, warm, naked place that was so familiar and so unexpected. He looked down the length of his arm, the one that had belonged to him for so many years and now seemed so alien. Simply because his fingers were cupping the sex of this woman whose eyes he no longer recognized. There was a burning intensity that scared him. He'd thought he'd known what to expect of this encounter. Looking at Corinna, he knew he was wrong. He was unexpectedly frightened. And exhilarated at the same time.

She held his hands there, against her responsive flesh. She didn't move. Neither did he. The heat zipping from her navel to the tip of her vagina was enough. For now. She moved away. Turned. Leaned against him, her inviting buttocks cushioning his penis, rolling small circles against him, leading him.

He moved then. As if jolted by an electrical current. His arms enfolded her, the crook of his elbows cradling her breasts, arms crossed, hands caressing her cheekbones, turning her face toward him. He kissed her deeply.

"I love you, honey," he whispered.

It wasn't what she wanted to hear. Not right now. She didn't want to be loved. To be his honey. She wanted to be desired, wanted, lusted after. She needed to know that he'd been as desperate for her as she for him. She wanted to be fucked. Not loved. Just fucked!

Corinna moved away from him, leaving him puzzled. She walked the familiar path to the dining room, noticing the beautifully arranged table, the scent of yellow and purple freesias lingering under the spicy smell of whatever was percolating in the oven. She was touched. Baz had bothered to get her favorite flowers. She turned toward him.

"You hungry, babe?"

"Uh-huh."

Corinna looked into his eyes and got the impression that he understood what she meant. But he held her gaze for a moment and then strode into the kitchen. Damn!

Baz knew that he was in the kitchen to give himself time to think. He couldn't work out what had gone wrong. He'd planned this all so carefully. He wanted, for once, to be like the Milk Tray man: suave, sophisticated, caring, devoted to his woman, taking his time to satisfy her every need. It happened so rarely. She deserved the wooing, the romance; she had waited so long for him. But somewhere, he'd taken a wrong turn. He knew that, but he didn't know when or where or how to navigate back to the starting point. And, goddamn it, there was no time to lose. He knew that, after an hour or so, the phone could ring at any time. He poured two glasses of wine and prayed that they would do the trick. He picked up a glass intending to take a surreptitious sip.

Corny though he knew it was, he had laid the table with coral roses as a centerpiece. Without a word, he pulled the chair from the table, indicating that she should sit. Baz tried to avoid glancing at her fulsome buttocks, knowing that they would distract his attention from food. He diverted his thoughts from her as he displayed the steamed asparagus on the plate. Baz could tell that she wasn't in the slightest bit interested in food, but he knew what he had planned. He dipped the succulent tips in the molten butter and smiled as he slowly raised the limp stem to his mouth and licked the butter from it. He could see that Corinna got the gist. She understood him so well. He watched, fascinated as the translucent liquid dripped from the fulsome pout of her lips, aroused as her tongue followed the path, rescuing the oily drop before it could fulfill its suicidal path. Almost unable to tear his gaze away from her probing tongue, he rose and arranged the next platter, deliciously anticipating the way in which she'd take the green banana into her mouth, tongue melting the creamy ackee, fondling the melting succulence. It only took a few mouthfuls before he cleared the plates away, turning to the sink for relief, clutching the stem of his wineglass.

Before he could turn round, he felt the prickling of Corinna's sharp nails piercing the fabric of his pants from his knees, up, up, along the inside of his thigh, nearer and nearer to . . . and then she stopped. She took the glass from his hand, leaving his now-erect cock unacknowledged. He heard her take a long sip of the wine, and then she held the cool, smooth glass to his lips. He drank. Fervently.

Corinna, his love, without a word unzipped him. He'd loved her from the first moment that they'd met. Wanted her. Instantly grown hard for her. And, despite the years, each time she touched him, he was transported back to that same moment: the wonderment, the thrill, the surging, the disbelief, the all-encompassing wait for what was to come.

He looked down at himself. His prick was hard. Straining against her slender, delicate fingers. Too coarse, too rigid, too demanding for such a delicate woman. But she was holding him, and now both hands were around him, the fingers interlocking, the nail polish on the finger that circled the head cracked and peeling. And then that same finger was tracking a path up the hairs of his abdomen, around his navel, painfully circling it and mapping a route up the center of his chest, then detouring to his nipple and touching it briefly to retrace its route back to his hopeful penis. Oh God Almighty! What are you doing to me, woman? I'm not sure I can hold on.

Why am I doing this? I'm looking at him and he's so hard. It's all for me. His cock is beautiful. Dark. Mysterious. Growing magically. Just because I touched him. That's what I can do to him. The power over him. I've got him where I want him. My womb is contracting, throbbing. My pussy is wet, desiring him. And I'm holding him, caressing him, when all the time he should be inside me. *There's not enough time.* And yet I'm loving the feel of him, the sight of his thick, beautiful, talented, powerful, demanding, fucking painful dick. He's leaning back, loving what I'm doing to him, and Lord, I don't know if I can wait to feel that beautiful dick inside my pussy. It seems like it's been forever and I can't wait. I want him. Now!

Baz straightened suddenly, pushing her hand away. Her touch was making him forget the plans he'd made. He didn't want to waste this rare opportunity. He couldn't let himself come too soon. This evening was going to be perfect for her. He turned away from her, zipped himself, and picked up the glass, his hand shaking, his head foggy, his body numb.

"To us, honey! To our time together."

He clinked his glass against hers, not daring to look into her eye, not sure that he would be able to resist the passion he knew he would see there.

Corinna didn't echo the toast, but Baz didn't notice. He

was absorbed in the effort to control his rising lust. Corinna shook her head slowly in disbelief. A slight murmuring of hurt and disappointment prickled at the back of her head, but she dismissed it and took a deep gulp of alcohol. She was being unreasonable and wouldn't let anything spoil this evening. But what was wrong with him? Didn't he understand how desperately she craved him? What if they ran out of time? Again? She just couldn't bear the thought of being interrupted, being left frustrated. Again. She finished the wine while Baz examined something fragrant in the oven and poured herself another glass. She watched his every movement, wondering how he could devote so much attention to the food when it wasn't her stomach that needed feeding. She looked down and there, tucked under a chair, was a bright, red, Minnie Mouse hair clip. Corinna sighed. She wished she hadn't seen it. But she would make herself forget about it.

Baz rose, turned to her, and took the glass from her hand. He placed it on the counter and took her hand, kissing each finger. Despite her irritation with him, she could feel the heat as each finger responded to the touch of his lips. She stepped closer to him and he took her in his arms, his lips forcing hers open, his tongue gently caressing hers until she pressed her breasts against his chest, thrusting her tongue into his mouth, savoring the sweetness of the wine and the delicious taste that was Baz's alone. Lord, she could drown in his kisses, could lose herself, forget everything else. But there he was, damn him, pulling away from her and leading her by the hand again. Please God let him be making his way to the bedroom. Though couldn't he see that he could take her right here and now?

He silently led the way up the stairs; at the top she stopped, pulling him back to her, impatient for the feel of his body against her. Corinna let her nails trail along the back of his neck. The other hand searched frantically for an opening in his shirt, needing to touch his skin. She raised one leg, wrapping it around his hips, forcing her pubis against him, rotating her hips, teasing his cock. He grabbed her ankle, pulling her closer. He dropped his head to her shoulder, sucking, biting the inviting flesh. He could feel his nipples hardening as she stroked and fondled them. He could never resist her touch and she knew it. For a moment he allowed himself to become lost in the musk of her scent, the delicious throbbing in his genitals, the heat from her wet, naked pussy. Then he remembered. They wouldn't have much time.

He reached behind him and turned the knob, opening the door, taking a step backward and pulling her with him.

"Baz, what are you doing?"

"I've got everything ready, honey."

Corinna looked around. Steam rising from a hot, fragrant bath. Tiny vases crowded around the bath, on shelves, on every flat surface. Yellow, purple, cream freesias, their heady scent intoxicating as it mixed with the sandalwood. Her heart soared and brought a lump to her throat. He'd gone to so much trouble and there she was feeling resentful because he wasn't willing to satisfy her at once. She couldn't dismiss the lust that had invaded her body, but she looked at him now, her eyes filled with affection and gratitude for his thoughtfulness. Tears threatened to mist her eyes. He'd remembered how it had been that first time. Corinna looked up into Baz's expectant eyes, then gently pulled his head down to her and brushed a gentle kiss against his lips.

He could see that she remembered and he smiled gently, relieved. He held her close, his fingers tracking a line down each ridge of her spine, every movement pulling her nearer. His fingers traced the round fullness of her ass, cupping her buttock, allowing himself the momentary sensation of her naked flesh, resisting the temptation to caress her crinkly pubic hair. He pulled away and gazed at her, still hardly able to believe that they were here, together, now, alone, glad that he'd been able to make the arrangements, pushing away any hint of guilt. She would be worth it.

He noticed the unbuttoned shirt and with one finger traced the curve of her lacy bra while the other hand opened the remaining buttons, pulling her shirt from the tight waistband. He couldn't resist planting a gentle kiss on the swell of her breast. He reached round and unfastened her bra, easing the straps down over her shoulders, releasing the heavy, swollen breasts. He knelt before her, trying to resist the dark, mysterious scent of her pussy so close to his face, to his mouth, to his tongue. He turned his head away and reached for the skirt button at her hip. She touched his face, lifting it as she bent forward, and offered her puckered nipple to him. He eagerly accepted the distraction, taking the pointed offering between sharp teeth and nibbling gently, sucking on the ridged flesh, flicking his tongue across the tip as he heard her sharp intake of breath and felt the pressure of her fingernails digging into his shoulders. He breathed deeply, stood, and unzipped her skirt, helping it across her hips, letting it fall to the floor, keeping his hands away from the roundness of her abdomen.

Corinna felt herself being lifted into his arms and she

clung to his neck as he carried her across the room and lowered her into the steaming water. He sat back on his knees as he soaped the sponge. She lay back and closed her eyes, allowing the lapping water to ease away the growing impatience, the tension of longing. She owed it to him to wait. He lifted her leg, soaping her foot, massaging between each toe, thumbs pressing along the arch, fingers smoothing the skin along her heel, kneading the calf muscle, snaking upward to her thigh, fingers wafting across the delicate skin of her inner thigh, a spider's touch heading toward . . . He moved to her shoulders, outlining the contour with confident fingers, the heel of his thumb brushing the side of her breast, awakening her from her stupor. Her flesh was alive to his touch, rippling, creeping toward him, craving the feel of his skin. She shifted slightly, edging her breasts toward his hands. He resisted her, taking his time, making her nipples wait their turn. The coarse feel of the natural sponge moved around her stomach, round and round. *For God's sake, move either up or down, one way or the other.* He chose to move upward, slowly, toward her breasts, and then his hands lifted the full globes out of the water, pushing them together, a look of reverence in his eyes. Corinna smiled as he held her breasts, dropping the sponge, allowing it to float away while his thumbs circled her prominent nipples, sending a surge of heat to her pussy.

"Honey, why don't you get in with me? You remember?"

He looked at his watch, hesitating for only a moment, and she looked from lowered lids as he unbuttoned his shirt, revealing the luscious expanse of chocolate skin dotted with dark, silky hair, layered with a film of sweat. Corinna's eyes widened as he unbuckled his belt, slid open the zipper, coyly turned away from her gaze, and slipped out of pants and underpants in one swift, agile movement. In less than a second he'd covered the space to the bath and she bent her knees, eager to make space for him.

Corinna looked around the room. There was no clock. But she felt the urgency again. She slid her bottom toward him, overlapping his knees with her own. She took the soap, rubbed it in her hands, and lathered his chest, allowing the heels of her hands to rub hard against his nipples, the friction making them swell into firm knots. She waited for a moment and placed one finger against each nipple, scraping them with long nails. He groaned and grasped her wrists, quickening the movement of her fingers. Corinna struggled to pull one hand from his tight grip. She couldn't wait any longer. Her hand disappeared into the opalescent water and searched blindly along his thigh, down and around until she held his balls that floated gently in the water. She caressed them softly, waiting to feel the tightening, the swelling. Her fingers searched upward until she held his penis, heavy and rigid even in the water. She watched his eyes dilate, becoming darker, dreamy, more mysterious, and she saw the narrowing at the corners as her hand circled him, moving up and slowly down, stretching the foreskin, exposing him, making him vulnerable. She twitched her hips closer, ever closer, running the pad of her thumb down the vein that pulsed in his cock. Oh, she was so ready for him, her nipples stretched and tingling, her stomach tight with wanting, her pussy hot, oozing, calling to him.

He let go of her wrist, bringing his large, strong hand to cradle the long, delicate fingers encircling his hard-on, guiding the motion, feeding her his own rhythm. He lowered his head to her chest, the flat of his tongue licking between her breasts, roving in diminishing circles as he neared her waiting nipple. His other hand was suddenly, urgently searching for her opening; she shifted minutely to allow him access and gasped when his thumb plunged into her, pressing down and back, dancing to the same rhythm as she let her head fall back and her mouth open and the sounds emerge into the expectant air. "Ooh, oh, ooh, mmm."

Baz raised his head from her breast and looked at her, about to cover her mouth with his hand, about to shush her, then realizing that there was no need. And oh, how the sound of her desire was turning him on. His cock was engorged, thicker, longer, harder than it had been for some time. He was almost ready to burst. His arms encircled her waist and pulled her to him while both her hands encircled him, guiding him. . . .

And then the phone rang. They were both silent. Praying. It continued to ring.

Baz couldn't look at her as he leapt from the bath, covering his erection with a large towel, and ran out of the room. Please don't let it be *her!*

Please don't let it be her! Corinna prayed, shocked, cold, shivering, away from his body. Please Lord, I'll do anything. Don't let it be her! She waited, wrapping her arms around her knees, the desire in danger of dying away. I can't bear it if we've wasted this time together. She could hear his muffled voice as if it were coming from thousands of miles away, but she couldn't make out any distinct sounds.

He came back into the room, the ends of the towel tucked tight around his waist. Not a good sign. He picked up another towel and held it out to her. She got out of the

bath and walked to him, leaving a trail of wet footprints in
the carpet. She took the towel and looked up at his disappointed face, a question in her eyes.

"It was her. She'll be here in half an hour."

Tears of frustration threatened to spill. She was disappointed too. She was angry with him. Why had he
waited so long? She hadn't needed food, or wine, or a
bath, or damn flowers. She needed a good screw, that
was all.

He looked at her and saw the familiar expression on
her face. Frustration, sadness, the tightening of the muscle in her jaw. He wanted to shout that this wasn't his
fault. What did she expect him to do? And then she
looked up at him, lifting those long, thick lashes, and he
saw the sultry look in her eyes. He knew what she was
thinking. He could feel a certain stirring as the towel
around his waist lifted, as if of its own accord.

Baz strode across the room and picked her up, feeling
the cool wetness of her skin against his as he almost ran to
the bedroom.

"We've still got half an hour, sweets."

"That's just what I been thinking."

He dropped her onto the satiny sheets, beads of water
staining the fabric. His body followed and he lay across
her, kissing her deeply, almost stifling her as he plunged
his tongue into her mouth, sucking, drawing the breath
from her. Corinna writhed against him, pushing her pelvis
against him, grinding her mound against him.

His hand grabbed at her breast as he raised himself,
squeezing hard, bruising her nipple until he took it between his teeth making her scream with pain and delight.
"Oh, babe," she muttered over and over as her senses
calmed and she was able to form words, but before she

could conjure more words, he was slipping down her body, his powerful chest rasping against her tender skin as she felt his cock against her stomach, his pubic hair against her legs, and then he was pushing her thighs apart. She looked down at him and his eyes were glassy as he stared at her pussy. She could feel the wetness flow from her as the red tip of his tongue emerged from between his lips and he lowered his head.

And then, oh my God, she had waited so long for this. Her clitoris pulsated as she waited for the touch of his mouth, but he headed lower and she felt his thumbs opening her further and his forehead, his eyes, his nose, his mouth rubbing against her, and then his tongue inside, briefly, unbearably, in and then out again and up and he was sucking on her clitoris, where every nerve ending, every fiber of her being was now concentrated. He stopped, pulled away, and his eyes met hers.

"I love you, honey."

She could feel the love, no longer guilty, surge with the passion as she looked into those oh-so-familiar eyes. Then his tongue was back, licking her, flicking left and right against her clitoris, sucking again as his fingers plunged inside her. She felt the slickness as they moved in and out raising her to dangerous levels of lust. She so wanted to come, to let him make her explode, but there was so little time, Corinna reached down and lifted his head, pushing him away, sliding down the slippery sheets until she was under him, his engorged cock pointing toward her lips. She held him in her hands for a moment and guided him toward her waiting mouth. She brushed the head against her soft lips, moving him from side to side, waiting for his moan before opening her mouth and taking him in, just the tip while her fingers spiraled a trail around the thick base, up to the soft, hard thickening.

He held himself above her for as long as he could, but the feel of her touch was too much as he felt the surge of heat to his groin. His balls tightened and his cock bounced slightly. She was so warm, so wet, so welcoming. He eased himself farther into her mouth as her lips encircled him, so tight. He moved himself gently, in and out, not wanting to hurt her, but hardly able to contain himself, feeling his brain empty as every sensation concentrated in his prick. *Oh Jesus. I can't take this. I've got to stop.*

*I can feel him tightening. I want to make him happy, but I need to feel him inside me, please don't come yet, sweetheart. My pussy* needs *you. Baby, wait. Please wait.*

Corinna pulled away, moving up to kiss him, so that he tasted the salty tang of his own flesh, and she, too, tasted her own scent on his breath. He reached under and clutched her buttocks as she angled her hips toward him, holding his prick and guiding it to the soft, fleshy opening. He rested there, preserving the sweet moment, and she held him there, savoring the delicious anticipation. Each heard the other's heavy breathing, gasping in unison. And then, at the same moment, the ticking of the clock intruded and Corinna thrust her hips upward as he drove deep into her as his fingers dug into the flesh of her buttocks.

*Aah, babe, I need you, want you, love you, love your pussy, need you, have wanted this for so long. Can't wait. Have to wait. Red, scarlet, hot, heat, liquid, honey, sweetness, lover, don't stop, take me, all of me, want to feel your cunt wrapped around me, taking me, accepting me, wanting me, loving me, loving my cock. Oh, honey.*

Oh, Baz, baby, baby, that's it. Take me. Love you. Never, ever wanted anyone as much as . . . oh, my love, oh, oh, oh, more.

Feeling as if life itself depends on this moment, nothing can intrude, you're everything, breath, feeling, life, love, pussy, cock, more, most, everything, now, fuck it, now, oh baby, that's it, aah, aaiiee!

The intrusive purr of a car engine. Right outside the door. Footsteps as Baz pulls out, rushes to force trembling legs into pant legs.

Hell, quick, get dressed. Tuck the shirt in. Forget the tights and panties. Legs trembling. No time to recover. Piece of green Lego on the stairs. Ignore it. Faster. Follow Baz down the stairs. Door opening. She hears his voice, still slightly husky.

"Hi, Mom. Thank you so much for looking after the kids."

"Well," she gazed disapprovingly and knowingly at Corinna's bare legs, "I have to do what I can to help, especially when you have to work *overtime*." The last word was stressed.

Baz quickly replied before Corinna could. "I don't know what we would have done without you."

She wrapped her children in a warm embrace, ignoring the chocolate ice cream clinging to their excited faces, happy to see them, though . . .

She glanced at Baz. "No, I can't *imagine* what we would have done."

## *About the Author*

Clare Ewell has a son and two daughters. She is married to a lawyer and lives in Balham, South London. She runs a small business making celebration cakes. "Snatched" is her first work of fiction.

# Scent of Vanilla

## Kwame Pitts

I never was one to follow those damned polls about what turns men on. In fact, I'd rather not even try to keep up with mags like *Ebony, Essence,* and *Jet*; they just make me depressed. I hate wearing makeup, I refuse to spend $10,000 on a boob job, and I do not screw like a porno star. In fact, I've been celibate for over two years now and I'm wearing out my vibrator.

So there's my life in a nutshell.

Breezing into work, I waved in greeting to the receptionist as I burst into my office, throwing down my bag and turning on the radio.

"You look cute today, Kay. Something smells good. Did you bring fresh bakery with you this morning?" Our receptionist who, no matter what else she was wearing, always had to have her leopard boots, smiled at me, leaning against my door drinking coffee.

"What? No, that must be the new spray I bought. Vanilla." I replied carelessly as I scanned through my e-mail.

My day was typical, nothing exciting except for the odd stressed-out student here and there. I'm one of the counselors at our university's CAPS program and was buried in paperwork from hospitals and outside providers. At about 11:30 I put my head on my desk and said "Enough!" and strode out for a break from my desk.

"Good morning," came from the deep-voiced Shawn Miller, one of the newest counselors here in the loony bin. He was a health nut, and I regularly watched him drink wheatgrass juice in the morning, while I sadly shook my head and downed chocolate chip bagels with honey butter and OJ. He was handsome even if just a tad thin for my taste. He seemed conservative, straight out of the old *GQ* with his neatly cut hair, Polo shirts, and Dockers khakis. Yet those brown, innocent-looking eyes weren't fooling me one bit. Why did I always feel I was being x-rayed every time we came in close contact with each other? For a brief second those eyes probed me, reaching out with transparent hands, brushing over any exposed skin, paying attention to the curve in my lips and the nape of my neck. His eyes were not friendly anymore, turning my otherwise clean mind into thoughts of wickedness.

"Morning, hon." I called everyone in the office "hon" or "babe." My voice held no trace of the curiosity I felt whenever we had one of these encounters. I was continuing my walk to freedom out the door for fresh air when he laid that muscular arm on mine.

"Kay, you smell good!"

I knew my face was flushed as I attempted to thank him for the compliment. His expression twisted into one of near ecstasy; just getting a whiff of my fragrance sent his mind into a flurry. Well, there was my laugh for today!

*There's nothing wrong with a man, even a married man, giving a woman a compliment,* I rationalized over and over in my head. Yeah right, so why did I walk into Walgreen's that very night and buy the matching shower gel, complete with glitter, and soak in the tub. The thought of Shawn kept a smile on my face as I ran a soft sponge over my legs, which splayed wide open as my eyes closed. His voice seemed to softly vibrate in my memory.

Another rainy day, I sighed as I tried to avoid being drowned by the torrential rain. It was going to be one of those days. I knew that, especially after reading the police report on the student who had ran out on the quad in nothing but a towel and olive oil smeared all over his eyes, ranting about how he wasn't going to wear glasses anymore; trying to encourage other students to do the same.

Heading back from the local hospital, I was suffering from a mild headache. I'd wasted my time talking to the student's parents, who were in complete denial. I struggled out of my car with my lunch, grumbling to myself about having to park the hell away from the office. All the damn money we had to pay for parking permits and the students eat up our spaces! Well, at least I was by the beach, even if the view was stormy.

"Kay. Kay!" There was Deep Throat again. I turned to see Shawn walking, at his usual fast clip, with an enormous umbrella.

I settled the fluttering in my stomach and smiled as usual. "Hey, hon, what are you doing out in this weather?"

"I was taking a walk until it really started raining. What are you up to?"

There was that inquisitive drop in his voice. As I glanced into his brown eyes again, my skin prickled.

"Oh, just came from visiting that student, the one they found running around the quad."

"Oh yeah, how is he?"

I briefly gave Shawn my opinion, though if I was honest, my mind wasn't on my work. We had stopped near a closed hot dog stand by the edge of the beach. The rain was pounding angrily on his umbrella and the wind had picked up. I was sure my food was getting soggy as I shifted the weight of the bag containing my lunch. I moved a little closer to him, partly to get out of the rain, but also because his strong musky cologne was intoxicating and so inviting.

"Mmph," was all Shawn said, nodding. He was looking into my eyes, but his concentration was somewhere else. *Something wicked this way comes now* had a whole new meaning.

Okay, so perhaps the wonderful new push-up bra I'd bought from Target had something to do with his staring, and the low, but tastefully styled, V-cut shirt and my breasts straining against the soft lilac cotton material.

"We'll probably have to wait here for a while, until this storm blows over. Want me to hold something for you?" Shawn extended his arm toward me while my heart began assaulting my rib cage, and not even waiting for my answer he freed me of my bag with a smile.

"Oh, thanks."

"I meant to ask you, what is that you're wearing?" He leaned in a little closer, still holding his umbrella tightly, his gaze zeroing in on mine. I could not tear myself away, and I knew I had to be blushing.

"Um, my body spray? Oh, it's just something I picked up at the store. I don't wear perfume, too expensive. It's vanilla." I was usually so steady and well-spoken; why in the hell was I rambling like a teenager? Shawn nodded, and I swore the skies darkened.

"Very nice," he breathed deeply.

The weather was not in my favor, as the wind seemed to pick up.

"Whoa! Ya know, maybe we should wait in my car!" I nervously spun around and began to head off, but Shawn caught my arm.

"Kay, we can wait here." Gone was the wickedness and his boy-next-door-smile returned.

"Um, no we can't."

"Why?"

"Uhh, never mind."

"Kay, did I say something wrong?"

"Oh no, Shawn, no, you didn't. No, why would I be . . . You're harmless . . . you . . . even give nice compliments."

Shawn grinned. "Well, I wasn't lying. Your scent is overpowering."

"Too much?" I grinned back. "You seemed to like it a whole lot."

Those brown eyes darkened again as he stood in front of me, curving his lips wickedly. "Yes, yes I do."

"Oh, I see." I smiled softly. The effect he was having on me was crazy. I lowered my lashes while strategically lifting my hair from around my shoulders. Resting my hand underneath my chin and glancing back at him, I flirtatiously caught my finger between my lips, fluttering my lashes at him. "Interesting."

Shawn seemed to tower over me ominously. Adding, "Just trying to shield you from the rain," he slipped an arm loosely around my waist. "I hope you don't mind." His tone was more commanding, his grasp tightening. He dropped his umbrella and slipped his other smooth hand under my chin, covering my lips with his.

* * *

"You kissed this guy?" My best friend Marylin's eyes widened over her coffee as she stared at me across the table at Starbucks as we chatted after work. I just grinned sheepishly.

"Yes, damn it. I need to have a real live orgasm any chance I can get!" I slammed the table for emphasis, laughing.

"Orgasm over a damn kiss? I'm going to ask you to quit!"

Well, what was I supposed to do? Go confess my sins to the nearest Catholic Church? Sorry, but I enjoyed it. The evening was overcast, and repeating in my mind like a broken record was that scene of his arms snaked around my waist, of his tongue firmly, almost forcibly, pushed into my mouth, wrapped around mine, sucking the kiss almost right out of me.

I couldn't look at him at work after that, but not out of shame. I knew that as I shared conversations with coworkers, whether standing right outside my office or in the hall, he was stalking me.

Downstairs in the office library, or what we liked to call "the morgue," it was quiet and that's what I needed. My heart rate was dangerously high these days. I was going to give myself a stroke thinking about Shawn. Deep near the back, near the very old and extremely dusty files, I pulled up a chair near a bookcase, closed my eyes, and sighed, my silk skirt barely touching the curve of my knees.

"Kay." Shawn's deep, commanding voice again, mixed with concern. He stood in front of me, his head tilted slightly to the side, those brown eyes probing my long legs, my black sandals curving around my ankles. I couldn't say anything, but bit my bottom lip and raked my teeth over it as I glanced up to him.

He slid his hands over my thighs, and I managed to laugh softly. "This would be the day I wouldn't wear underwear."

Shawn's mouth dropped open.

"Kay." His steadied voice was cracked and he leaned into my neck, hungrily devouring whatever skin I was going to have left. My legs shifted lazily as I caressed one sandal against the other, almost uncomfortable as the wetness lightly began to ooze through the damp curly hair and trail down my thighs. My clit was throbbing, and at this point I was too far gone to care. He dropped to his knees and kissed my knees, trailing his tongue over my thighs as I stroked his beautifully carved head. I was shaking as he pulled me forward, pushing apart my knees, working that beautiful tongue of his, lapping at my pussy lips. I was losing control of my breathing and vision, the scent of vanilla mingling with the heady aroma of overwhelming lust.

I sat back in a tub full of steaming water and perfectly curved bubbles. The only disturbing noise was in the hallway as my cat zipped back and forth. This was not an enjoyable experience for me. I couldn't get thoughts of Shawn out of my head. I sighed and glanced out my tiny bathroom window at the beautiful golden moon. The vanilla steam coming from the water wove its way over my only exposed arm and brushed my face with warm kisses.

I couldn't believe that I had sunk to the level where I let a colleague cock my legs open and suck me into a couple of orgasms in the basement of my office! I wrapped my arms around myself and closed my eyes, remembering my shamelessness. I sank deeper into the water for comfort, my fingers drifting over my thighs, teasing. I wanted to feel his smooth face against mine. "So sweet and spicy at the same time," he'd growled as he nipped my ear. The water was slippery, pulling at my clit, working in between my fingers moving more in frustration than anything else.

As usual the phone always seemed to know when to interrupt me at the wrong time. I got out and rushed to my bedroom. I didn't recognize the number flashing on the caller ID, but hey, who knows? Maybe I'll get lucky.

"Hello?" I offered my very best Kathleen Turner impression.

"Mmm. Sounds like you're busy."

Shawn? How in the heck did he get my number? My face flushed as I sat up straight.

"Um, no, no. Just surprised to hear your voice. On the telephone, I mean." Damn, was I losing all cool points or what? Shawn's laugh rumbled and he sounded pretty relaxed himself. From the monotonous hum in the background I assumed he was on the road.

"So, what are you doing if you aren't busy?"

"In the tub, thinking how nice it would be if you could tuck me into bed." Now where in the hell had that come from? The smile curved on my face as I caught the challenge in my voice and him sputtering on the other end. I tightened my favorite fluffy blue towel around me, laughing softly.

"I'm about fifteen minutes away from you, you know that?" Shawn's tone was playful, but with an animal, growling undercurrent. I lay over the side of my bed, grabbing the body gel that was made for cute little babies but was extremely effective on my skin.

"You had nothing better to do than to drive around with your hand on your dick trying to peek into my windows?"

"Go unlock your door." Shawn's voice sounded a little irritated, but oh, so excited. I'd caught him off guard. I smirked and reached for my vibrator, letting him hear me turn it on.

"I think it will be too late by the time you get here, hon," I purred low into the receiver and hung up. Laughing, I sashayed naked through my house and, shocking myself, unlocked the door and wandered back upstairs. My skin was prickling, full of goosebumps. I hoped I'd got him so worked up that he'd come busting through the door. How cute that he was trying to order me around! But hadn't I just gone downstairs and unlocked the door? In Chicago?

Come on, Shawn, I whispered as I lay back on the bed, my legs open, my hands touching, drifting over my stomach, tugging at my breasts, my toes dug into the carpet. I reached for my vibrator again. A hand slammed down on my wrist. I hadn't heard him. An adrenaline rush of fear and excitement flooded through me.

"You won't be needing that." Shawn covered my body with his, biting at my ears and my neck. I wrapped my legs around his. He growled low into my neck, kissing me, grabbing both my arms and twisting them above my head. My eyes widened at the pressure, and I licked and nibbled at his lip, pulling him closer. He returned my kiss with a fiendish smile as he stripped himself of his shirt.

"Give me back use of my hands."

He snickered. "No, that's for you being flippant with me."

He was not joking, and I narrowed my eyes at him. Who did he think he was? I watched him slip on a pair of black gloves, never letting go of my hands, and my heart jumped, my legs betraying me as they involuntarily widened. I whimpered softly. He leaned down and kissed me, so, so gently.

"Damnit woman, you can get a man so worked up."

"Quit talking and fuck me, if that's what you came here to do." I growled back at him, disobedient, seeing how far I could push him. Those brown eyes narrowed and his whole expression rippled into one of pure lust as he stroked his leather-clad hands over my sensitive skin. He licked the nape of my neck, leaving a trail of warm air as his hands continued their assault down my sides. My hands struggled in their bond as I gripped the sheets, my throat swelling with moans. Shawn kissed my sides until his lecherous tongue found its way over to my breasts, almost swallowing my brown nipples whole.

I couldn't take it anymore, my voice hoarse, demanding, "Fuck me."

Shawn chuckled softly, ignoring me and paying more attention to my breasts as he seemed to savor each one. His jogging pants felt so cool against my skin, but his cock apparently was pissed off it was not in the action and began to protest angrily. His eyes were closed, enjoying the soft, soapy scent of vanilla and the warmth that rose from my body. The room spun, and I half closed my eyes, imagining tendrils that probed his senses. My legs wrapped around his and my hips began to grind against him. He dove his tongue into that part of my body that he seemed so drawn to—my natural scent.

Did he know, subconsciously, how badly I'd needed this? The way I'd walk down the hall, my hips curving into my stride, eyes that seemed to follow him, challenging him every time he spoke, inviting him to whatever he wanted from me. I seemed to float, watching my face contort into a scream, my bound hands banging against his back, repeatedly. His own breath caught in his throat, harsh moans coming. He pushed me back onto the bed, finally releasing my hands. I hungrily slid them from his back into his pants and boldly grasped his cock. Shawn moaned softly, almost losing control. I pushed him up and away from me, backing him against the baseboard of the bed.

"If you won't fuck me . . ." I wrapped my legs around him, losing control. What started as my taunting quickly turned into cries as I rode him, his arms so comforting, curled around my back and my waist, responding with taunting thrusts of his own. He kissed me openly, pulling on my tongue, drawing it out, as I attempted weakly to return his affections, his moans vibrating against my lips, my pussy overflowing with wetness, covering him, trickling onto his groin and down the inside of his thigh. His eyes half closed, he gazed into my eyes and slipped his hand underneath my chin, forcing me to look at him.

"No," I whimpered. My vision was clouded. I was past arousal.

"Yes," he demanded. He grabbed my hips and increased his torture, making me bounce on him. I lost control and screamed in what seemed to be endless waves of orgasms.

I hung limply against his shoulders as he kissed the top of my head.

"Good God," I managed when I could finally speak. He laughed and kissed me again.

"Who do you think you are coming in here, just jumping all over me and, and . . ."

Shawn laughed. "Who said I was done with you yet? You did put in a request, right? Or were you bluffing?"

I stuck my tongue out at him. "I wasn't! You just couldn't handle me!"

"Uh-huh?" Shawn rolled me over playfully and kissed me all over my face, gently kissing the tip of my nose before he drove himself deep into me. Holy shit! I was caught off guard and squealed weakly as I entangled my legs with his, his rhythm mocking, slow, intense. Damn it! His moans spilled out of his mouth, driving him insane with self-torture. I groaned faintly, my face leaning toward his, our eyes locked.

I managed an evil grin, whispering "Fuck me." I was screwing with his ego, messing with him again, seeing how far I could push him.

Shawn bit my bottom lip, snarling as he slipped out of me and flipped me over on my stomach, slamming into me, intensifying his thrusts, repeating his punishment until our moans seemed to mix together, filling the room.

The sun seemed overly cheerful as it streamed into my windows. I looked around my rumpled room and crumpled sheets. What the hell had happened to me last night?

There was my damned phone again.

"This better be good."

"Hey, girl!" Oh Lord, it was Marylin. "What's wrong with you? I thought we had an early morning date at Curves!"

"I already had a workout," I mumbled. Why did I smell food in the house and I wasn't in the kitchen?

"What? Girl, did you get drunk last night?"

Before I could answer, Shawn appeared in those same cute jogging pants. They were blue too. I hadn't noticed that last night. Last night? Oh my God, that wasn't another one of my intense dreams. It was real. He grinned and kissed the side of my cheek.

"Now tell your friend good-bye and get downstairs for breakfast," he whispered.

My mouth dropped open. He twisted his face into an evil grin. "Now!"

"Uh, Marylin? I have to say good-bye now. The handsome stranger who stole into my bedroom last night and screwed me silly has made me breakfast and I have to go now." Shawn winked at me and sauntered out of the bedroom.

"What?"

"Girl, I'll call you later!"

I curiously, carefully made my way down the stairs; cinnamon, brown sugar, and vanilla wafted through the air. Shawn was standing at my kitchen countertop, whistling.

"No 'good morning, hon'?" he mimicked as he turned around, smiling.

"I'm just . . . um . . . amazed at what we did. Oh my God, what we just did!"

Shawn laughed and came over and wrapped his arms around my naked body, kissing me. "Do you always walk around like this, or are you trying to go for round two?"

"But, but," I sputtered, "you're married! Holy shit, I just screwed a married guy!"

Shawn nodded. "Yes, married. But in name only."

"Oh, don't go pulling that stuff on me. Okay, so you lusted after me. We screwed and you're supposed to disappear in the morning and we just remain good colleagues or friends . . . with benefits even!"

Shawn actually looked hurt. "I'm sorry, Kay. I guess I assumed there was more between us."

I was surprised, shocked. "Whoa, Shawn. Wait a second. No, no. I enjoyed this, all of this. Good Lord, but you're married. I can't let my emotions get riled up!" I held out my hands helplessly, palms upward. Shawn's eyes lowered and he sighed softly. There was that painful silence.

"So this was all a game for you?" he finally asked me, a touch of anger in his voice.

"A game? Isn't it for most men? Shawn, listen . . ." I was caught off guard, but I was not going to be made the bad guy in all of this. "You're extremely good-looking and I just broke about a zillion rules about screwing married men. I would be lying if I said I wasn't attracted to you, but none of this is fair to your wife, is it?"

Shawn hesitated but nodded. "There's no passion between us anymore."

"Did you talk about it or at least try? Counseling, maybe?" He shook his head. I sighed and slipped my arms around his waist.

"Kay . . ."

"Shawn, I am really flattered that you seem to like me on so many different levels, but maybe your friendship is more important to me than anything else."

I spent the next several weeks buried in work and bottomless pints of Chocolate Chip Cookie Dough and Chocolate Brownie Frozen Frappucinos. I couldn't look at Shawn because I was trying to reestablish that friendliness that we'd once had. His eyes now followed me sadly around the office.

My birthday came that Friday, and among the silly cards that covered my office desk was a beautiful bouquet of flowers. Astonished, I read the card.

"Happy Birthday, hon." Shawn's voice floated into

my ears as he gently kissed me on the cheek. I half spun around. "I miss you," he added, burying his face in my neck, hungrily smelling me. "Still the same sweet vanilla."

## About the Author

Kwame Pitts lives in Chicago, Illinois, with her husband and two children. This is her third published short story. Her sci-fi erotica piece, "Controlled Corruption," was included in the *Erotic Tales* anthology published in 2003. She is currently working on her first (nonerotica) novel, *Libations*.

# Office Politics

## Lani Douglas

Some of those women were looking fine as I walked out of the office. I never looked at them straight up, but out of the corner of my eye. Don't want to make it look as if you're desperate, or even slightly interested. You have to keep an air of mystery; make them do the running. There was a cute little blonde with curly hair, Shirley Temple dimples, and shapely legs over by the filing cabinet. And a skinny, dark-haired woman behind one of the partitions. Couldn't make out what her legs were like under the desk. A sista with braids and a nice round ass walked past me and out the door. I wanted to check out a bit more of her. I speeded up, but by the time I got to the elevator, she'd disappeared from sight. I skipped the elevator and ran down the stairs. There was a definite bounce in my step and I felt as if I were walking on air, or at least brand-new Nike Air Zooms. I'd gotten the job, offered to me on the spot: Assistant Publicist with an indie label. I could have danced down the street, I could have run, but I got sidetracked by the car showroom, checking out how I was going to spend the wads I was sure to be earning in a little while. There was only one downside. I would

have to go back to the insurance company I was working for and hand in my notice. A lot of the women
working there were going to be disappointed. But, hey,
those are life's breaks.

Now my first day in the office is here. My friend Nick's
sister braided my hair yesterday and I put in a request for
some intricate styles at the back. I asked if she could spell
out the name of the record company, but she just kissed
her teeth and slapped me in the head with the back of the
brush. So this morning, I shaved with extra care and
slapped on some Hugo Boss aftershave, the pain making
me wince for a few seconds. I checked my hair in the mirror. "Looking good," I mouthed, smiling at myself. I
dressed carefully, pale blue linen Paul Smith suit (the only
one I own) and a black cotton T-shirt. This was going to be
my first day in the new office and I had to get the look
right. I knew how important image was, and I wanted to
make sure that those girls were in for a treat. I took one last
look at myself and I was satisfied. I was looking hot.

I checked my three-year-old black Peugeot 206 on the
way to the subway, waving good-bye to it, promising myself that I'd be trading up very soon. I got to the office a
little early, not because I was feeling nervous or anything
like that, but I thought it would be good to show some en-
thusiasm.

I can't say that the day was the most exciting I'd ever
spent. I had my own cubicle in a prime position—right
next to the photocopying machine. And my own secretary,
Patti. Okay, I shared her with five others, but I could still
get her to hold my calls, not that I had that many today.
My first, and only, task was to get to know all the contacts
in the media. Well, I had to update the list, so I was basi-
cally chatting on the phone, repeating the same questions

over and over, until I didn't even have to think about what I was saying anymore. Managed it on automatic pilot. So I had plenty of time to check out the talent. And when I said that I was in prime position, you have to know that being right by the photocopier means that you soon get to know most of the women working in the place. I got to thinking that Cheryl, the little blonde I noticed the day of the interview, was looking for any excuse she could find to copy more pieces of paper. And it was supposed to be a green office too. Anyway, the chick was soon flirting with me, batting her eyelids and asking all kinds of questions designed to find out if I was single. I wasn't giving away too much. You need to keep them guessing, have a mysterious air about you.

You could tell that the sista was getting a little bit jealous every time I stopped to have a little bit of a conversation with Cheryl. Them black women can sure get up themselves when they're a bit superior to a brotha! Just because she's been there longer than me and got herself a little promotion. Turns out that she's a full-fledged Publicist, looking after some of the bigger names on the firm's roster. And you know that as a black guy you can't let the sistas see you even glancing at a white woman. That's when they get all political and start their history lessons about slavery and the struggle, as if they were even alive during all that civil rights stuff. So when she wasn't glaring at me, I had a chance to check her over. I'm never sure about the way girls like to dress themselves in men's clothes. She was wearing a pants suit outfit and even a striped shirt. I wondered if she had a tie in her drawer. I knew she had to be one of them ball-breaker types, trying to compete with the men in a man's world. Her name's Darlene and she's got a pretty enough face. I found myself wondering, in between phone calls, what kind of body she had underneath that severe suit, but my attention was soon distracted by Cheryl and her miniskirt and high-heeled pointed shoes.

I waited to see what everyone else did at lunchtime; it was a sandwich-at-the-desk job, so Patti did the honors, going to the local Italian delicatessen. They were a pretty relaxed bunch, but I could tell that I was going to have to work hard to keep up with them. Work seemed to be the first thing on their minds, that's with the exception of Cheryl, who was cute, bubbly, and ready to joke about nearly everything. I got a little bit nervous—well . . . not exactly nervous, just concerned—when I looked at my watch and realized that the day was nearly over and I still had more than half my list to get through. Maybe Cheryl was just too distracting. I took off my jacket, draped it over the back of my chair, and got down to some serious effort that lasted for, oh, fifteen minutes before Cheryl was back again.

"Hey, Chris, I can see you work out." She sat on the edge of my desk and lightly ran her fingers over my biceps. Now, I'm a three-times-a-week man and none of them sissy women's weights either. I take my training seriously and have developed a pretty convincing eight-pack. I knew that in my tight T-shirt I was looking fit. Cheryl must have agreed because she crossed her legs as she leaned over to clasp her hand around my muscle, gauging the size. There was a slight motion from Darlene's direction and I looked over to see her biting the end of her pen and rolling her eyes to heaven. I don't know what that was about. Probably nothing to do with me, but damn if Cheryl wasn't making me feel uncomfortable. The heat rose from my groin straight to my face.

Anyway, I did eventually manage to get the job done, just as everyone was switching off their computers and tidying their desks. Seems like they regularly go to the bar after work, and when Darlene invited me to join them, I knew she hadn't been as immune to my charms as she pretended. The designer suit must have done its job.

I bought the first round, even though that made a pretty big dent in the cash that's supposed to see me through to payday. As I got my change, I realized that everyone was talking about some crisis that had occurred the previous week and I was standing next to Darlene who, I could tell, was affected by my presence. You can tell by the body language. She was forcing herself to keep her distance, but I knew by the edgy way she played with the stem of the glass that she was having trouble keeping her hands off me. I made her nervous and she kept looking away from me, pretending to be interested in something right on the other side of the bar. She was getting through her drink pretty rapidly, too, so when I asked her if she wanted another and reached for her glass, I let my fingers brush against hers. I knew she felt the electricity and she looked flustered as she refused. I could hear her deep sigh, though. Chris, boy, you ain't lost any of your powers! I just wish she would take that jacket off, or even unbutton it. How can a guy make any kind of judgment? So things are definitely looking good. I've made the right move with this job.

This was the last thing the company needed. An office stud! For Christ's sake, we already had Cheryl, the blond bimbo, and now, for the sake of political correctness, we had to have the dark-skinned himbo. The guy walked into the office as if he owned the place or had already been promoted to chairman, chief executive, and managing director rolled into one. He was cocky and, as far as I could tell, with little reason. He obviously didn't know that he'd only got the job because the competition was nonexistent. And that's not me putting him down. I got that from the horse's mouth, from Terrence, who is in charge of hiring and firing and happens to be a brotha too. Now Terrence and I have worked together for a long time and I can trust him to give me the real deal.

"The guy's all front, but he'll get the job done," he'd reported back after the interviews, a definite sneer in his voice. I was only interested because I'd probably have to deal with any fuckups coming out of the department. I think I noticed him on the day of the interviews, but I can't be sure. There's nothing much to distinguish him from the herd; his own mother would probably have difficulty identifying his corpse!

So, as I said, he walked in looking as if he owned the joint. Flash new suit where the rest of us made do with last-year's sale bargain. And, of course, Cheryl immediately made a beeline for him. We'd been through the same routine many times with guys who could give the brotha a run for his money and, sooner or later, they'd all succumbed to her "charms." With this new guy, it was sooner. He didn't know that we'd started an office sweepstake last week (without Cheryl knowing, of course) to see how long it would take before he shifted in his seat, trying desperately to hide his predictable hard-on. The day I meet a guy who can resist the blond hair and short skirt, I think I'll marry him. To be fair, he lasted through the morning, and I might have won if only Cheryl hadn't crossed her legs right in front of his face. Stephen, one of the guys in A&R, happened to be looking through his office window at the time. His thumbs-up made me want to puke, especially as he waved the winning ticket at me. I could only roll my eyes to heaven.

And the new guy has the sensitivity of a clam! We'd all been hoping that he'd have the decency to go out to lunch so that we could dissect him, but no, he has to join in the sandwich round. So I had to spend most of the afternoon listening to his pathetic routine with the pseudo-American accent. And his voice dropped an octave every time he got a woman on the phone. He was obviously too green to understand that these were cynical journalists he was dealing with.

When it was time to go, it would have been too obvious to leave him out, so I had to invite him to come with us for a drink. And there he was, all eager and goofy like Bugs Bunny flashing the cash. And then the rest of my so-called pals must have thought it was hilarious to leave me standing alone with him—they know what I'm like with these arrogant, self-satisfied jerks. I couldn't get away from him fast enough.


I've been there for nearly two months now and the gods are certainly smiling on me. The day of the brand-new BMW M3 Convertible is hurtling toward me. I know I'm making an impact with my boss, but more especially with the *laydees* . . .

I've got Cheryl eating out of the palm of my hands. She brings me little treats with my sandwich every day— crisps, a drink, or a chocolate bar—and she still finds more photocopying to do than the rest of the office put together. I know the girl is mine for the plucking any time I want. I'm just keeping her in reserve while I check out all the options. I notice that Patti gives me that certain smile whenever I ask her to do a little job for me and she always makes sure she gives it priority. I make sure I treat her to some of my best lyrics as a reward. She's a good-looking woman too. The kind you hardly notice at first because she's a little . . . well, mature, but then her attraction kind of creeps up on you and bites you on the backside. She's got long, silky hair, all black and shiny, and every time she leans over my desk, deliberately revealing the creamy tops of those full breasts, I can feel some sensation in the groin region. I've noticed the way they jiggle when she walks across the room, and sometimes I get so hot and horny that I can barely stand. Patti flashes her diamond engagement ring sometimes, but I can tell that her man can't be keeping up with his business because it seems to me that she's on the lookout for something else. You can be damn sure she notices every time my cock stands to attention for her.

And, of course, there's Darlene. It's hard to figure that one out. Sometimes she seems so standoffish, but I know that she's got her eyes on me. Whenever I look up and catch her off guard, she's staring at me, a hungry look in her eyes. Lord, it must have been a while since the chick has had any 'cause I know from that expression on her face that she's got some down-and-dirty thoughts about me going on in her head.

I wish the brotha would show a little restraint. Each and every day the same thing: his tongue hanging down to his knees when he looks at any one of those white girls. He's almost panting after them and doesn't even realize how everyone is laughing at him behind his back. Even Cheryl finds him a little too easy for her liking. Says she prefers a bit of a challenge.

Patti, about to be married in just a couple of months, can't escape his attentions. You can see her trying to stifle the laughter when he tries another one of his cheesy chat-up lines. I've seen her and Cheryl giggling together about him. On top of all that, he's one of those men who are forever fiddling with themselves. I don't know whether he's got a permanent hard-on or is just checking to make sure that it's still there. Whatever, he does draw attention to himself, and your eyes can't help turning to the region between his legs. Doesn't do diddly-squat for me, so I don't know why he doesn't just put it away.

And don't get me wrong about the "white women" thing. I don't have a problem with all them brothas who, as soon as they find themselves a little two-bit job, have to turn their backs on us black women. I don't feel nothing about that. Honestly.

I've noticed, too, that, since that first day, he doesn't turn up in any sharp suits, just the same old black denim jeans, leather jacket, and a T-shirt. I must admit that he wears those T-shirts well. You can tell that he works out and looks after that body. I wonder why he doesn't have a regular girlfriend. At least I don't think he has. The way he ogles every single woman under the age of a hundred, especially when we're all in the bar together, you can tell that he hasn't been getting jiggy. Wouldn't even surprise me if he was still a virgin.

The BMW's gonna have to wait if I'm forced to spend like this all the time. With the drinks after work every day, regular office lunches to celebrate something or other, and all the new gear I've had to buy to keep up my fine appearance, I'm getting short well before payday each month. Today it was Patti's birthday and a Greek restaurant that looked relatively cheap until I started to count up the number of empty bottles of retsina. I surreptitiously checked the bills in my wallet and noticing my credit card, decided to stop worrying. What difference could a few more dollars on my overdraft make? Once I forgot about the money and had a few glasses of wine, I began to relax. Patti and Cheryl were sitting opposite, laughing loudly at my slightly rude jokes, their faces getting redder and redder as the minutes ticked by.

I looked down at the other end of the table as if my eyes were drawn to her. Darlene. Staring at me again. The sista just can't get enough of this sweet thing. I raised my glass to her and drained it. Then suddenly I shot bolt upright. I could feel a warm, stockinged toe on my leg, easing up the leg of my pants. A tickling ran all the way up to my thigh, circled my balls, and instantly woke something in my cock. Across the table Cheryl and Patti were chatting and laughing with each other. And still the fleshy pad of an instep was crawling up my calf, my thigh, pressing against my balls, but I couldn't tell whose foot it was. The heat rose to my face and I reached for the bottle to fill my glass. Darlene's curious stare burned into the side of my face, even though I wasn't looking at her. I knew my face was getting red. I grabbed a menu, trying to concentrate on anything but the waves of delight spreading from my crotch area. I was only saved by a hat going round with a request for $75 for tickets to the annual charity dinner. That certainly brought me down to earth. Seems like, every year, the firm takes a table. The way things are going, looks like I'll be paying *them* for letting me work there.

I knew there was a reason why I hate these office lunches. Sometimes they can get way out of hand with the amount of alcohol that goes down people's necks. There's always someone who makes a fool of himself—and it usually *is* one of the men—and then has to go around apologizing for the next week. That's if he can remember what he actually did.

Today, for a little while, I thought Chris was going to surprise me. For about an hour he was quiet, hardly drinking a drop, looking as if he wanted to be somewhere, anywhere else. I almost felt a wave of sympathy for him and was beginning to think he looked quite cute in a boyish sort of way. And then, for no apparent reason, the boyishness disappears, taken over by obnoxious, immature behavior. He's downing glasses of wine as if the place were about to run dry, telling the most awful sexist jokes. I must have been looking daggers at him because he turned to me with this curious look, and then that stupid smile came over his face as he tried, unsuccessfully, to be all suave and sophisticated. Ended up looking more like he was constipated. Then I don't know what was going on at that end of the table, but Chris suddenly looked as if he'd been poked with an electric cattle prod, and the next thing he's grabbing a menu and you knew he wasn't even reading it because he looked like . . . God, I don't know how to describe it. Well, yes, I do. To tell the truth, he looked just like he was about to have an orgasm, right there in the middle of the restaurant. And our whole table is quiet, staring at him until Patti and Cheryl start giggling together like naughty toddlers. Funny thing is, I don't think Chris knew what was going on either. He was in some kind of trance and only came out of it when, to disguise the awkwardness, Jeremy started talking about the charity dinner.

"Must have been something he ate," Stephen whispered to me.

God, just imagine what he's going to be like at the dinner. I might die of embarrassment. The guy is such a turkey. Don't know if I can bear to go.

You know, none of them guys in the office paid much attention to me before. And now they're all being so friendly and making a point of coming up to me and asking if I enjoyed the lunch. You know how it is in these firms: They must all think I'm going somewhere and want to stay on the right side of me. That's office politics for you.

Still, I'm trying to keep a bit of a low profile. Running so short of cash that I have to stay away from those after-work sessions in the bar. So I've kinda had to invent a girl-friend. Not that it's a complete lie because there are plenty of women out there who would give anything I wanted to be with me. It's just that I'm picky about whom I'm seen with. That last money for this dinner just about broke the bank. And I'm going to have to borrow the cash to rent some threads for it too.

You know, though, there's a funny thing about women: as soon as they think you have someone else, they're all over you. Even Darlene, normally so standoffish, is always asking me about my girl. She must be wondering how she could have let a fine thing like me slip through the net.

Boy, he's thick! Can't even tell when he's being teased mercilessly by the guys, and doesn't notice that the whole office collapses at the mention of "dolmades." Of course, Cheryl eventually confessed what she was doing under the table. I guess he finally had the sense to be embarrassed, though, because he's stopped joining us in the bar after work. Finally, he takes the hint! But now he's come up with some shit about a mythical new girlfriend. As if! He can't even keep his story straight. One minute she's a blonde, the next she's a redhead. Doesn't remember her name from one day to the next. Does he think we're all idiots?

The more I think about it, the more I'm going off the idea of this dinner. Normally, I really look forward to it, but I can see "disaster" written all over it this year. All because of Chris! Even Professor Higgins couldn't turn him into the belle of the ball in only a couple of days.

Strange, though, those drinks after work don't feel the same without Chris and everyone leaves a little earlier. I can't put my finger on it. I suppose it's just that he's not there to be the butt of everyone's jokes. That must be it.


I knew I'd need a lift home, otherwise I'd be walking. No money for a cab. I spent the last of my cash on renting this damned stupid tuxedo with one of those bow ties you have to do yourself. Some time ago I must have learned to tie one, but I was struggling. I stopped for a moment and just stood looking at myself in the mirror. I'd been to the barbers that morning and had my hair shaved into a dark skullcap knowing I wouldn't be able to keep paying to have it braided. The dream of the BMW was fading. I don't want to be no sad old gray-haired geezer before I can afford one. But still, I grinned at myself, I was looking hot, hot, hot.

I ran a hand over my scalp, checked for my wallet and keys, then set off for the subway.

\* \* \*

The long, bronze sequined dress was lying across the bed just looking at me. I'd bought it months before, knowing I'd need something new for this evening and it had been a perfect fit, lifting and separating where it needed to, slit almost to the thigh. I knew from experience what those other women would look like all glammed up, especially the sistas, and there was no way I was going to let the side down. I'd felt a shiver of excitement every time I opened the wardrobe and heard the tiniest tinkling of the sequins. Now, the edge had been taken off any anticipation I felt. I was nervous of what the night might bring. We would be at the same table, so people would be bound to pair us together in their heads, and Lord only knew how many ways Chris would find to humiliate himself and, by implication, me. I was reluctant to put the dress on. Instead, I spent far too much time on my makeup, delaying the moment. Finally, I looked at my watch and knew that if I wasn't going to play into all the stereotypes, I'd have to get a move on. No doubt Chris would be late, so I'd have to make sure that I was on time. I stepped into the dress, pulling the tiny straps up to my shoulders. I looked in the mirror and couldn't help smiling. I was looking hot and there was a tiny glint in my eye.

Park Lane couldn't have seen anything like it in . . . well . . . in a year, since the last charity dinner. I've never seen so many cool brothas and fine sistas together in one place. There was only a sprinkling of white faces and most of them came from my firm. And wow, if the women weren't looking good in those long dresses that hide a lot and reveal even more. I was just checking out Patti in a shimmering green something, her hair all soft and long, when I heard everyone gasp. I looked around to where they were all staring. A taxi had pulled up and Darlene was getting out and the split in her dress revealed long, silky legs that started at her toes and went right on up to heaven. I couldn't breathe and ran a finger around the inside of my collar. In my horniest dreams I would never have guessed what was lurking beneath those suits Darlene normally wore. She looked around searching for us and as Cheryl waved, she smiled and walked toward us. I'd never noticed before how brilliant her smile was with those soft, full lips all pouting and red. Something deep inside me shouted hallelujah as she stood on tiptoes to kiss my cheek. I wanted to take her hand, but something in her eyes stopped me. Goddamn, I was scared.

Wow! And wow again. I had to look twice. And then three times more. The brother was looking fine. He'd got rid of the pretty-boy cornrows and looked somehow more mature. Damned fine! And the tux sure wore him well. I hadn't realized before quite how tall and broad he was. Suddenly I was glad for the dress. As I leaned against him to kiss his cheek, his arm came up to brush against my hip and a small, distant whispering of desire began somewhere deep inside. But a deeper, more authoritative voice argued that when the taxi had drawn near to the hotel, I'd watched him leering at Patti's chest. He made a tiny move as if to take my hand but I moved away, throwing my wrap across my shoulder. The boy might be looking good, but that didn't change the way he was. I'm definitely not into those guys who are too easy.

Of course, we had to be sitting next to each other. I admit, though, that somewhere along the way, Chris must have found some lost manners. He helped remove my wrap and I laughed out loud when his eyes popped out. I'd known exactly what I was doing when I wore a dress that plunged almost to the waist. I couldn't wear a bra with it but, as I said, it was designed to uphold. I sat down. Chris was still standing, his mouth open. I poured him a glass of water and handed it to him. With one simple, tried-and-tested technique, he was mine for the taking. And now that he was there, I was beginning to think I might even want him. Just a little. I took my time to look at him, the long, lean body, finely tuned muscles, and a promising hard-on that was spoiling the outline of his trousers.

"I think you should sit down," I murmured to him. He was in danger of embarrassing himself again. This time, though, I didn't feel my previous annoyance.

I really couldn't breathe, let alone speak. My heart was pounding fast against my ribcage and I felt a tornado swirling in small concentric circles where my stomach should have been. I could only stand there, staring like an idiot. But who could blame me; nobody had warned me that there could be this kind of transformation.

I couldn't move until I felt her tugging at the hem of my jacket, her glance and her gesture making it clear that I should sit. I couldn't hear a word that she said. All I could think about was those glorious breasts, that soft, dark glistening skin, and under the white linen table-cloth, hidden from view, that high slit revealing those fabulous, silky legs. I didn't know how I was going to survive the evening with my hands only inches away from her naked flesh.

I don't remember too much about the meal; I could have been eating cardboard. That's what it tasted like, and it was all I could do to get my jawbones to move, they were clenched so tight. I know a lot of people stopped by the table, but I can't remember who or why or what they said. I couldn't concentrate. Couldn't see anything above the gleam of her skin, under that white tablecloth. I know Cheryl was on the other side of me and she kept touching my arm trying to get my attention. I know I said words to her, but I couldn't tell you what they were. I was fighting to keep my hands in my lap. They were clenched tight, the knuckles white.

I struggled to hide my amusement. The poor guy looked completely dazed, and I was beginning to feel a little warmth spreading across my stomach when I thought about the effect I'd had on him. *Still got it goin' on*, I told myself. That's until I woke up to the fact that a lot of other women had it goin' on too and quite a few of them were flocking to our table, finding excuses to talk to Chris. I sat back and looked at him more carefully than I'd done before. High forehead and beautifully sculpted head. Dark, soulful eyes that looked as if they'd been outlined in kohl. Straight, narrow nose and full, soft, cushiony lips that were crying out to be kissed. I shook my head. What the hell was that about? This was Chris, the office dork, that I was thinking those thoughts about. What had changed? Well, nothing much had changed where Cheryl was concerned and she was still flashing those deformed tits of hers at him. And if one more sista came along and bent over to whisper in his ear, shoving her backside in my direction, I was going to scream. By the time it was nearing midnight and the lights were low, I'd had enough. I looked across at the crowded dancefloor, back at the latest bimbo heading toward our table, and I took Chris's hand and led the way to the center of the room.

For a moment it looked as if he didn't know what to do,

so I pressed my body against him and wrapped his arms around my waist. If he really hadn't known what to do, he was a fast learner because he was soon holding me tight, running his hands over my ass as I felt the heat swirling around, settling itself in my pussy that was suddenly feeling deliciously wet.

The scent of her perfume was making me dizzy, and when she tilted her hips toward me, I thought I was going to scream. I had to fight to hold my erection away from her, but every way I swayed my hips, she followed, molding her body against mine. I ran my hands over her ass, the sequins rough against my fingertips, but they couldn't hide the voluptuous softness of her behind. I was so turned on that I was grateful the music was slow enough for a gentle grind. Any faster movement and I might have come there and then. The tip of my cock was on fire, feeling the warmth from her body, crying out for release. In the darkness of the crowd, I caressed the soft, smooth skin of her thigh, moving down her leg, lifting it slightly as I stroked the hollow behind her knee. She leaned against me, her breasts pressing into my chest. I watched her eyes close and let my hand rise farther, farther inside the slit, expecting to find the lace of her panties and finding none. I must have gasped because we were both still and she looked up at me and whispered something incomprehensible about visible panty lines. Lord Almighty, give me strength, I breathed, feeling my cock twitch as she slowly licked her lips. My fingers tingled, electric shocks sparking through my whole body as they rounded the soft globes of her buttocks and plunged between the cleft. I was floating somewhere between heaven and hell, not sure of which direction I wanted to go in. Panic overtook me and my body turned to ice. I couldn't move.

I was enjoying the slow, languorous grind, my body glued to his, the feel of his steel-hard penis pressing into my belly. I moved against it, making small figures of eight with my pubic bone. I was in control and loving the feelings generated in my sex, the heat, the ripples of anticipation. I had the upper hand, teasing, torturing. Until I felt his touch on my bare skin. I stopped moving then, my heart pounding, wondering how far he'd go. My mind was racing, formulating a plan, but all the time silently begging him not to stop. I heard his gasp when he realized that I was naked under the dress, and then he stopped moving too. The crowd of dancers brushed against us, but we were like stone. And then his fingers danced around the swell of my buttocks, one finger plunged between them and I froze, my decision made.

I grabbed his hand and walked fast across the room, almost running in desperation. There were people in both directions in the corridor. Which way to go? I took a gamble and turned left, almost dragging him along behind me. I turned left and left again, striding in whichever direction seemed most empty. Then we were running, hand in hand, almost blind to where we were headed, turning doorknobs, making fast exits, searching, searching until we almost fell through an unlocked door.

We were in the kitchen. Cold, gleaming, brushed steel. Empty, sterile surfaces. I hardly noticed as he kicked the door shut and tugged at me, crushing my lips with his, bruising me as his tongue delved into my mouth. I was gasping for breath and pulled away. I backed up against the cool of the metal sink and parted my legs. I slowly lifted the slit in my dress to one side, revealing the triangle of pussy hair. I licked my lips and beckoned to him.

Darlene just stood there, legs wide apart, and slowly, oh my God, so painfully slowly lifted the dress to one side. The sequins gleamed brightly like embers of fire shooting out around that dark, mysterious mass of pubic hair. I could only stare. My cock was screaming commands at me, but my feet wouldn't listen. Then she crooked her finger, calling to me, and it was like she was pulling on an invisible leash. The next thing I knew, I was there, right in front of her, and she was tilting her ass toward me, lifting her leg around my hips, and I could see the glistening, red wetness of her pussy lips. I needed rescuing. I needed help and Darlene provided it, unzipping my pants and reaching inside, tugging, pulling to release my monstrous prick. I wriggled to help her, loving the feel of her fingers around me. I looked down to her chocolate fingers gripped around the base, stroking upward to the angry bulb at the head of my cock. I wanted to pull away from her, to think about times tables, motorway junctions, train-spotting, anything to pause the shafts of pleasure rippling out from wherever her fingers touched. I wanted to move, but she grabbed my behind with her other hand and pulled me closer to her. Still holding my cock, she placed the head just where she wanted, against the tiny seed of her clitoris and rubbed me back and forth, the juices from her pussy making me slick and slippery. She moaned deep in her throat and I felt a tightening at the root of my prick. I shivered and she held my balls, squeezing gently, then harder until the wave passed over.

Before I could recover completely, she held the soft head against her opening and moved it round and round in small circles, tracing the outline, pushing upward against the walls of her sex.

His cock was making me so wet that I was dripping. I loved the soft-hard feeling of his prick teasing my opening. My pussy was hungry for his hard shaft. I'd been torturing him but I was the one who couldn't bear it any longer. I raised myself up, hovered above him for an exquisite moment, and then forced myself down on him as hard as I could, his cock buried right up to the hilt inside me. I raised up and let him slide all the way out before drawing a slow circle with my pelvis and then slamming down against him once more. He gritted his teeth, grunted, and reached for me, sliding his hand inside the straps of my dress, finding my breast and massaging, kneading. I shuddered with instant lust as he found my nipple and bent his head to blow cool air on it. And then he took it into his hot mouth and sucked hard. The sensation was magical, but I didn't need the distraction. I needed to concentrate on what was happening between my thighs. I pushed him away, resting my hand on his stomach, watching his hard cock as he thrust in and out of me.

Her hot fingers pushed against me as she held herself over the head of my cock. The woman was looking so sluttish, her dress up around her waist, tits hanging out of her dress, hair falling down from where it was piled on top of her head. I almost creamed then and had to look away. I couldn't stand the painful slowness of her soft pussy walls teasing me. I reached for her, clutched her buttocks, and lifted her, wrapping her legs around my waist. I looked around and walked her over to a metal counter. I pushed her knees wide, holding on to her thighs as I slammed hard into Lani and held myself there, rotating in circles against her womb, winding my hips, rubbing hard against her clitoris. I started a regular rhythm then, pulling out, slamming back, holding steady for a while, over and over, round and round, in and out until her breath was coming in rapid gasps and she let her head fall back, her mouth wide open, mouthing ooh, ooh, ooh silently. I lifted her legs up over my shoulders and leaned over her, ramming into her hungry pussy with all my strength. There was a rushing in my ears and I heard her moaning, *aah, aah, don't stop, give it to me,* until I felt her muscles tightening around me, clutching, releasing, clutching, releasing, and I didn't have the strength to fight it anymore. My balls tightened, the tension unbearable, and then, oh glorious release, I was coming, spurting fiercely into her.

He was so strong, so hard, so deep inside me. The fluttering started and I couldn't stop it as it grew and grew, taking over, clutching at his hardness, and as he plunged a final time my body erupted in waves of pleasure and I came with a million, tiny, rippling orgasms melding into one as I bucked against him, taking every last drop of his sweet thing.

We held each other for a while and I stroked the curve of his head as he nestled into my shoulder, his hand softly caressing the satin of my breast.

There was a sense of loss as he pulled out of me and I held him for one more second before letting him go. He gently kissed my lips and turned away, looking for something to clean himself up with before we could return to the ballroom. It could have ended like that, a delicious memory, but he just had to turn back to me, an undeniable smirk on his lips.

"Hey, sweet thing, daddy gives good lovin' don't he?"

Why on earth does sex make men speak in a foreign language? I slowly looked him up and down, lingering on the shriveled penis along the way.

"I've had better. And much bigger."

I left him behind trying to cover his prized manhood.

The following Monday, Chris wasn't in the office. Stephen teased me mercilessly. "What the hell do you do to these guys, Darlene? Looks like there'll be yet another office vacancy."

## About the Author

Lani Douglas works as an office administrator for a West London company that her husband hopes is far duller than the one in her story. The character, Chris, is based on someone she worked with in a previous incarnation who will remain unnamed, but will probably recognize himself. Then again . . . there are quite a few like him out there! Lani is thirty-three, lives in Acton, and has two young sons.

# Roots Thing Dirty: You Make My Body Slink and My Tail Fall Rounded and Crooked into the Shape of a Heart

S. P. Brown

When Tamara Gates arrived at the hotel lobby earlier than all the others, she sat and wondered was she really here or even supposed to be here. This was about 2:00 P.M. The boys should arrive at 4:00. Butterflies cage-wrestled in her stomach. Who could ever imagine? Skinny little Steven, and bad little Tam, and somehow the 5thand6th. Steven and Tam met at a 5thand6th concert; well, they were formally introduced. They had been conscious of each other for their whole lives.

At 2:30, Tam and another sister sat and daydreamed as a tall, handsome, brown-eyed woman approached smiling and embracing. The brown-eyed woman was sharp like Tamara's grandma said sharrrrp, with the sound of extra *rrr*s rolling in it. In fact, Tamara noticed, both of these black women were dressed very nicely. Tam became self-conscious of her clothes. Examining her rolled up jeans, Jimmie Hatz T-shirt, and the socks that the flea market man told her would make her look like a clown, Tamara considered changing into her backup outfit.

"Tamara?"

Tamara's head popped up.

"Hi, Sweetie. I'm Claudia." The tall, handsome woman introduced herself.

"Oh. Mrs. Bass." Tam stood.

"Sit down, girl. This is Angie . . . uh, Mrs. Drum." She pointed to the woman who had been sitting next to Tammie for the past half hour. "We have heard quite a lot about you. And you are just as precious as Drum said you were."

"Thank you," the plain-faced girl replied. People always thought Tammie was so cute. She certainly had some neat little proportions. She was a petite woman. Since she began wearing heels, she had stopped clutching that extra half- or three-quarter-inch that separated her from being five three. She never got much smaller than a 27-inch waist, but she maintained a 40-inch C cup, and a bigger ass. Back in high school, when Technique was just Steven, and he saw right over, around, about her, Tammie was 50 lbs curvier all over. She stopped plenty traffic way back then. Now, Technique would say she was just fly. Cool and hot at the same time—tomboy, sweetheart, contradictory, and attractive as friction—she was bright eyes, rich brown skin, thick black hair, dimpled ivory smile, and all over ease.

Tamara had charmed Claudia and Angie to death with her nervousness, and before 3:45 the women had insisted Tamara change her outfit, her hair, and her nail color. They had glossed and polished her so that now she looked like she was waiting for someone important.

Walking in, Technique knew a headache was coming. His thoughts were moving at a frenetic pace. The synapses were throwing off sparks. Damn smoke was clouding his eyes before it escaped through his ears. It could have something to do with spending the last six months high. Ha. Drunk. Ha. Ha. Getting . . . ha . . . fucked . . .

What is she going to look like to me, Tech had asked Mind and Tongue—the lead lyricists. They had the least to do, so he was around them the most. And they was quiet, and that was usually good. They was on some, "Tamara is beautiful. She still gon' be fine. You don't want her, I'll take her." Fuck-ass niggers. Whatever happened, Technique knew Tammie was loyal to the end. She was too hood to abandon him. That is why he called her and asked her to come to New York this week. "Shit, Ma coulda come. Tamara wouldn't have minded, and . . ." He must have really wanted to see her, he thought, and he looked up as he thought of it.

Tamara stood up when she saw how Steven had grown. His eyes dropped when he saw Tammie; memory blinding like a glance at the sun. Tamara's jaw dropped. Steven had gained at least 15 or 20 lbs. Good pounds. He was no longer her little boy–sized man. His chest was deeper and his arms were much bigger. He had grown this mustache and this little beard. His locks, cornrowed backward, met his shoulders. When he'd left, his locks were too short to braid. Realizing she was gawking, Tamara smiled.

Everything that made men desire Tamara, Technique thought, is eclipsed by her smile. His dick twitched at her dress. Well, not totally. He seized her hips as soon as they were in reach. He pulled her until his lips met her forehead. He whispered, "Damn, Tammie. I missed you."

Even his voice was huskier. And he smelled like cologne, Burberry cologne. Tammie knew because it was an ex's fragrance. *Whatever. I guess that's cute,* she thought. A deep sigh gave way to a deeper sigh.

"Let's go to the room," Tech said. He tightened his arms and an electric charge tickled Tam's toes and the nape of her neck.

"I think . . . I think they want to go to dinner." She took a breath and her ribcage rattled. Part of her wondered if she wanted to be alone so soon with him, the other part wondered, was there anywhere she wouldn't want to be with him.

"Let's go to dinner," pleaded Mrs. Bass to her husband. She tugged at the handle on his giant guitar.

Bass smiled and twirled the tall, black case with hips as wide as his wife's. "Baby, I think some of us have other things to do." Tech had asked Bass and Drum about Tam too. They had just laughed. And then every time they looked at him afterward, they looked at each other and laughed again.

6th said, "I ain't got nothing to do." 6th was new at the time. They picked him up just a month or two before Tech came along. But Tech was just a DJ; he wasn't in the group. 6th was really trying to make some friends. Lonely ass.

Drum finally spoke. He was the drummer, and the biggest, so he usually got last say. He didn't want to go. Well, he got last say on the road, because at home the wives had the situation on lock.

Mrs. Bass insisted, "Everyone doesn't have to go." This prompted Drum to ask Mrs. Drum. She did want to go.

"Come on, Drum," she chided, "don't be a stankbutt."

Drum pointed at Mind, Tongue, and 6th. "Let me say what's not being said. See these three? These three gotta find some pussy. See this one?" He pointed to Ivory, the keyboardist, who had a wife and some kids way out somewhere that he was always rushing to. He never wanted to do too much extra, so no one ever bothered to ask him. "He still got to get to his pussy. And these two," he smirked at Tech, and didn't even glance at Tam, "bound to sneak off during the middle of the meal and have the whole place stinking like pussy."

"Damn. We can sit through dinner," Tam piped up. "I got home training. You just . . . he just . . ."

Mind interrupted, probably up to something, but that's how it went. "I'll go. Tongue'll go." Them two were connected; Mind didn't go without Tongue. And if either spoke to you, which was a big if, it was Mind. So, it was fair, Mind speaking for Tongue. "6th done already admitted he ain't got shit to do."

"I ain't got shit to do," 6th confirmed. That's why 6th was Tech's favorite. Honest as hell.

So Tam and Tech sat through dinner, ankles barely touching, then resting alongside each other, then intertwined. By the time Claudia ordered dessert, Tech was fingering each of Tamara's toes as she rolled the arch of her foot against his fleshy, expanding crotch. They skipped dancing.

The two walked back to the hotel in silence.

An empty elevator. Technique grabbed Tam's waist and pulled until their hips met. He swiveled their hips, side to side. Each gentle swing took Tamara by surprise, and the tickle of Tech's new beard as he kissed her ear elicited something part giggle part moan. He quickly unbuttoned and unzipped her dress, and then, hmm, he slid his hands underneath her bra. His warm fingers tickled her nipples. She was nervous for him to know how wet he had gotten her already. He tickled her neck again with his beard, as he tugged with two fingers at the ribbon knot of her bow-tie bikini panties. Their room was on the sixteenth floor. By the tenth floor, one of the bows had been untied and his fingers were buried in the fold of her fat, wet pussy.

"You so hot, baby," he whispered. The tickling breath and the tickling chin hair produced more giggles. "I'm gon' knock them giggles out your ass tonight." Silence. He dug deeper inside her with his two probing fingers. Tamara untied the other side of her panties. Ding.

In the open doorway, Tech unfastened Tam's bra. She wiggled out of it somehow keeping some of her dress over her breasts. "Let's let the neighbors see just a little." He kissed into her neck, tugging her protective handful of fabric from her fingers. She moaned; he slowed and deepened the kisses on her neck. Her feet stumbled backward but Technique held her up. Technique dropped kisses down Tam's earlobe, down her neck, down her shoulder blades. He scooped her up in his arms like a little girl. Her little Technique scooped her up into the room and flipped her gently on the bed where he began kissing up and down her spine. She scrambled higher on the bed; he crawled with her. It was like he was hungry, hungrier than he'd ever been. Anxiety tensed Tam's back. Tech sensed it and drew back. He went to the tiny hotel fridge and took out a bottle of cold water.

"Boo, that costs."

Technique smiled. "I forget shit's not free anymore."

Tam giggled. "We can buy one at the grocery store and replace it."

"I missed you, Tam."

"I missed you too."

He sat down on the far corner of the bed and drank the bottle in one swallow.

He reached back and grabbed Tam's closest leg, slid her across the sheets—swvvvt—"We need satin."

"Satin?"

"You scared of me, Tam? You tense up like you scared." He pulled her to straddle his lap. He whispered into her earlobe, his new goatee just barely touched her neck. She instinctively pulled her head into his. He reached down and tickled the arch of her foot. A gasp and a scream raced out of her mouth in a dead heat. He whispered, "You didn't forget me, did you? I know you didn't forget me."

He turned her around, again. He could lift her before he left, but not so easy; and he must have been enjoying this show of strength. He tilted her off his lap, over the edge of the bed, until in a panic she locked her legs around his back and braced her arms against the mattress box spring. Her back stretched in front of him; her tits swung back and forth, about three feet above his toes. Then he kissed between her shoulder blades with his ice-water-cold tongue. She lost strength in her arms and folded over the end of the bed. He pulled her up, kissing from just above the crack of her ass to her neck. Tam felt wetness itchy on her thighs, loose in her ass. He lifted her off his lap and stood her up. Her dress was the only clothing she still wore, and barely that. Tech pulled the dress off slowly and the seams tickled her crotch and hardened nipples. She shook first from the vulnerability of her sudden nakedness and panting desire. The next shock was from the cool chill of hotel air against her sweaty back, which tightened her nipples even more.

"Is that me or the cold that made your titties do that?"

"Uh," Tammie stuttered. Steven didn't talk like that.

Her mind instructed, *This is not Steven, Tam. This is not Steven.*

"Uh. You, and the cold air. Both."

"Hmmmm." Technique stood up, and Tammie kneeled. She unbuttoned his pants, unable to break her gaze from Technique's dick standing straight out. The slacks fell with a *ffft* to the floor. Tech pulled his boxers to his feet. Damn, if Tammie didn't look like she was trying to give him head. Tech didn't know if he liked that. Tammie was kind of wild tonight. She always had been, but she was down for whatever tonight. He didn't know if he wanted to know everything she could do, least not right now. Already he was learning that being with Tammie was like dancing with her. She was light on her feet, and she anticipated everything. He'd only watched other men dance with her as he DJ-ed. Now, he was seeing what was so sexy about it. All he had to do was touch her and she twirled into the right places. And now here she was on her knees, pulling his pants and boxers off. Just the sight of her down there made him want to bust, and the thought of busting in her hair, and in her face, all over her tits, with those flame-shaped areolas and stiff nipples, both fascinated and horrified him.

The last thing he wanted her to do was suck his dick. He had his shit sucked by some real pros on tour. He had fucked some pros, too, but fucking came long after the head. Shit, for the first month the manager gave him head every night he DJ-ed. Vapors. Tam had potential, though. She had wet, full lips. And her tongue was just visible in her hot, open mouth. "Tamara. Grab a condom out my pants. You know how to put it on?"

Tam smiled and laughed breathily. She was such a silly girl, he thought. "Yes, I know."

"Okay, well, I just never asked—"

"I didn't know you'd want me to . . ."

"I want you to do whatever moves you, Tam. Don't be afraid, or inhibited. Don't hold back from me." He reached down and pulled his girl up by her armpits. She pulled her knees up high around his back, beneath his shoulders; her hot pussy wet his muscled stomach. She squealed. Had Tech forgot about the noises? How could he forget the noises? They'd keep whispering to him for days after sex. The voices were right here in his ear.

Between deep sighs, Tam poured, "Tech. Steven. Tech. Steven. Tech," into his ear canal. With her still clinging to him, he climbed onto the bed. There she fell. He split her thighs gently and began to penetrate her. She was wet all over but she was so fucking tight. . . . She was making this hard for Tech. It had been so long since he had been with her—and she was so hot—but Tam was going to take some rocking back and forth, and he was real close. He slid farther in her anyway, and she cooed so deep and low in his ear that it vibrated in his balls. Damn, baby. He slapped the side of her ass. She giggled and squealed.

"Oh. Shit. Shit. Oh, Tam. Shit. Tam. I'm sorry. I'm about to . . . bust. Aaaaarghh!"

Tam gasped. He just came. Whoa! And she didn't. And . . . whoa. This was really not like Steven. He was the best lover. He wasn't the biggest, strongest man. And sometimes he was awkward, not like some lovers who could do the shit folks do on TV. But he was attentive and patient, and he always waited until she came. And if this was all she got in exchange for better game and bigger muscles, she was not pleased. She knew she never wished for it. Steven was perfect the way he was.

"Tech . . ."

"Baby. Baby. I know. I'm sorry. I just. God, you had me so turned on. Please, just give me fifteen or twenty minutes. You know what you can do is pick out some music. Look, I got my MP3 and you can—"

"You pick out the music." With that Tam pulled the condom off Tech's limp dick, picked up the wrapper, and proceeded to the bathroom. Tech lay back on the pillow, anxious for Tamara to return so he could explain more.

Soon he heard water running in the tub. Just give her space, Tech, you'll make it up to her later on tonight.

Tam was just in there crying. What happened to Steven? He used to be so sweet and gentle. Now, he was so rough. It was good in a way, she guessed. He was more aggressive, but . . . She got into the tub. She always felt nauseous after casual sex. She felt nauseous now. Steven never made her feel this way. She got in. The water wasn't hot enough. She turned the hot with her dark red toes, red for him. The crying slowed a little as the warmer water pushed its way up. As she turned the bathroom fixture off with Steven's red toes, she resolved to just sleep in the tub. If she drowned, whatever. That was how she felt.

Technique's head snapped up. How long had he been asleep? It felt like hours, but when he looked at the clock only fifteen or so minutes had passed. Tam must still be in the bathroom. He scratched himself, rose, and crossed from the bed to the bathroom door. He knocked softly. Waited. No answer. Damn, she was mad. He knocked louder. Still, no answer. Tech wouldn't have imagined Tam would get this mad about him coming too quick. She wasn't a diva. She was pretty cool. He cracked the door and poked his head in. There she was asleep in the tub. That's dangerous as hell, he thought, as he sat on the toilet stool looking at Tam.

Here was a woman whose face was always filled with tension. She was a school teacher, just like her mom, and they both had the same smile and frown lines. He knew both faces well because Tam's mom was his ninth grade social studies teacher. Lots of times Tam made faces that made him want to look for his homework, but when she was asleep her face was perfectly still. There were only two times when Tam was that relaxed. Tech kneeled next to the tub and kissed Tam on the forehead. Then he kissed both her eyes, then Eskimo kisses on her nose. Finally, as he kissed her lips, he slid his hands underneath her back and her knees and lifted her out of the tub. She woke in his arms and struggled a little bit to get onto her feet. He grabbed a towel and wrapped it around her.

"Tech." Tam looked into his eyes, grabbed his ears, and pulled him into a long, deep kiss. She parted his lips with her own and gently sucked at his tongue. She fingered his ears and pushed her breasts up until just her nipples met his chest. "Tech. Are you ready yet?" And, just like that, he was. It was back on, steamier because of the sweaty heat of the bathroom. Tam liked her shit on hell, all her shit on hell, hot like that. Tam kissed him all over his face, all over his neck. Then she started to lick and kiss gently through the hair on his chin, all over his hairline. She stroked his growing dick. Tech could feel himself growing again, too fast. "Tech. Oh, Tech. I waited so long for you. I waited . . . I've been so cold and . . ." Then again sucking his neck, the crook behind his collarbone, back up behind his ear, and then finally her tongue in his ear.

"Shit, Tam." Tam got hotter and hotter. Tech knew this wasn't going to happen, and Tam was gonna blow her top. She had waited fucking six months for him. He hadn't waited six days before he gave in to the manager's eager lips. No wonder Tamara was so tight. He thought she was just nervous, but six months? And if Tam masturbated, she would do that with her fingers, nothing big. She barely masturbated at all when he was around, cuz she was always with it. Damn, all this thinking about Tam and who he never knew she was and who she was right now, shit. He got onto his knees in front of her and pulled her until she was sitting on his face. He began to eat the hell out of her pussy. He was pulling with his mouth, while he probed deep with his tongue. He rolled her clit around and Tam mapped him with rolling, curving, roller-coaster moans. Sounds came from as deep as where his tongue tried to penetrate her, and higher, quick sounds came when he fingered, licked, and kissed her clit. And Tam came, and came, and came, begging and moaning constantly. She was loud now, and he wanted everyone to hear. Then the panic came. She began pushing at his shoulders, scratching his fingers; her legs shook, her chest heaved, and she screamed his name, Technique! Technique!

Technique sucked and swallowed as fast as he could, and Tam's knees buckled. "Tech. Tech." And for a second it was over. He stood up and pushed Tam against the bathroom door. Tech pulled one of her legs to rest on his hip. They were perfectly sized for each other. He pushed inside of Tam and she took a bit more of him each time, with a moan that made him imagine he was pushing sound out of her. As soon as his whole dick was inside her, Tech yelled, "UUUAAHHH! SHIT." He pulled out as fast as he could and came all over the bathroom floor.

Tam couldn't lift herself off Tech's shoulder. "Tech." She couldn't look at him but she had to let him know she wasn't satisfied.

"Tam, I know. This is the second time."

"Not just that. And you didn't wear a condom."

"I forgot. I'm sorry."

"You forgot. Who . . . I ain't . . . you . . . you ain't never forgot before."

"Sorry. I forgot. I only forgot cuz it's you and I don't see why we're using these things anyway. We don't need this. And you so tight, Tam. The condom's making it worse, and you so tight. Just squeezing inside you is almost enough. Plus, you look so good. You look better, feel better, smell better, sound better, taste better than anything I've come across in the past six months. I promise you, Tam. Just give me about ten or fifteen more minutes. I promise."

Tam knew. She looked at him for a long time, wondering where that baby-faced Steven went. How he became this man. As if the changes hadn't been enough, this speech made everything painfully clear. Whatever else he saw, felt, smelled, heard, or tasted had made him a man. Her baby was gone. She had to take or leave Steven, but now and forever after he was going to be this man. Tech wrapped his arms around Tam and guided her in this embrace to the bed. She plopped down and climbed into the sheets. He climbed in, after her. She tucked him in, kissed his ear, and turned her back to him. How would she ever accept this new Tech?

Tam began dreaming vivid, colorful dreams instantly. Tech's mind was completely gray and still. Tam dreamed Tech like Voltron, Tech a Superfriend, Tech racing toward her, around her, Tech like Speed Racer, Tech like R2D2, Tech on somebody's mission, coming to her. And in every episode, she was Genie, and he was in her bottle hiding. As Genie, Tam poured Tech a drink. Simultaneously, the dreams in Tech's head switched from gray to television fuzz.

Tam couldn't sleep long, and he had said ten or fifteen minutes. This was going to happen tonight. Even if this was the last time, it was not happening like this. Maybe Tech didn't want her no more. Maybe all them other girls had excited him so much that she wasn't enough. Or maybe it was all the shit he said, she didn't know. Whatever. Tech was going to handle his business tonight. She shook him. "Tech," she said in her best you-are-not-going-to-fall-asleep-in-my-classroom-young-man voice. He awoke from his brief, intense sleep to find Tam on her knees next to him. She was wiggling and squirming. "Tech, come on. Tech, I need it."

Tech thought, look at this good girl. Look at what you could pull out of somebody if you give them space. Tam was about to come just begging for the dick. This was priceless. Oh, he was gonna eat good for some time, cuz after he put the thing on this hot-ass little girl, she was gonna wake up wanting to cook. But he knew she wasn't wet enough yet, she was just excited. Tam got a secret spot, he thought. "Come here." He pulled her back into his arms so that the crack of her ass was just over the top of his dick. He reached over his head for his water, and took a big drink. "Finish this, Tam." She sat up to drink and he kissed the back of her neck, right at the top of her spine with his cool water mouth.

Her back arched to absorb the chill. "Ooooh," she sang. He kissed higher on her neck. She "ooohed" an octave higher and melted into his chest. He kissed at the nape of her neck. "Oh," two octaves lower than the first note, and she collapsed onto the bed.

He thought, satin. "Put me in, baby."

"Put a condom on, Steven. That's not sexy."

"I'm sorry, baby. I really keep forgetting. But all this fussing, that's not sexy either, Tam."

"You not acting like Steve."

"I know. Steve is a little older now, baby. Can you understand that?" He surveyed her face as if acceptance were a distant traffic signal at the end of a road the depth of her eyes. He waited. And Tech had these big old eyes. And Tam always fell in. "Let's decide, after. Put me in, baby."

"I better come this time," she warned.

Tech laughed. She guided the head of his dick to her pussy lips. He pushed in just a little, and upon penetration Tamara hummed loudly. "MMMMmmmm." Side to side. "Aaauuuu." Around, and then he was really rocking her back and forth, side to side, and after a few minutes of shivering and trembling, her hips began to match his. She laughed. Technique could make anybody's hips move, at any time, especially hers. Only some people got to learn how many ways he could make a woman's hips move. She relaxed her pelvis, and he slid farther into her. Now completely impaled, she rode his hips side to side, back and forth, round, round, round. Just the sensation of fucking Tam could keep his soul satisfied for hours, but he wanted to get to work too. Before he could change positions, the moans changed to stutters. It sounded like she was trying to say something but it wasn't words. He must've hit her G-spot, and he must be on it good. Every push, she gushed around his dick. Oh shit. Tammie, Tammie, Tammie, he thought.

"Lift your legs up." Tammie held both legs straight in the air. This simple change in position electrified everything. Every stroke banged just right. She opened and closed her fingers, screamed, moaned, and begged. Called him by all his names, "Tech," "Steve," "Stevie," "Steven," "Technique," "Technique," begging, "have mercy, Technique."

"No mercy, Tammie. You don't have no mercy for me. Look how you holding me. Goddamn, you so tight. This pussy so goddamn tight and wet, Tammie. You don't have no mercy for me." And the strokes lengthened and slowed, then built to a heightened pitch. Tech! Tammie. Tammie. Tech! Her knees, first her right, then after a minute or two her left fell over his shoulders. Sweat stunned his eyes, he blinked. Tammie's body quaked. Sweat covered them both completely. His locks fell from the careful braids all over her shoulders. He reached over his shoulder and tickled the arch of her left foot. She screamed, clawed his back; she pulled and pushed and cursed, and her pussy shuddered around his dick and a flood came so warm he could feel it distinctly through the condom. Her pussy got even looser, he really went to work then.

He pulled her legs straight up and spun her onto her knees while he locked his hips against her swirling ass, so he could feel her moving against his balls. He remembered he used to have trouble getting in her from the back cuz she was so tight. She'd push him out. Some Senegalese girl taught him how to get around that, or was she Ghanaian? Damn, Tammie was loud. She had come already so she was extra sensitive. The veins on one of her smooth, neat hands stood out as she gripped the bedpost with it. He kept pumping steadily, slowly increasing his pace. He was just enjoying the feeling of fucking this tight-ass pussy so much he didn't want to come.

He warned her, "We gon lean back, okay? Just let me rock you backward." Confused, she just expelled sound and air and leaned back into his chest. Simultaneously, he shifted their weight over his feet. Then he asked, "Can you just balance like that?" She locked her knees and folded the bottoms of her feet up to her ass. She braced herself on her arms, making a plane of her body descending from head to knees. She rested the back of her neck on his shoulders. "Good girl. I knew Tam could. I knew Tam could."

He slid in and out of her by rocking forward and backward on his hip until he had to clutch her hips and pull her all the way to him. This was always his favorite part because no matter how many times Tam came, she would always come again when he came. She got off on having made him come. It drove him crazy. He loved hearing his loud groan mixed with her frantic cries. And true to form he bust with a force like water pushing the cap off a fire plug, Tam tightened, quivered, surged into him, and held her pussy tight around his dick long after they had both come before falling drained and completely still.

"Who," she asked him as sleep that had sealed her eyes rushed to close her lips, "Where is my baby? Who," she mumbled as Technique fell into musing, "is this hungry ass man?"

In her sleep she dreamed of a dark figure following a woman down a wooded path. In her dream knowledge, she vaguely knew the woman was herself. She wanted the figure to follow when they were walking through the big city market, and she did not mind when the path turned quieter, and more intimate, but he had slowly and consistently been closing the gap between them. Now they were nearing her cottage door, and she was barely two or three strides in front of him. She felt his hand reach for her neck, she turned back before she could scream. She peed on herself.

Her eyes opened. In the same moment she felt the tickle of Tech's hair against the top of her thighs, and she felt the hairs of his chin between her ass cheeks. Tech looked up. "Good." He dropped himself next to her on the pillow. "Sit on my face."

"You ready again?"

"Too soon?"

"No. No. I—"

He pushed his fingers in as she crawled over his lips. "You hotter than before."

"I get like that."

"Glad to learn it."

Tam laughed. She hovered for a second too long. Tech

tilted her hips and pulled her to him. A series of rapid, short moans, then long, deep kisses on her clit. Like mangoes, like all the deep people say. Who was this hungry ass man? She went to nowhere and came back as he slurped her like a mango. Eventually her legs were too weak to hold her and she collapsed onto his face. He rolled her off. She scrambled to her knees to reciprocate. Here she goes with this again. He didn't know Tam got down like that but she was so insistent. And she was coming like she knew what to do. He slowed her down again. Let that wait. Tech tapped Tam's head; she plopped back confused and frustrated. "Tech, please let me show you," she panted.

"Shhhh." He lowered his head and kissed the nape of her neck. Tremors of anticipation charged her body. She wished she could be cool but she was so hot for Tech right now. She was almost scared of herself. Tech lay on the bed with his arms pushing at the headboard looking at Tam suffer from the demand of these deep sighs pushing out and deep charges pushing through her. She was covered in goosebumps, and her nipples were hard. She turned and crawled toward Tech. She kissed his lips once or twice, then back to the hair on his chin. She liked the feel of hair on her tongue. She slid onto her side so that she could kiss his Adam's apple and underneath his chin. She licked each collarbone like it was covered with creamy hot fudge. Then back up to his ears, then in his ear. She liked ears. She stayed there a while, before she moved down to his left nipple. She licked it and rolled it around with her fingertips, then she licked it some more. She moved onto the other one, repeating the same process. Then she rubbed her body across his chest as she began to kiss the bicep on the opposite arm, then up and down his forearm, into his armpit, licking and sucking. She loved hair on her tongue.

Back to his nipples, sucking and licking. Nipple to collar-bone, and back. He attacked her neck and she cooed.

"Get on top of me." Tam straddled him. "Condom, girl. Get a condom. I don't want to hear no more shit out of you."

She giggled. He laughed, "What's funny?" She opened the new box of Jimmie Hatz, tore the wrapper off one, and set the wrapper back in the box. She pinched the tip of the condom, placed it securely against the head of Tech's dick, and rolled carefully, gently, so that the condom just touched the base of his penis. "You make that feel kinda nice, girl."

She laughed more, and came back up to his face so she could put her tongue back in his ear. She kissed his collar-bone, his Adam's apple. She wiggled her ass so that her pussy barely touched his fully erect dick. "You wanna play, Tamara?" She smiled and wiggled her ass a little more. He surged forward and planted himself deep inside Tammie; she said his name slow and long, "Tech."

"I got this." And up and down, up and down inside her. She just cooed and purred. Her breasts swung back and forth over his head. Sometimes he'd lean forward and take a bite or lick at her. Then Tam did the wildest shit. She cupped her breast in her hand and began to lick it herself. Oh shit! Technique felt a surge in his balls, he doubled the pace rocking Tam back and forth like a blow-up doll. She was wet, and soft, and flexible in his arms. She just kneeled over him, concentrating on taking all his dick. Pussy quivering, and nearly in tears, she said, "Stevie. Please, Stevie. Please."

"Please what? Please what? Please what?"

"Please don't stop," she begged.

"No mercy?"

"Please, Stevie. Stevie. Stevie. Stevie!"

And there it was. In a short dramatic burst everything was twenty-five times wetter, slicker, hotter. He slapped her ass. From deep in her chest she made a sobbing sound with no tears. "Relax," he whispered hoarsely. And she fell onto his chest, completely onto his dick. "Aaaah. Now I'm all the way in there. I wasn't all the way in before. You were pushing me out before."

"I didn't mean to."

"I know you didn't, baby." He rolled the two of them over onto her back. "I know you didn't."

Then he was right there on top of her again. "You like it this way, Tam."

"Uh-huh."

"I can tell. You always let me in deepest this way. You like to feel me right there." And he pushed right onto her G-spot. It was too late for words. She just stuttered and muttered. "Speaking in tongues, Tammie? I wish I knew what you was trying to tell me, Tammie. I wish I knew what you wanted to say."

Stutters, yielding to cries, "Jesus." Tech pushed farther back. She started to struggle from him. He loosened his grip slightly, but continued pushing fast, far, deep inside her. She trembled everywhere over him. "Oh, God." She was screaming. "Oh, God. Tech. Tech. My Tech. My Tech."

And Tech yelled, "Tam! Uuuaaaghh!" He kneeled over her for a second, as all over Tam closed up like a little sea crab around him. "Tam. Tam." He pulled out of her slowly and carefully. She curled up on her side shaking. He fell behind her and kissed her neck, she moaned. He kissed her shoulder, she moaned. He kissed right above her ass at the small of her back, and then buried his mouth and fuzzy chin into her neck above her shoulder. She leaned into the kiss and drifted off to sleep.

Her dreams were bright and vivid again, but easy. She was Smurfette, and she skipped to and from Tech Smurf's hut, making her skirt flutter for the enticement of his eye. She was the kitten chasing PePe Le Peu. Tech stayed awake and watched Tam's peaceful sleeping face. Right before he drifted away he heard her whisper through her dreams, "You make my body slink and my tail fall rounded and crooked into the shape of a heart."

### *About the Author*

Writing under several names including S. P. Brown, Sweet Potato, 53935, and occasionally her real name, S. P. Brown has published several poems and essays and has written a number of full-length and one-act plays. She is a Minnesota-born, Missouri-raised playwright who teaches, writes, and lives in Chicago, Illinois.

# Shadow's
# Discretion

## Sonya Michele

"Hey, baby, what you think of this? Is it cool? It's not like we're going out on the town or anything," Shadow said sarcastically to April, tucking in her white button-down oxford into her Levi faded straight-leg jeans.

"You look fine, Shadow, baby. We accepted this invitation over two weeks ago, sweetheart. Now, going to dinner is not going to hurt either one of us. I'm not that keen myself seeing as Cher's married to Marcus, who is a bit of a smart-ass, and they're a heterosexual couple with a child, but hey, what's the worst that can happen? Come on now, baby, let me just hop in the shower so we can go and be civil. Let the heteros know that we're just as normal as them. I wanna get my grub on, come home, and get my loving on with you. Is that all right with you, cutie? You know I love you so much," April said, giving Shadow a gentle kiss on the lips.

Shadow watched April disappear into the bathroom. She lay on the bed and stared up at the ceiling thinking how naive and precious her lover was. They had been together for a year now, and Shadow adored April. She just couldn't understand why she was so accepting of people.

Shadow was a stud. She was used to the criticism that outsiders threw at her when they saw her on the streets, but April, being a femme, had no idea of the outside world when it came to how they viewed the two of them together. The few times they had been out together were to a gay club where they were among "family," where they were accepted. Shadow had a few reservations when it came to having dinner with the perfect couple next door, but to please April she stayed quiet. But she would damn well be on guard, 'cos a heterosexual couple might just have invited them out of curiosity. Shadow damn near fell asleep listening to Maxwell's "This Woman's Work" softly echoing throughout the room. She woke to the shower running in the background. She slowly rose and walked toward the bathroom. Shadow listened at the door not knowing whether or not to enter, but wanting so much to take her lover. She backed up and carefully undressed, exposing a white wife beater with a matching pair of white cotton boxers. She entered the hot, steamy bathroom with the thought of seducing April. She pulled back the shower curtain exposing the seductive body of her angel as she lathered herself with a bar of soap. White, sudsy foam covered her body of dark, sensual chocolate. All Shadow could do was stand and be mesmerized by her beauty, her clit growing harder by the second. April was a bitter chocolate statuette with a picture-perfect face. Deep brown eyes, dimples, a smile to die for. She could have been a model. Breasts, round and supple, nipples dark and erect, a resemblance to a Hershey's kiss. Her stomach was smooth and delicate. Shadow loved caressing her skin, and it was a turn-on for April to feel her fingertips running all along her body.

"Baby, what you doing in here?" April asked.

Shadow licked her lips in a way that only April understood, and in that split second she climbed into the shower to stake her claim on that oh-so-sweet, chocolate body. Shadow considered April's body her own sanctum. She worshipped her body just as much as she did her mind.

"Oh, baby. You know I was waiting on you. I thought you'd never come," April whispered, looking intently into Shadow's deep brown eyes.

Shadow said nothing, she just reciprocated with a kiss that melted April's heart, and they held each other as if they were the only two souls left in the world. Shadow's kiss was deep, intense as their tongues engaged in a sexual orgy, Shadow's hands ever so gently exploring her lover's body. April was weak with the wanting of her lover's expertise. Shadow carefully sucked on April's hard, erect nipples, paying each one special attention, with April's soft moans coaxing her to continue, to take her to the point where she could find release. Shadow bent down only to look up at April, wanting her permission to take her to that place. She breathed deeply and inhaled April's fragrance as if it were to be her last breath. April's pussy was neatly shaved with soft, curly hair. Shadow slid her tongue in between April's luscious lips gliding over her engorged clit, which tasted like chocolate sponge pudding but yet was as hard as a marble. Shadow reached behind to take her full ass in the cups of her hands pulling her into her mouth, which yearned to devour her womanhood. April was holding on to the showerhead with one hand; the other hand on Shadow's head, guiding the movements of her erect tongue. They were in total accord, moving together to achieve the perfect orgasm, each lost in the other. The hot water beat against their bodies, the steam rising to the ceiling. April began bucking hard against Shadow's consistent tongue-lashing, Shadow holding on to her tight, wanting to take her to that brink of ecstasy as her moans became louder, her hips rotated faster, matching the rhythm of Shadow's tongue.

"Shadow . . . baby . . . baby . . . you feel me? You feel my clit throbbing? It's calling your name, baby girl, I'm cummin . . . baby, I'm cummin . . . oh damn, baby . . . your tongue's the shit . . . oh . . . oh . . . oh . . . Shadow . . . I love your sexy ass . . . you know how to give it." She fell, exhausted, against the wall, the hot, stinging water steadily beating down on both of them.

"Hey, Shadow, April. How are you two doing? Glad you could join us," Marcus said self-consciously as he answered the door.

"We're fine, Marcus. Thank you," April answered politely, she and Shadow looking at one another with caution in their eyes.

"Come on in. Cher's in the kitchen," he said, eyeing the both of them, not sure of this encounter. "Would you like a drink?"

"I'll take a Hennessey on the rocks. The lady will have a White Zinfandel," Shadow said, looking Marcus squarely in the eyes. Marcus cleared his throat, making it clear that he intended to challenge Shadow.

"So, Ms. Shadow, if April here is a lady, then what would that make you?" His tone was sarcastic.

Shadow looked at April seeking permission to answer. April shook her head "no," trying not to be too conspicuous.

"Well, Marcus, that would make me more of a woman to April, my lady, but more of a man than many of you when it comes to loving and satisfying my lady."

Cher glided into the room as if she were walking on air, carrying a tray of appetizers. She was, unquestionably, a beautiful woman, a thought that entered Shadow's and April's minds simultaneously.

"Shadow, April, it's a pleasure having you here," she said, not knowing that she was interrupting what might have been a very interesting conversation, but she sensed the tension in the air. "You all doing okay?"

"Why sure, Cher," Shadow said. "Your husband and I were just having a little debate about the weaker sex."

Cher looked puzzled and glared at Marcus but managed to change the subject. "So, anyone for appetizers? Shadow, April, you both look great. Come take your drinks. Have a seat. Dinner will be ready in a few minutes." Cher was velour picture beautiful. A majestic coat of deep, dark ebony, a perfect piece of eye candy for the soul, Shadow thought to herself. There was definitely an air of sexual tension in the room. A conversation about the effects of the war and Kobe Bryant provided a welcome distraction until the foursome headed for the dining room.

Dinner was elegant and simply delicious.

"Cher, you outdid yourself. That was superb," Shadow commented as they retired to the deck outside.

"Thank you. Do you cook?" she asked Shadow.

"Girl, I can throw. Ask my baby. She'll tell you," Shadow said, taking April's hand looking her in the eyes wanting so desperately to kiss her, but letting her know just through her body language just how much she wanted her.

"Yea, my girl can burn. She keeps me well fed," April

said, laughing, wondering if anyone, besides Shadow, picked up on her play of words.

Marcus and Cher definitely did but they decided to ignore the remark. Cher couldn't deny the attraction she felt as she watched Shadow's affectionate gestures toward April. Shadow could feel the presence of Cher's desire. The conversation was flowing and the Apple Martinis were kicking in.

"Shadow, would you join me in the kitchen to get dessert?" Cher asked.

"Sure thing," Shadow said, following Cher.

There was a moment's awkward silence. "You and April have a very loving relationship. It's so . . ." Cher couldn't find the words to finish, so Shadow completed her thought.

"So 'different.' Is that what you wanted to say? That's because of April. She makes loving her so easy, so natural. Yea, we're both women, but aside from all that, she's the one who gives me the strength to be me, which is what makes our relationship."

Cher stood back and looked at Shadow. "That's beautiful. Your love is visible. Something most people rarely get a chance to feel."

"Yeah," Shadow said. "Well let's take this double-layered chocolate cake out here before Marcus has a panic attack."

"Now, baby. The evening wasn't so bad now was it? Although I couldn't help picking up on this vibe from Cher," April said, unbuttoning Shadow's shirt.

"I don't know, sweetheart. You know how some women are when it comes to a couple like us. She was just a little curious. I kinda think we turned her on in her own little way," Shadow said, smiling devilishly.

"Yeah, whateva! You just make sure you watch yourself with that one, sweetheart. 'Cause I could tell she had her lil eye on you!" April said, kissing Shadow gently on her lips, her hands unbuttoning her jeans. 'Oh, baby, you feel a little wet down there," April said, touching Shadow's pussy. Shadow moaned lightly against April's mouth.

The bedroom was glowing from the lit candles, and the smell of sex was beginning to fill the air. Shadow's heart was beating fast, feeling April's intensity.

"Lie down, baby," April demanded.

Shadow looked at her lover, curious as to what she had in mind but apprehensive for she was always the aggressor.

"I said lay down!" April forced Shadow down onto the bed. "Now stay there and wait for daddy to come back!" April said, leaving the room. *Daddy*, Shadow thought to herself but not moving a single muscle, making sure that her girl would find her exactly the way she'd left her. The sounds of April's humming filled the dimly lit room, and Shadow shivered, anticipating what was going to happen next. The door opened and there stood April sporting a red slip-on lace bustier with detachable garters and a G-stringed thong. She had on matching feather glamour-girl marabou slippers. She was freaky girl fantastic.

Shadow took a deep breath. "April, you're beautiful."

"Oh no. No, you didn't call me April. Tonight I'm *daddy*. That's who I am. You got that? Don't let me have to . . ." and she smacked Shadow's thigh with a red leather whip.

"Oh, shit, baby. All right. You daddy tonight!" Shadow said, thinking she might just enjoy this little game.

April walked back toward the bathroom, tantalizing Shadow, exposing an ass so round and luscious. She twirled, dancing, gyrating to nothing but the beat in her head, her body glistening under the moonlight shining through the window.

Shadow sat up on the bed enjoying every minute of the burlesque routine. April pranced back to the bed exposing a shiny pair of handcuffs. "Lay back, baby girl." She pulled Shadow's hands above her head and handcuffed them to the bedposts.

"Oh, baby. Damn, girl!" Shadow moaned. April flicked the whip against Shadow's thigh. "I will not tell you what my name is again. You fuck up one more time and you won't be getting none of this! You understand?" she said, letting the whip run down Shadow's chest.

"Yeah, daddy. I understand. No more fuckups."

April reached down under the bed, exposing her plump breasts and erect nipples that protruded out of the bustier. She reached for the scarves. She took the first one and covered Shadow's eyes, tying it tight enough so that there could be no peeking.

"Daddy, that's not fair," Shadow complained until she felt the warmth from April's mouth lingering above her lips.

April touched her tongue to the underside of Shadow's chin and licked her way down to her navel, lingering there for a moment to tease that spot. April heard Shadow's moans as she struggled to remain still. April licked down to the waistband of Shadow's boxers and pulled the drenched undergarments off with her teeth. She blew at Shadow's pussy teasing her to an oblivious shudder.

She spread Shadow's legs, tying each one to a bedpost. "Oh, baby, if you don't look all nasty lying here all-body beautiful."

Shadow could feel April positioning herself over her.

"Prepare for the fuck of your life, my baby, my Shadow." April began licking and pulling gently at the erotic spots on Shadow's body. Shadow twisted and writhed from the wet strokes of April's tongue as she licked and sucked her taut nipples, pulling at them, igniting heat. April sucked, licked, and bit every inch of Shadow's body.

Shadow lost herself in the wet tongue bath. April bent up and over to kiss Shadow's neck, something she knew would drive her crazy.

"Oh, daddy, I want you to taste me, I want you to feel me."

April gently lifted the scarf from Shadow's eyes and looked at her with a want that was intensely arousing. She kissed the love of her life and let her tongue trickle a path to Shadow's destiny.

"Oh, Shadow. I almost forgot how wet daddy could make you. You want daddy to slowly fuck you? You want daddy to taste your juices?" she whispered, all soft and seductive.

"Oh yeah, I want daddy to take me. Do me, baby. Do whatever you want."

April blew onto Shadow's belly and skilfully tongued her pierced navel. She slowly fingered Shadow's hard, wet, hot clit. Shadow moaned in pure ecstasy. April spread Shadow's lips slowly and inserted her index finger deep into Shadow's pussy, finger fucking her into a frenzy.

Shadow was bound by the handcuffs and scarves and that increased her excitement. "Oh, April baby! That shit feels too damn good!" At that moment Shadow realized her mistake.

April pulled her finger out. "I thought I told you my name was daddy! Why'd you do that, you dumb stud? You can't play the game!" April began taking the handcuffs and scarves off while a dumbfounded Shadow wondered what the fuck was going on.

"Turn that ass around, Shadow!"

Shadow obeyed like the little sex slave she was. She was startled as her hair was yanked back and she felt the warm breath of April's mouth sucking on her neck as she covered her eyes again. Once more, her wrists were handcuffed to the headboard.

"Oh, daddy, you are so bad, and I am loving every minute of it!" She felt April leave the room and noticed the soft seductive sounds of Beyoncé's "Speechless" playing in the background. Then she felt April's body climbing up to her wet palace. She felt the hot air as she blew on her pussy, bringing a sensation that was unbelievably good. Shadow shifted down to feel April's tongue reach up to lick her delicate spot. She was lost in April's desire, busily grinding on her tongue as April smacked her ass, a stinging feeling that hurt so damn good.

"Oh, daddy . . . daddy . . . oh . . . I wanna let go . . . I want to cum all in your mouth," Shadow moaned over and over.

April could feel her getting ready to release and she didn't want her lover coming so soon, so she slowed down and started to talk to her, mentally seducing her. "Baby girl. Your pussy got my heart trembling. I feel the hardness pulsating through my tongue, making it the key to your heart. I feel you, Shadow. We are one."

"Oh, baby. I want you so damn bad," Shadow screamed.

April bent over Shadow's body kissing every inch of her back, licking down to her ass. "Stay still for a minute, baby, I want you to totally feel this. Relax, let me make you all mine." Shadow couldn't wait for what April was about to do. April spread Shadow's legs so that she was in a doggy position. She then inserted what felt like a hard, frozen rod into Shadow's pussy. Shadow let out a loud gasp. "Oh, baby. Oh, baby. You got me all in!"

April pumped Shadow's pussy hard, in and out, deeper and deeper. "Oh, daddy . . . give it to me . . . you got me open . . . fuck me, daddy . . . fuck me, daddy . . . You feel me? You feel me? I'm about to explode! You feel me? Oh shit, daddy, here I cum . . . here I cum!" Shadow exploded with a series of gyrating spasms, her body in a sexual trance. April held on to her tightly, lost in her own world of seductive shudders as her body succumbed to the intense lovemaking. They lay there for a minute breathing rapidly. "Oh, baby. That felt so damn good," Shadow said looking into April's eyes.

April smiled and said, "Hold on, baby, I got one more thing."

"Oh no, I don't think—" and before Shadow could finish her sentence, April pulled out the cherry popsicle she had inserted in Shadow's pussy and engulfed it with her lips. Taking a bite, she then bent over and kissed her lover, exchanging the popsicle in her mouth. "I love you, Shadow."

"I love you, too, baby."


"Honey, did you enjoy yourself tonight?" Cher asked, turning off the bedroom light.

"Well, it was quite interesting, apart from their choice of each other, they are two very attractive, intelligent young women. I must say that Shadow does have a way about her, though."

"Yeah, she does," Cher said, reminiscing about the night and Shadow's confident air.

"Baby, you sure outdid yourself tonight; dinner was simply delicious. Just like you. And I've been saving my own little dessert for you," Marcus said as he kissed Cher lightly on the neck, his hand caressing her breasts. Cher purred softly with thoughts of more than Marcus on her mind.

His manly scent and strong masculine hands had Cher melting with desire. She pulled Marcus closer to her warm, naked body feeling his manhood hard against her stomach. She placed her hands around his member, slowly stroking up and down.

"Oh, baby girl, feels so good," he groaned into her ear. Cher moved down and took him in her mouth, slowly sucking at a pace that would arouse her husband to the hilt.

"Damn, girl. You kinda freaky tonight. Wonder what's gotten into you?" he said, pumping her mouth faster and faster. Cher embedded her nails in his ass rotating his dick in and out, round and round. She was aroused, wondering what was going on next door. Marcus slowed down, not ready to release, slowly pulling out of Cher's mouth. He bent down and kissed her open mouth, which was warm and inviting. He slid down sucking on one of her dark succulent nipples while pinching the other, bringing a sound of sweet ecstasy from her.

"Marcus. I so want you to fill me up. I want you to give it to me, daddy!"

Marcus wasn't used to Cher being so vocal when it came to making love. *We need to have those two over more often*, he thought to himself. He reached down and felt between Cher's legs. It felt like a warm river of creamy juice, and he wanted a taste. Marcus caressed Cher's body and parted her lips, her pussy inviting him in. His tongue plunged deep inside, sending Cher into a frenzy. She placed her hands on Marcus's head rotating her body to the movement of his tongue. "Oh, Marcus baby boy. You the shit! I want to cum all in your mouth."

Marcus was lost in Cher's wet river of love that tasted sweeter than honey.

"Oh damn!" Cher said bucking to the rhythm of Marcus's mouth. "Baby, I'm about to cum. . . . You got me about to explode!" Cher shouted with her fingers deep in Marcus's scalp. She was trembling from the tongue-lashing she had just received, her body shuddering from the contractions of coming so hard. Marcus inhaled her sweet fragrance for the last time, and while looking up into her eyes he entered her slowly, his hardness meeting her wet and tight juicy pussy. He plunged deep inside not skipping a beat; Cher's nails deep inside his back were a pain that felt so good to him. His rod thrust deeper and deeper as he felt the muscles of Cher's pussy contracting against his manhood, driving him crazy. "Cher . . . you got me all in. I'm bout to drown in this good-ass pussy you got on you . . . baby . . . baby . . . oh my . . . shit, girl," he repeated over and over as he released his love juice inside of her. They both lay there exhausted for a moment until their shudders subsided.

"Whew, baby. That was good. I love you," Marcus said as he gently kissed Cher's forehead before he fell fast asleep.

\* \* \*

"Honey, breakfast is getting cold. Come on, baby, you're going to be late," Cher yelled to Marcus while pouring Tiffany's milk over her cereal.

"Mommy, are you taking me to school?"

"No, baby, your daddy will be taking you this morning," she said with a sigh of relief.

Cher peered out the window while washing dishes to watch her, Shadow. She was busy wiping off her Cadillac Escalade EXT. There was something about this woman that intrigued Cher, and after the little dinner party last night the temptation she felt was more than a little on her mind; it almost made her uncomfortable to think about her neighbors. She watched them every morning each going their own way. Shadow had a way about her, sexy as hell, but with a touch of masculinity that many a woman would love to get to know. Cher watched as April looked around to make sure no one was looking before she planted a long, passionate kiss on her sweetheart. Cher was lost in their world when Marcus snuck up on her and lay his own little mark of sexiness on her neck. Cher jumped. "Damn, baby, where you at?"

He caught her uneasiness and looked out the window. "Oh, I see the neighborhood dykes have sure gotten your attention. Sweetheart, last night wasn't enough to satisfy your fascination for those two? What are you so intrigued about? Baby, don't let your curiosity get the better of you!"

"Marcus baby, Tiffany is right at the table."

He laughed and played her off jokingly, saying, "Now don't you go getting no ideas."

"Boy, you crazy, you know I'm lovin' on Big Daddy Marcus's long, hard, hot rod," Cher whispered, laughing as she kissed her baby and husband good-bye. As she made her way back up the driveway, she couldn't help but look over at Shadow, who was still busy wiping off her pride and joy. It was a beautiful morning, kind of muggy for it being so early. Shadow was gleaming, her golden tan body glistening from the hot sun. Cher couldn't believe how Shadow turned her on in a way that she had never experienced before.

Shadow looked up and noticed her standing there. "Hey, Mrs. Duncan, how you doing? Beautiful morning, huh?"

"Um yea," Cher replied. She was suddenly shy.

"See you got your beautiful family off," Shadow said, walking toward her.

Cher couldn't get over how captivating this woman was, so beautiful, with a honey brown complexion and long brown hair, soft and shining down off of her neck. She had dark brown eyes that looked as if they were peering into one's soul. A smile that was infectious, with deep dimples that could make anyone fall in love with her at first sight.

"Hey, Mrs. Duncan, you aiight?" she asked in her slang type of talk.

"Yes, I'm fine. And you know you can call me Cher. How about a cup of coffee?" she asked, not believing that she was inviting this woman from around the way back into her home. What had come over her? Shadow looked at her with those sexy eyes of hers and rubbed her six-pack abs as she responded, "Well, I ain't too much into coffee, but a nice cold glass of orange juice sure sounds inviting."

Cher watched her as she glanced around and then down at her gold Rolex watch that was dangling on her glimmering, caramel golden arm. *Oooh, this girl is damn fine*, she thought to herself. Shadow followed Cher into the kitchen. She opened the cupboard and pulled out a long decorated drinking glass, filled it with ice, and poured the orange juice. "Hope you like ice in your OJ."

"That's fine with me, the colder, the better it goes down. I really meant to tell you last night what a nice place you have here."

"Yeah, it's okay, but there is a lot of work to be done. Let me show you around, because I lost all sense of my manners last night." Shadow followed behind Cher wondering what was to come of this little visit.

Cher was having her own doubts as the tour of the house made its way upstairs. A sense of guilt came over her as she entered the master bedroom.

"Damn, Cher. You have a very nice bedroom. I guess Marcus be tearing it up in here."

Cher looked at Shadow in disbelief, reminding herself that she and Marcus had gotten busy the night before but surprised that Shadow would refer to the two of them together in that sense.

"I'm sorry, I shouldn't have gone there with you. We hardly even know one another. My bad, it won't happen again."

Shadow stood motionless, looking deep into Cher's eyes, and it seemed as if her heart just melted right there at that precise moment. There was definitely a magnetic pull between them. Shadow broke the uneasy silence. "Cher, I noticed last night that you . . . me . . . well, we kinda . . . dig one another. I know the circumstances between the two of us makes this unrealistic, but I can't help but feel this attraction toward you. Do you feel me? 'Cause I feel you, I feel your vibes when you look at me from your kitchen window. I saw how you looked at me this morning, last night. You want me, you want me to touch you. You want me just like I want you." Shadow moved closer toward Cher, running her finger down the side of her face.

Oh, how Cher wanted her! Not knowing whether or not to give in to her feelings, she was nervously biting her bottom lip. She felt so weak at that moment, not knowing how to react. They looked at one another until Shadow made the first move, gently pulling Cher's face close to hers. Cher could feel her warm breath on her lips tasting the Big Red that Shadow chewed religiously. Cher let down her guard, closed her eyes, and let herself go. Shadow kissed her, all soft and gentle, on the lips, slowly sliding her tongue deep into Cher's mouth. It was a warm, sensuous kiss, just like the kiss Cher had witnessed earlier that morning, except this time she was on the receiving end. Shadow's hands caressed her body and she wanted to surrender in her arms, but something about this encounter frightened her, and Shadow sensed it. She pulled Cher close to her, holding on tightly, giving Cher a sense of security. "Cher, let it go, trust me, I only want to make love to you, rescue you from that little fantasy you have. You know you been thinking about me. This is just between you and me, no one else has to know."

Shadow had Cher's head spinning, her body in want of her touch and the moistness in between her legs was becoming unbearable. Shadow began taking off her clothes, revealing a body that was a chiseled masterpiece, athletic, brown skin glistening from the heat of the early morning. Cher didn't think it was possible to fall in love with another woman's body, but Shadow was beautiful all over. She had never known a woman's body could be so perfect. Cher began to undress when Shadow abruptly stopped her. "No, let me." And Cher just stood there as Shadow gently took off her long, white, cotton button-down shirt. She look surprised, noticing that she had nothing on underneath but a black thong. Shadow stood back and gazed at her body. Cher could see in her eyes that Shadow was just as astonished with her body as she was with hers. Deep chocolate skin, breasts that were full, nipples, round, supple, hard, and erect. Shadow took a deep breath and, looking deep into Cher's eyes, pulled her close to her naked body, both of them high on one another.

Shadow began kissing Cher's neck, sucking, tonguing, licking all the way down to her breast. She sucked long and hard on each nipple. Cher was lost in her mouth, there was a Love Jones forming in her soul. Cher had a want for Shadow, her body trembling out of control. Shadow sensed this and lay Cher down on the bed, all the while continuing to suck madly on her nipples, pulling hard, nipping with her teeth. Cher felt as if she might orgasm on that sensation alone.

Shadow reached down and felt between her legs. She felt the warm, creamy nectar that was calling out to her.

"Cher, you're soaking wet."

Cher let out a moan that let Shadow know that she was surrendering. She caressed her clit with her two fingers, sending Cher into a sexual frenzy. It felt oh so good. Shadow slowly inserted one finger into Cher's drenched pussy and stroked in and out, driving her crazy, finger fucking her to near climax.

"Shadow, take me. I want your mouth on my pussy. I want your tongue to fuck me deep, come on, girl."

Cher heard her snicker, like a little kid, making her

mother angry. Shadow began pulling Cher's wet thong off with her teeth, licking each thigh as she finally removed the last stitch of clothing from Cher's body. She looked at Cher's lost soul, which was all into her, and she slowly placed her face onto her wet mound of loneliness that was so wanting for a woman's touch of love. This woman was rescuing Cher, and she wanted it. Shadow inhaled Cher as only a woman could. She raised up and admired Cher's delicate brown pussy. She smiled up at Cher and gently kissed her clitoris. Cher thought she had died and gone to heaven as she felt her tongue plunge deep inside her. This was sweet ecstasy. She was losing control, gyrating with Shadow's mouth, fucking her back, and Shadow was bucking hard against Cher's leg. Cher could feel her wetness, she was moaning and fucking her leg just as hungrily as Cher was grinding her pussy on her face. They were in a motion that was like a wild river running out of control, their motions becoming faster, their hearts racing, both feeling lost in a sexual fantasy ride.

"Cher, your pussy tastes so good. Cum in my mouth, let it go, I want to feel you explode." Cher obliged and grabbed Shadow's hair, pumping her pussy deep onto her tongue, as she let herself go. Cher heard the erotic sounds of screaming and moaning. Her body was shaking out of control.

"Shadow, you are working this pussy, Shadow, I am cummin, baby girl, fuck me, I am loving this shit!" And with that she came in an intense orgasm. Cher felt her juices flow into Shadow's mouth, she felt the contractions in her pussy. Shadow's lovemaking had taken over her body, which still trembled from the orgasm. Cher could never, ever remember feeling like this before, nor would she ever feel this way again. She had never come this hard. There was no way she could explain what had just happened to her.

Shadow got up quietly and put on her clothes. She looked down at Cher and gently kissed her on the mouth. Cher smelled her own fragrance on Shadow's breath and instantly fell in love with the scent of herself on another woman. Shadow said nothing to Cher, she just stared at her with that look of hers.

That evening as Cher was busy washing dishes after dinner she peered out the window just as she had done earlier that morning. Shadow and April were busy planting flowers in their front lawn. They were engrossed in one another, playfully fighting with each other. Cher saw Shadow tenderly caress April's back and gently kiss her on the neck. She felt a warm rush through her body. Cher smiled to herself.

"Girl, stay out of those lovebirds' business. You know good and well you can't handle that type of loving. You know Marcus here got what you need," he said, hugging her from behind.

"Oh, you do, do you?" she said to him as she turned and gave him a deep kiss.

## About the Author

Sonya Michele's writing addresses the lifestyle of the African-American Lesbian community. "Being a lesbian was not a choice. It was a feeling that was embedded in me by nature. I always knew there was something differently unique about me and I was comfortable with this feeling as long as I kept it hidden within myself." It was at this time that Sonya turned to writing. "It's how I found myself."

# Hourglass

Kiyra B. Holt

*H*is gaze was unflickering, his concentration intense as he plucked each crimson petal from the bud, laying the trail, the fragrance of the roses evoking sweet memories of a summer past.

The hotel concierge walked with Quinn to the elevator lobby.

"Mr. Broderick, I trust that your stay here will be more than pleasant. Please call the front desk if you need anything. Anything at all."

"I will."

The concierge pushed the elevator button and shook Quinn's hand. "Have a lovely stay here."

Quinn returned the handshake. "Thank you."

The concierge walked off. Quinn was settling into his thoughts as he waited on the elevator when he heard the concierge's booming voice reverberate through the lobby.

"Mrs. Houston, hel-*lo!* We have several messages for you."

"Can I pick them up later? I'm exhausted and I need a nap."

"I'll send one of the desk clerks up with them, if that's okay with you?"

"That's fine. Just have them do it soon, before I fall asleep."

"Will do."

The elevator pinged and Quinn moved to step in when he heard the woman's voice, tinged with urgency and exhaustion, "Hold the elevator, please!"

He pressed the "hold" button and as she stepped inside a familiar fragrance assaulted his nostrils. He looked at her and she glanced back at him, barely acknowledging his presence. "Thanks—" She turned her head slightly to the left, her tone a question.

"Kylie?"

She looked at him, blinking, her gaze becoming more intense. "I'll be *damned!* Quinn."

"Kylie. What a *pleasant* surprise!" Quinn stared at her, secret reminiscences flooding his mind.

"I'll say. You're looking good!" She smiled at him.

"You too," he said, his eyes taking in all of her. "In fact, you look superb. Love the new haircut."

She wriggled unconsciously; his voice was deep and smooth like warm chocolate. It seemed to envelop her and she took a moment to respond. "Oh yeah, well . . . the nappy shit was getting on my nerves, and I need every one I've got."

"It looks good on you." His caramel eyes traveled over her face and body like hands, taking in everything from the page haircut to the Dolce & Gabbana pantsuit and Manolo Blahnik shoes. He remembered a time past and she shifted from one foot to the other as his dulcet tones became an auditory magnet, drawing her closer.

The elevator pinged again and the moment passed.

Quinn still had his finger on the "hold" button. Exhaling, uncertainty and pride intermixed in her tone, Kylie extended her hand for Quinn to inspect her rings. "I got married." She shifted her weight between her feet and clarified, "To Keidron. Two years ago."

"Just six months after you took me to the airport." He looked at her platinum rings, then at her. They were both silent.

The elevator ping broke the silence and Quinn tore his eyes away to punch his floor and ask her, "What floor?"

"Twenty-five."

"So . . . you got married." His eyes held her enthrall as he spoke.

"I know I was worrying about marrying him . . . but I decided I didn't want anyone else." There was a determined edge to her voice and she held his caramel gaze, defiant. Meeting her stare head-on, he countered, "You don't need to be without a husband, Kylie. Not a woman like you."

She lowered her eyes, losing the tug-of-war. That voice, his voice . . . even after all this time . . . it was still auditory seduction.

Kylie shifted. "I always hoped that you were doing well, Quinn. I remember the things we talked about."

"I hope you remembered *everything* . . . because I do."

Kylie went still, remembering the kiss he'd laid on her at the airport. Her attraction to him had been a fierce, tangible thing, but she never said anything to him. He was married and a father. He was *forbidden*. She didn't want Quinn thinking she was a whore or unworthy of respect, flinging herself at a married man. Everything about him had been ingrained into her mind, everything. Six feet tall, skin the color of roast almonds, broad-shouldered and physically fit, with a slender waist and hips, a beautifully shaped bald head, and that deep, seductive voice. His voice alone had nearly been her undoing.

She hadn't known that Quinn had felt the same attraction until he'd given her that kiss at the baggage check-in. Kylie's emotions hadn't been worth shit after Quinn's transfixing kiss, and she had relived it over and over and over in agonizing detail. She never forgot the feelings it evoked, never forgot how weak-kneed it had made her. Never forgot him.

Quinn's recollection of the kiss hadn't been much different. He'd kept the experience of Kylie's sweet lips and the soft, sensual feel of her body locked in his mind's vault for the past two and a half years, taking it out to ruminate and savor it. Even though he adored his wife, he'd found himself, on more than one occasion, reminiscing about Kylie, the kiss, and what *might* have been.

The elevator stopped at the twenty-fifth floor. Kylie shouldered her Coach purse and smiled at Quinn, checking him out one last time. He was wearing the hell out of that Armani suit. "Well, I'm here for another day or so. Maybe we can do lunch or something."

Quinn allowed himself the barest hint of a smile. "Or something. Good day, Kylie. Enjoy your nap." The elevator doors closed.


Kylie was in the hotel observatory on the fortieth floor, watching the sunset, shrouded in thoughts of her husband, staring at the majestic views the observatory commanded. To lay eyes on Quinn Broderick after two and a half years brought to the surface the swirling miasma of forbidden thoughts that had been laid to rest the day she'd pledged to love and honor Keidron Houston. Or so she'd thought.

Quinn . . . Quinn . . . She had been sure she would never see him again. Had she wanted to? She had no answer. The idea of a man like him had been enough to make her put off Keidron's advances for years; the reality of him was potent, dangerous . . . and married. So now what? Things had changed since their first meeting.

They met at the wedding of two college friends. Kylie was a bridesmaid and Quinn a groomsman, and the prewedding celebrations had thrust them together. Their initial meeting had been at the family picnic where they'd noticed each other at the condiments table. He had been wearing a pale yellow shirt, open at the neck, and loose-fitting khakis, the light colors doing wonders for his chocolate skin. Not every man could make a yellow shirt work, but what Quinn did for that shirt should have been illegal. Even now, her breath caught in her throat when she saw him again in her mind.

Quinn extended his hand and she took it, bewildered as he raised her fingers to his lips in greeting, closing his eyes. The bride was talking, but Kylie heard nothing except the beat of her own heart and she was unable to say anything. Even then she was aware of the electricity sizzling between them. It was in his eyes.

One of the dying rays of the sun reflected off a sky-scraper and the blinding light illuminated the observatory. Kylie stepped back, one hand blocking the light and the other instinctively cupping her belly. After a moment, she removed her hand, blinking, afterimages dancing across her field of vision. She sighed as the sun sank below the horizon, lighting the sky one last time with its brilliant rays.

Later on, when everyone had broken up into different groups, Kylie was sitting at the table watching the sky when Quinn came and sat beside her. In just a few moments, they were engaged in deep conversation. An hour passed and neither noticed.

Kylie sighed and left the observatory. She turned the corner that led to her suite and stopped in front of the door. A rosebud was taped to it. Kylie shifted and looked around, then back at the flower, as the barest hint of a smile curved her lips. She glanced down and noticed the trail of rose petals leading down the hall. She looked around again. No one there. Curious, she began to follow the trail, picking up each petal. She found herself in front of the elevators and another rosebud was next to the "up" button. Kylie pressed it, and within moments an elevator arrived. She got in and saw another rosebud taped to the button for the thirtieth floor. Kylie smiled slowly and followed the unwritten instruction.

She stepped out into the hallway and more dark red petals invited her to continue. Kylie followed, the pit of her stomach beginning to flutter as she walked down the hall, stooping to pick up each petal. The trail ended at suite 3030. Her hands were now full of rose petals. She brought them to her nose and inhaled their fragrance, savoring the invigorating scent. She loved roses. Keidron knew of her passion and had a dozen roses sent to her on the twelfth of each month, their wedding anniversary. The thought of her husband brought a fleeting tender moment. She crushed one of the petals between her fingers. *What am I doing?*

Kylie stood outside the door, hesitant, thinking. There were only two things to do: knock or walk away. Knock or leave. Give in to him or give him up. Knock or walk away. She could, she *should*, remind herself of her vows to Keidron. Recite the vows. *Love. Honor. Cherish.* Turn around and walk away. She almost did just that. But . . . but then she would never *know.* Her stomach hurt in anticipation. Her nerves tingled. Forbidden memories of Quinn and his kiss resurfaced and she closed her eyes, feeling light-headed from such a potent recollection, wondering how much more there could be. Kylie inhaled deeply, weighing her options. Whatever happened would happen because it needed to happen and needed to be put to rest. But if she opened this Pandora's box of temptations, the ensuing memories could never be banished to her subconscious. How could she ever look her husband in the eye with such fiery memories of another man forever in her mind? Should she even be doing this? Would she be able to put her illicit desire for Quinn to rest if she knocked on this door? *Could she . . . should she . . . would she?*

She stood outside the door for maybe five minutes. Kylie took one final deep breath and, remembering the power of his kiss, raised her hand to knock. Before her knuckles could touch the mahogany door, it swung open. . . .

Quinn stood before her, wearing black pajamas, the jacket unbuttoned. His killer eyes engulfed her; not even the barest hint of a smile relieved the deliberate intensity of his gaze. Kylie's breath caught in her throat. He silently moved aside to let her enter.

His suite was decorated with the full intent to seduce. Lights turned low. Rose petals and candles everywhere. The room smelled of sandalwood. On the table, a bottle of sparkling juice and a crystal bowl full of fat, succulent strawberries. At the foot of the luxurious king-size bed lay a lingerie set in Bordeaux silk. How had he known that she would indeed come to him? How could he have been that presumptuous? For an instant, Kylie regretted the impulse that brought her to his room. How could Quinn have been that sure of her? She took a deep breath. What in the world was she doing here? She turned toward him, half meaning to flee. Kylie looked again at the elegant lingerie, wetting her lips. Truth be told, she hadn't been seduced in a damn long time. Quinn's elaborate setup was a painful reminder of what her husband wasn't doing. Especially now, when she was craving physical intimacy and the comfort of his arms. Kylie looked at the dark red silk again and then down at her clothes. She was dressed in black tights and an oversized T-shirt. Certainly nothing even remotely sexy. She smiled slightly; Quinn must be seeing something that eluded her.

Quinn took the petals from her hands. Kylie looked at him. She had not realized she was still holding the roses. He sprinkled a path to the bathroom and beckoned her to follow. As if hypnotized, she obeyed. The bathroom, too, was illuminated with candles. The tub was filled with hot, steamy water fragrant with bergamot oil, and more rose petals rippled along the surface. Kylie's breathing became tight. Quinn slid off his jacket and Kylie looked at his muscular brown chest and one word popped into her mind—*damn!*

She opened her mouth to speak and he brought his index finger to her lips, shaking his head. He reached down and touched the hem of her shirt and made to pull it off, but stopped suddenly. He seemed to be thinking. Then he ran the flat of one palm over her belly, pressing it just a bit before bringing his other hand to it, cupping it almost reverently, and then running them both over her breasts and up to her shoulders. Kylie shivered, gasped as her nipples sprang up. She wasn't wearing a bra; her breasts were so tender and sensitive now that she went without one whenever she could. Quinn's hypnotic fingers encircled her neck, gripped her shoulders, and slid down each arm, until he held her fingers, squeezing them. He brought both of her pretty hands to his mouth and kissed her fingertips, one by one. Kylie inhaled sharply and thought she would need to exhale at some point but when didn't really seem to matter.

And then his hands were on her stomach again, caressing her gently, thoughtfully . . . almost lovingly. His beautiful caramel eyes were riveted to the curve of her belly.

Kylie's breathing quickened. "Quinn, I shouldn't . . . I . . . I . . ."

"Shhh," he said, his tone quiet but firm. He seemed to be concentrating. She shivered as the words escaped her in a fluid rush. "Quinn, I—I'm p—pregnant."

"I know."

For a millionth of a second, there was silence and the only motion was the flickering of the candles and the rippling of the bath water.

Quinn closed his eyes as he began to rub Kylie's stomach, triggering desires that lay deep within her. "So beautiful," he murmured, sliding both hands around to the small of her back and running them over her ass, pulling her closer. His fingers smoothed over her hips, gripping slightly. Then his hand was trailing down her leg to her knee, then around, and then up the inside of her thigh, up, up, up until he reached her crotch and cupped his palm and squeezed.

Kylie moaned, surprising herself. The sensation was so new, so unexpected, so unfamiliar. "I'm going to come if you don't stop," she warned.

"So what do you think I intend?" His tone matched the intense heat in his eyes, but there was an undercurrent of laughter. Kylie stared at him, swallowing, not the least bit amused. Was she going to have any control in this at all?

Before she could think any further, he caught hold of her T-shirt and removed it, tossing it aside. Her tights followed. Reality invaded the room again as Kylie realized how she looked. She stood before him, her eyes closed in mortification as he stared at her. Kylie was wearing a pair of unflattering, unsexy, white cotton panties. Worn for comfort, not seduction. She blushed as red as the rose petals, but Quinn didn't seem to notice or care. He slid off her panties and flung them over his shoulder.

Quinn knelt before her, his eyes level with her belly. Kylie stood there, giddy from his nearness, minute quivers beginning to wrack her body. He leaned forward and placed both hands, and then a warm kiss, on her stomach. She got wet, suddenly and willingly, in spite of herself. Quinn stood, scooped her up, and lowered her into the tub. The water was steaming and Kylie relaxed instantly, closing her eyes and deciding to shut out all thought and apprehension. She exhaled and moaned softly. When she felt his strong hands on her foot, she opened her eyes. Quinn's hands were lathered and he was rubbing her foot and massaging her ankle. He was going to bathe her. And she was not going to stop him. The heat of the water, the scent of the roses, the luxurious ripples had her in a trance. She *couldn't* stop him.

Quinn stopped at her thigh and re-lathered with the glycerin soap and lifted her other foot. Kylie's toenails were painted a sexy shade of red that brought out her tawny skin. Quinn had begun planning her seduction from the moment he saw her in the elevator, but the seeds had been planted long ago. Over the months following their friends' wedding, the thought of Kylie had almost become a constant, and he knew if he ever saw her again, he would do more than just dream about making love to her. She had affected him in ways that had lain dormant for years, then slowly bubbled and now were preparing to erupt.

The memory of her sitting at the picnic table in snug white capri pants and a lime green looped top with sandals that showed off her flawless feet, watching the colors of the sunset, still brought him to his knees. Hers was a smoldering, seductive beauty and it drew him like a moth to the flame. Soon, they were laughing and touching each other like old friends. In the days after, they had been subconsciously drawn to each other. All during the wedding events, they were never more than ten feet apart, whether by design or by intuitive intent. In the background, they both felt the unspoken mutual desire. It was practically tangible, but remained unacknowledged. He had a wife. She had a boyfriend.

During the reception, they danced, weaving an invisible, sensual cocoon around them, keeping the rest of the world at bay. They clung to each other, oblivious to everyone and everything. Then Kylie gave Quinn a ride to the airport when the wedding was over. Exhaustion had gotten the best of him and he'd fallen asleep on the long ride. He dreamt that they had made love in her SUV and it was so vivid that he didn't know he was dreaming until she woke him up.

When he'd gotten to the baggage check, he'd been overcome with the desire to kiss her full, sensual lips. And he did. And thus laid the foundation of his subconscious plans to seduce her if the opportunity presented itself. He *had* to. Everything about Kylie inflamed him, from the beauty of her toes to the seductive slant of her chocolate eyes; from the camber of her gorgeous legs to the width of her hips; from the grace of her back to the sexy curve at her waist; from the elegance of her hands to the mystery of her mind, and now this extra, profound power within her . . . he was gone. He had to have her at least for a day . . . just twenty-four hours.

Seeing her in the elevator—with a foxy new haircut at that—had brought his dormant desire raging violently to the surface. It had come bubbling out with a vengeance, robbing him of his sanity, leaving him with nothing but the need to give in to it. It was insane, but what could he do? Sure, he was married. He wasn't planning to abandon his family. And now Kylie was married too. And pregnant. But none of it mattered. God, but she was everything . . . luscious, desirable, tempting, *forbidden* . . . he couldn't *not* take advantage of this opportunity.

He ran his soapy hands over Kylie's stomach, looking into her eyes. She held his gaze as his hands continued their deft rubbing. Up Quinn's hands went, soaping her breasts. Kylie winced and Quinn eased up on the pressure, but the sudden, momentary pain had felt so good. It had been far too long since . . . she covered his hands and moved them back to her nipples, biting her lips as she welcomed the sweet twinge again.

"Turn on your side," he commanded. Without a word, Kylie rolled in the water. Quinn soaped her buttocks and the backs of her calves. The water was cooling and he turned her back over, rose, and picked her up. He stood her on the fluffy bath mat and gently dried her. Her skin was pink from the heat of the water.

Kylie stood there, her legs parted, watching this physically perfect man pat her down with the plush towel. He lifted one foot and rubbed it dry. Then he ran his fingers over her pedicured toes and brought them to his lips, kissing each toe. Kylie was quivering. Before her pregnancy, Keidron sometimes began romantic evenings by bathing her. Even though she adored him, she had to admit, with a certain amount of guilt, that his pampering had never quite made her feel the way Quinn was making her feel at this moment. She pushed the thought of her husband out of her mind. Quinn took her hand and led her out of the bathroom. Kylie followed him demurely. If he wanted to lead, so be it . . . the man could have his way with her.

"I bought this for you," he murmured, picking up the Bordeaux silk set. It was a two-piece, a lovely dark red cami with matching hip-cut panties. "Will you wear it?"

She nodded and he slipped the camisole over her head. It was snug in the bosom, but flared out over her mid-section, allowing for a loose fit around her waist. He had judged perfectly. The dark red matched her fingernails precisely. Quinn sat down on the bed edge with the panties in his hands. He brought them low for Kylie to step in and slid them up in place, tucking the front waist-band under the swell of her stomach. Once again, he kissed her there. She moaned softly, gratefully, fingering the silk. "I love Bordeaux. You remembered."

"I told you I remember everything."

Quinn stood to his full height, kissing her forehead. He went over to the table and poured two goblets of sparkling juice and picked up the dish of berries and brought them to her. He handed her a stem. "I'd love to give you champagne, but I thought this would be best, considering . . ." He raised his glass. "To you, Kylie . . ."

Kylie raised her glass. Her throat was suddenly dry with suppressed emotion and she downed the juice in one long swallow. He took the glass from her and walked over to the CD player and turned it on. After a moment, Kylie recognized the song as the one they first danced to at the wedding reception. Her stomach began fluttering like crazy and she closed her eyes, recollections flooding her senses. That song had been deleted from her life because it reminded her way too much of Quinn and those forbidden feelings. She hadn't allowed herself to listen to it since the reception. Now, Kylie let the music float through her and, once again in control of herself, she opened her eyes to look at Quinn. He held out his hand.

Her body had a will of its own and she found herself walking toward him, her hand reaching out to his. As he pulled her in and the vocals emanated from the speakers, she was back inside the bubble of time created at the reception. Quinn's caramel eyes locked with her mocha ones and there was nothing that needed to be said. It was all right there, between them and within them.

Looking into her eyes, her pretty face, time stopped. "Kylie," he said, touching his forehead with hers, "we have twenty-four hours. That's all."

"Beginning when?" she breathed.

"Now."

"What do you want to do?" She felt she should ask.

"I want to do everything. All you need to do is hold on."

Kylie's insides twisted and her toes curled at his words. Shit, the man's velvet voice could turn her into a weeping, seeping, dripping pile of feminine goop in a matter of seconds. "I think I can do that," she murmured, pressing her thighs together to shield her wetness.

"Good," he said. "Because now we have to establish new memories. Hence the song." He tilted his head back in the direction of the music. She nodded in response. He released his hold on her and took one step back, his caramel eyes sliding over her body, from head to foot. "You are so . . . *sexy*. No, don't say anything, just let me . . ." Slowly, achingly, his eyes traveled from her red toenails, up, up her legs, her thighs. She was beautiful, early in her pregnancy. He wanted to be all over her in the worst way imaginable, and yet he wanted to look at her, take all of her in, preserve the memories.

"Come with me," he murmured. He took her hand and led her across the suite to the bed. It was turned back and rose petals were strewn over the sheets and pillows. She closed her eyes, a secret smile crossing her lips. He remembered *everything*. What a man!

Kylie lay on the bed, closing her eyes. She had no words for how she was feeling at the moment. She was warm, soft, and hornier than she'd been in months. Her hormones were off the map and her pussy lips trembled in expectancy. Quinn lay beside her, resting his chin in one crooked palm. He raised a strawberry to her lips and she bit into it. Some of the juice ran down the center of her lower lip and she unconsciously slid the tip of her tongue out to catch it. Quinn's eyes were riveted to her mouth as he ate the rest of the berry. Kylie chewed slowly, her dark eyes held captive by his gorgeous caramel ones. "You're beautiful," he said, his voice low.

She smiled at him. "You don't mean that. Not . . . *now*."

Quinn fed her another berry, running the tip of it over her lips. Kylie stared at him, getting lost in his inviting brown irises.

"You don't think pregnancy makes you desirable?" he asked, finishing off the berry.

"I mean . . . it's just . . . I'm so uncomfortable sometimes. I feel so . . . well . . . unattractive." He stroked her cheek, his finger tracing the contours of her cheekbone. "I am still getting used to the idea of being a mother. Why do you find me so appealing now?" Her husband didn't. She wondered if it showed.

"I found you appealing *before*, Kylie." He put one hand on her stomach and began to make slow circles. "Nothing has changed. Let me show you."

The circles moved lower and she closed her eyes, breathing slowly. At this rate, her panties would be thoroughly unwearable and he hadn't really done anything to her.

"I am sure your husband finds you irresistible." There was a mischievous glint in his eyes.

"Uhh," she breathed, "I doubt that." She did not want to say that since learning about her pregnancy, Keidron refused to make love with her because of his fear that he would hurt their baby.

Quinn stared at her in utter disbelief. "Really?"

"It's okay, though," she lied, wondering if he saw through her.

"Kylie," he breathed, seeing the sadness in her eyes. He pulled her close. "I can't tell you what it does to me, seeing you like this. See, I'm so hard for you. . . ." He took her hand and placed it over his erection, warm and alive underneath his pajamas. Quinn groaned. Her husband was an unbelievable fool. She sighed against him, relishing the comfort of his strong arms. Quinn released her and let her lay back down. He moved around, parting her legs, sliding between them. He began to rub the insides of her thighs. "Relax. Everything will be all right."

His velvet voice mesmerized her, and the searing warmth of his hands relaxed her. Quinn's hands found their way to her belly again and he continued his warm rub. He raised his eyes to meet hers and she found that she didn't want to look away. She would not be ashamed, she would bask in the adoration of this sexy man. She wanted to be cherished, she wanted to know that she could still make a man hard with desire. Feeling such a response from Quinn made her shift involuntarily. He then moved close to her, his lips bare nanometers from hers. They kissed.

Kylie closed her eyes and cradled his head, wanting to feel his body atop hers. She wrapped her arms and legs around him. He hesitated, and then gently pressed his body down on hers. The kiss deepened and she moaned against his mouth. Quinn's hands glided toward her pussy hair, enjoying her softness. She felt so good, so right.

When his lips moved over to the side of her face and neck, she groaned. Her pussy was aching and she was squirming from her desire. Quinn kissed her neck and throat as he massaged her breasts underneath the camiset. Her nipples were pebbles under his hands, and he could feel the pulsing of her vagina through his pajama bottoms. He began trailing kisses down her sternum and over her belly, and then kissed his way down between her thighs. Kylie moved to take off the panties but he stopped her. "No, I intend for you to keep this on . . . for now."

"But—"

"Lie still and lock your legs around my head . . . that shit turns me on."

She made some strangled sound of agreement as he lowered his head between her legs. He fingered the silk of her panties, edging nearer and nearer to her clitoris. Kylie moaned in response, enjoying the anticipation, yet wanting him to hurry. Quinn slid the crotch of her panties to one side and inhaled her scent, then licked her clitoris like a cat would lick milk. Kylie tried to move, but Quinn, expecting it, had locked his arms around her hips and held her fast. She wasn't moving. Not until he allowed it. He had a magnificent, long, pointy tongue and he played Kylie like an instrument, alternately flitting his tongue tip over her clitoris and sucking it with his full, gentle lips.

She was groaning and, at his request, had locked her thighs around his head and was squeezing every time he made her throb. Quinn groaned. She tasted so good, just like he knew she would; he didn't want to move his head, not even to take a breath. All he wanted to breathe was Kylie. He rubbed his face in her pussy and pulsed his tongue inside her rhythmically, hitting notes that made her sound off. God, she tasted so good . . . she was like strawberries, or peaches . . . or what he imagined ambrosia would taste of—all things delicious. His dick was harder than vector calculus and Kylie hadn't had to do anything to him. He pushed his face in as far as he could and when she tried to move away again, he clamped his hands down on her thighs and spread them back, angled his head, and went to town. She was lush, she was sweet, and for the next twenty-two hours, she was *his*. Kylie trembled as he licked and sucked, her hands guiding his sleek bald head back and forth over her dripping folds. "Oh God!" she cried, not caring if she was heard. "Quinn . . . Quinn, please . . ." she panted, begging for more, mercy, a ceasefire, she had no idea what her words meant. He was actually nibbling on her clitoris and labia and Kylie, drawing on inner reserves, slammed her legs around his head again and bucked savagely, and climaxed. She felt it deep within, a mega-tsunami rumbling up from the depths of primitive desire and the wave slammed against her internal shores, causing her to thrash and shake violently. And her lover held on, riding out her wave, baptizing himself in her moist heat. Kylie screamed a warning and tried to move, but Quinn tightened his hold again and she came, drenching him. Kylie was moaning, the sound escaping her like a deflated balloon while Quinn sucked up her honey, rubbing his face back and forth over her swollen vagina, enjoying the trap of her thighs.

She was shivering and by degrees, her muscles relaxed; she released Quinn's head and dropped her legs on
the bed. Quinn, his face damp, buried it in her belly and
she cradled his head.

"So . . . sleepy," she whispered. He didn't want to wear
her out before time ran out, so he kissed his way back up,
ending with her lips. Kylie kissed him deeply, her arms
around him, and when the kiss broke, she was out of
breath. She turned on her side, her back to Quinn, closing
her eyes. Her body still shuddered spasmodically and
Quinn drew her close to him, running his hand idly over
her belly, spellbound. He would not sleep.

Kylie woke suddenly, a gasp on her lips. Quinn was
crawling over her body. This time, they were both fully
naked. He'd let her sleep undisturbed for as long as he
could bear. Quinn leaned over her chest and began to lick
and suck on her breasts, and she felt his erection pressing against her swollen vagina. Gently, he kneaded her
breasts, running his tongue between them and over her
nipples, barely nipping one of them and causing her to
draw a sharp intake of breath. And damn it if she wasn't
wet again. He kissed his way back up her throat to her ear,
catching the lobe between his teeth as he inhaled her scent
again. It had been with him for two years, and now it
would never leave him.

He shifted and her thighs parted unconsciously, making room for him to enter her. "Ohh," she breathed, wondering if he was going to go all the way this time. She
wanted him so bad, she needed him more than she wanted
him and she craved the feel of him within her body.

"I want you so bad," he whispered, almost to himself.
He raised himself off her, noticing the look in her eyes,

and started to caress one of her thighs as he took himself in hand. Quinn pressed himself forward, touching the moist tip of his penis to her clitoris. She exhaled, bringing her thighs closer together around him, trapping him with her long, graceful legs. He placed his palm over her mound, his thumb pressing her clitoris as he gently traced her pussy lips with his dick. Slowly, he massaged her clit with his thumb as he moved around her labia, gliding his penis over and between her folds, his eyes closed as he imagined the heat of her body enveloping him. It was sweet, painful ecstasy as he stroked himself.

"Quinn," she breathed, her hands massaging her breasts, nipples between her fingers. He felt so good, so hard, too, too good. She shuddered. Her orgasm was building deep within. Her pussy lips seemed to spread, to open like a mouth, and it was all he could do not to oblige and feed it.

"I want you inside me now!" she cried.

He held himself away from her.

"Quinn, please . . . now, right now!"

He continued to caress her with his hands, a finger sliding over the curve of her belly. She pressed toward him, clutching him, digging into the muscle of his thighs, reaching for the delicious hardness of his dick, meeting a tender, unexpected, unwanted softness.

"Quinn?" She was on the verge of tears. Puzzlement was in her voice and her eyes.

"Shh!" He probed, the friction, the movement delicious, making her gasp in sudden shock. Her pussy clenched around his fingers, wanting to draw them deeper . . . to feed the hungry mouth that was her sex. She wanted to move away, to make room for his dick, but it felt too good. His thumb reached her clitoris, stroked it gently, moving faster and faster as his fingers continued their hypnotic motion within her body. Kylie watched Quinn's fascinated eyes as he inched closer to her pussy, unable to tear his eyes away from the sight. He inhaled her, breathed her in, acknowledging her scent as the breath of God. And then his tongue darted out, touching her clit, encapsulating it, sucking hard as her orgasm built up from somewhere deep within and she climaxed again as she held his head, forcing his lips hard against her.

Sometime later, she was eating fresh fruit with mascarpone cheese, proscuitto, crusty baguettes with butter, and drinking more sparkling white grape juice. He was eating Beluga caviar with trimmings and drinking a fine chardonnay. They were listening to John Coltrane's "Equinox." Kylie's feet were in Quinn's lap and he was massaging one of them as he ate. It was after six A.M., thirteen hours to go. They ate in companionable silence for most of the meal. After finishing off his caviar, he took a sip of wine.

"I wanted you like crazy the moment I laid eyes on you."

"I couldn't tell." Kylie was eating shreds of the baguette, wrapping each piece with proscuitto. She was starving.

"You couldn't tell even though I was never more than a few feet from you the whole time?" He smiled, the act lighting his handsome features.

"Well, I noticed that, but I thought it was because of me not wanting to be too far from you." She forked a chunk of watermelon into her mouth.

"I wanted to follow you wherever you went. I was so attracted to you. I still am. Watching your lips around that melon does nothing but make it worse."

"Quinn—" She licked her lips, reaching for another piece of baguette.

"Yes, I know that we are both married. But I can't help what you do to me, how you make me feel."

Kylie bit into a strawberry. "I haven't been able to forget about you either, Quinn."

"I've never cheated on my wife before. I don't want you thinking that . . . that this . . . is a habit with me, because it isn't." His expression turned serious, his lips formed a harsh line. Then it softened into a rueful smile. "I'm crazy about you, Kylie. I just don't see how I missed you the way I did." Quinn massaged her feet, sliding his fingers between her toes. He looked at her. "I'll never be able to get you out of my mind. Not after this. Come sit in my lap and finish your meal. I want to feel you next to me."

Kylie dutifully rose and sat in his lap. He shifted in his seat. "Mmn, woman . . . mmn mmn mmn . . . you are exquisite." Quinn's hands made large, slow circles over her thighs. Her skin was like satin, flawless. She was radiant. Quinn buried his face between her shoulder blades and brought his hands up, splaying his fingers on her stomach. He moaned, closing his eyes. After nine hours of being with Kylie, he wasn't sure about the life he currently led.

Kylie sensed his consternation. "This could get difficult, Quinn."

"I know."

"We just have to control ourselves."

"Yes, stop talking." He didn't need to be reminded of the path his thoughts were taking.

Kylie let her lips fall shut. Quinn pulled her back gently and adjusted her so that his penis slid right up between her thighs, against her vulva. Kylie groaned again.

"It's what you do," he said in response. She arched her back and squeezed her thighs, moving just enough to generate a sinuous friction between his hard dick and her wet pussy. Quinn groaned, pressing his face into the soft, warm flesh of Kylie's side. She was everything he had always wanted and more. Too much more. But now he didn't really know if he could just walk away from her when their time was over. Hard again, he rose from the chair, scooped her up, and took her back to the bed. He lay beside her, rubbing her belly.

"Quinn, dammit . . ." She was horny again.

"Now you see the effect you have on me. Are you still hungry? I'll order more for you to eat but all I really want to eat is you."

"Quinn . . ." Her body was tingling again.

"If you're tired," he teased, "I'll let you rest." One hand slid over the curves of her form, down and over, then between her thighs, to cup her sex. She exhaled.

"I'm not *that* tired."

"I feel it, getting tight and hot. You want me to eat you again, don't you? Tell me, how do you want me to do it? I feel it and I want it, Kylie. Let me eat you, let me get my fill of you . . . even though you make me insatiable." Quinn lay beside her, using the pillow to cushion his head. Kylie rose up to a sitting position so she could turn and look at him.

"Quinn, the way you talk . . ."

"I should be with you," he murmured.

Kylie moaned. The man had turned her into liquid heat, she knew it. She was horny all over again, and hungry, too, but the desire for food was no match for the hunger of her sex. She wanted him desperately. She kissed his lips, his face, stroking his smooth bald head and his cheeks. She couldn't get enough of him, he couldn't get enough of her, could not, probably would never be able to get enough. And Kylie wanted her fill of this incredible, wonderful man. She reached for him again, her fingers caressing the hard strength of his dick. It had been *so* long. She wanted to feel him deep inside her.

"Lord, Kylie . . . what you do to me . . ."

"Oh, I can feel it, baby." She smiled secretly, savoring her effect on Quinn. "Is all this mine? You're so hard!" Her tone was light, playful, but she was dead serious. She wanted to feel that hardness inside her.

"God, woman, yes!" His eyes were closed as she stroked him. She wrapped her legs around his hips, edging her desperate wet pussy nearer and nearer to his erection. Closer, closer . . . she tilted her hips, ready to suck him in. "Now, right now . . ." she murmured to herself.

And instantly, Kylie knew a sense of loss as he imperceptibly drew away from her as he continued to massage her skin, maneuvering her onto the bed.

"Quinn, what is it . . . what's wrong?"

But he stopped her with his lips, pinning her arms down to her side, roughly probing her with his strong tongue, licking, flicking down across her nipples, biting, making her wince in pain and in ecstasy. He continued down, flitting kisses over her abdomen, stroking down, down . . . hitting the spot, his tongue now gentle, probing, his lips tightening, squeezing until Kylie forgot the question she'd asked and, unable to hold it in a second longer, erupted in violent, convulsive paroxysms of pleasure.

\* \* \*

When their time was almost up, they stood together in the foyer. They held on to each other and he rained baby kisses on her face. So many words were in mind, so many things he wanted to tell her. About everything. About all the reasons why. He sighed. She looked at him, seeing the consternation on his face, and closed her eyes.

"Quinn, circumstances are what they are."

"Are they? Do you know what I'm thinking right at this moment?" Quinn looked into Kylie's eyes. His unspoken words were reflected in the deep mocha of her irises.

*How do I find you again?*

He said nothing but ran his free hand over the curve of her face and lips, pressing his thumb on her lower lip. She said nothing as his other hand caressed her rounded belly. Words weren't necessary.

*About the Author*

Kiyra B. Holt is a thirty-year-old American chemistry instructor. She lives and works in Atlanta, Georgia, and is single. She is currently working on what she hopes will be her first published book of fiction.

# Hotel Room

## Saran Thornton

I've traveled much of the world on my own. It goes with the territory of being single. And as a lone female, you learn the etiquette. No eye contact with any stray men. No treating hotel staff like your long-lost, dearest buddy, never lift your head from the ever-present book that you devour over a solo restaurant meal. I've used the same techniques on vacation in Britain, in Europe, in Africa, and in the Caribbean, although the warmer climates make it more difficult to maintain that frosty exterior. One or two joints too many, and all the practiced aloofness disappears down the drain.

The plane landed only twenty minutes late at the enormous Aeropuerto Internacional Benito Juárez in Mexico City, my first time in Latin America. I was planning on just a few days there before heading for the lazy, mindless pleasures of Cancun's sandy beaches. Mexico City was where I planned to *do* culture.

"*Bienvenida a Mexico*" greeted me at several stages from the plane to passport control. I'm hopeless with languages, but even I could work out what that meant and I was grateful for the friendly, welcoming smiles. I've noticed in many places that I'm singled out for special attention, particularly in Scandinavian countries where I seem to stand out from the crowd. I take it all in good spirits, though. Most often, they really have never seen anyone who looks quite like me before.

I had made the effort to learn a few useful Spanish phrases, and with those, I managed to negotiate the hazards of baggage claim and customs. I was traveling relatively light, having learned how to pack for vacations: the minimum amount of clothing and toiletries plus a relatively large amount of traveler's checks and a major credit card as backup. So, with my one case, handbag, and security belt strapped around my waist, I headed off to the money changing counter, converted some cash, and looked around for signs to the taxi line. I was hoping for one of those little pictures with a word like *taxi* above it that might offer a clue.

*"Bienvenida a Mexico. ¿Puedo ayudarle?"* I didn't understand those last words, but the tilted head and the questioning look in the eyes of the young man made it clear that he was offering help.

I scrambled in my bag for the handy phrase book that I'd been foresighted enough to buy and flicked through the pages to the Travel section. I struggled with the words, *"¿Donde está el taxi?"*

"Señorita, if you come this way, I will show you." He was kind enough not to laugh at me. He took my bag and, on the way, explained the system of official taxis and paying in advance and getting tickets. His English was flawless, though spoken with an American accent.

"Where are you from?" he asked. I'd thought about that one before setting out on this trip. I'd wondered about long memories and decided that I didn't want to be implicated in any involvement in the Falklands or Las Malvinas depending on which side you stood.

"Jamaica." I couldn't think of any country that could possibly have any resentment against Jamaicans, unless they'd been brainwashed with the reports about drugs and yardies.

"You have wonderful hair, yes?"

I was used to this. "Yes," I replied. Quite simply, my hair *was* wonderful.

He showed me to the ticket window, then led me to the line of waiting taxis. He opened the door for me and handed me my bag. I fumbled in my purse for some notes and handed them to him, not sure of how much I was giving. He waved the money away, though, and just smiled brightly at me.

"*Muchas gracias para . . .*"

He reached out and gently touched one of my shoulder-length locks. "*De nada.*" And he was gone.

I knew I would enjoy Mexico.


The taxi driver nodded at the scrap of paper on which I'd written the address of the hotel, and within moments he'd screeched away from the curb, headed west into the heart of the city. It was just past midday and I searched in my bag for sunglasses as the blinding light bounced off the windscreen. You could see shimmering waves of heat rising from parked cars. The driver switched on the radio, and though my heart lurched each time he swerved sharply to overtake a slower vehicle, screaming abuse as he passed, the sound of the rapid, unintelligible Spanish helped to distract my attention.

Even from the air I hadn't been able to grasp how huge

the city was and I stared out of the window as corrugated shacks reminiscent of South African townships flew by giving way to colonial mansions followed by fantastically surreal modern skyscrapers. The taxi tore at breakneck speed down the wide, multilaned roads, seeming to ignore every traffic light along the way. Eventually, and I thanked God, it was forced to slow to accommodate the bustle of the city center and fairly soon ground almost to a standstill in the chaotic traffic, hemmed in by scooters and green VW beetles. I looked at my watch. I'd been in the car for nearly forty minutes. It took almost as long again to cover the mile or so to the hotel. I was glad to finally escape the confines of the vehicle and stood for a moment, enjoying the feeling of just being on a different continent, breathing a different air, seeing different colors. I turned from the huge monument that dominated the center of the square and looked up at the hotel. I might be on a different continent, but it looked much the same as many others I'd stayed in. I picked up my bag and headed up the steps.

The receptionist wore a badge that read INES.

*"Bienvenida a Mexico, Señorita."* Her smile was brilliant, gleaming white teeth with the slightest of gaps. But it was her eyes that drew you. Large, sweeping upward like oversized almonds, fringed by the longest, thickest lashes. She wore only a trace of makeup, yet it was as if her eyes were outlined with a soft brush of kohl. She was, quite simply, stunning in that dusky Latin way. Hair of the blackest black, shiny like varnish, smoothed behind her ears.

I couldn't help returning her smile, even if I hadn't wanted to. But I was excited, like a child. I just couldn't help it. Despite the regulation hotel décor, easy chairs grouped around low coffee tables, dark paneled wood, and gaudy flower arrangements, I still knew that, beyond the glass doors, there was . . . Mexico!

There was a hint of amusement on Ines's face, as if she had encountered this reaction to her city many times before and knew exactly what the progression of emotions would be.

I dropped my bag. "Thank you. I'm really glad to be here."

I completed the formalities of checking in and Ines rang for a bellhop to take my bag. As I followed him toward the elevator Ines called out, "Miss . . ." I turned back and she was studying the registration card. She struggled over the name. "Miss Maclaren . . ." She looked up at me with those warm eyes, "If there's anything you need . . . My name is Ines. Please, just let me know."

"Thank you, Ines."

I hardly looked at the room, just glanced at the neutral walls, the flowered cover on the queen-size bed, the narrow wardrobe and matching dressing table with stool. There was a tiny shower and a television in the corner. I unpacked as quickly as I could, took a quick shower, and dressed in a simple cotton shift and leather sandals. I slathered suntan lotion over my skin and grabbed a hat. In less than thirty minutes, I was back down in the reception area, studying the map, trying to decide which of the city's treasures to sample first.

"Hello, Miss Maclaren." Ines was just emerging from a cubicle somewhere in the back and she leaned across the reception desk, her dark hair falling in a curtain across her face. She pushed it behind her ears and, unconsciously, I mirrored her gesture, sweeping back the wavy locks that covered my eyes. We smiled at each other.

"Call me Helena."

I walked over to her and turned the book so that she could see the page that I was studying.

"I was thinking of going to the National Anthropology Museum. What's the best way to get there?"

"It's in Chapultepec, the park. It's quite a distance from here."

"Can I get a taxi?"

"Yes, but it might be quicker and certainly cheaper to take the subway. It's easy. I'll show you."

Ines's scarlet-lacquered nail traced a snaking path along the map.

"The metro station is only minutes from here. Once inside, you follow the colors, take the train to Auditorio, and then there is only a short walk through the park. It is very quick and quite safe, but the trains will be crowded at this time of day. Take care, Elena." She pronounced it "Yelena," the stress and intonation making my name sound more seductive than it ever had before, as if her lips were caressing it. I looked into her eyes and something passed between us that was like friendship, but it was too soon to tell.

"Thank you, Ines."

"Will you be back for dinner? I can book a table for you."

"I don't—"

"Don't worry. We would find you a table not near the kitchens. Somewhere where you can watch without being watched. Around seven o'clock? What do you say?"

I laughed. "That sounds great. I'll see you later, then."

"See you later."

I walked out into the burning heat and followed Ines's instructions to the metro. She was right, color-coded signs pointed me in the right direction to the platform. Within minutes a train had arrived. I was tired after long hours of traveling and should probably have gone straight to sleep, but I was determined to make the most of every single minute in the city. I kept my eyes glued to the map, determined not to miss the right exit.

I strolled through the luxurious park to the museum, declining the offers from the vendors along the way, everything cheap, cheap. I bought a guide and was tempted to just lounge in the huge central courtyard reading it, listening to the background noise of the tinkling, umbrella-shaped fountain. I knew, though, that I'd just drift away. So, turning the guide to orientate myself, I pinpointed where I wanted to go and headed that way: The Teotihuacán gallery.

The room was dark, skillfully lit to highlight the brilliant red and gold Tlalocan mural and the ceramic pots and masks. I made a detour around the groups of schoolchildren sitting on the floor taking notes from the guides. I stood in front of an enormous, elaborately carved stone monument. The legend was in Spanish but I knew that this had to be a goddess, she was so imposing. I stood there for a long while imagining her standing before the Pyramid of the Sun, wondering about the story behind her creation. I rubbed the back of my neck, stiff from craning upward and made my way back to the courtyard. I sat on the cool floor and flicked through the pages of the guide until I came to the section I wanted. I began to read, but my eyelids soon began to droop and I knew that, unless I kept moving, I'd be fast asleep within seconds.

As I stood, I became aware of a young man staring intently at me from the other side of the courtyard. In the way of non-Englishmen, he made no attempt to hide his fascination. I was about to turn and walk away when he nodded at me, smiled and began to walk in my direction.

He had the same dark coloring of Ines, and the Spanish edition of the guidebook that he carried might have given some indication of his nationality. He stopped about three feet from me and gave a slight bow that was curiously archaic.

"Excuse me for approaching you, but you were at the hotel, no? I noticed you there."

"Um . . . I'm not sure . . ."

"You would not have noticed me, Señorita, but I could not help seeing you." He made a gesture that took in the flow of my hair. "You are indeed beautiful."

I might have blushed. The look on his face was serious, matter-of-fact. This must be a culture that was used to giving and receiving compliments.

"I think you arrived just this afternoon. I am on my way back now. I wondered if you would like to share my car."

I was so tired that I was beyond caution, and besides, I liked his old-fashioned politeness, the way he kept a respectful distance.

I nodded. "Thank you, that's very kind of you."

"Not at all."

He led me to the car, guiding me with his hand hovering an inch away from the small of my back. The driver opened the door to the backseat and I clambered in, grateful for the tinted windows and the air-conditioning.

My rescuer sat in the front and gabbled something in very rapid Spanish to the driver. And then he turned around, leaned over the seat, and extended his hand. I took it.

"May I introduce myself. I am Emilio Duran."

"Helena Maclaren. Very pleased to meet you, Emilio Duran."

His smile was slow, but made him seem even more

youthful. It was impossible to guess his age, but the hint of gray at his temples suggested that he might be a little older than I had at first thought. Emilio turned away, watching the road ahead, and I stared out of the side window, knowing that I might have been physically awake, but my brain had gone into sleep mode. I dimly recall Emilio telling me that he was from Hermosillo right in the North of the country, in the city on business, taking the opportunity of a free afternoon to visit the museum.

Before I was really aware of my surroundings, we were back at the hotel and Emilio was opening the door for me, taking my hand as he helped me out of the car. He still held my hand as we walked into the lobby and as I thanked him again he lifted it to his lips and kissed it.

"No thanks required, Elena. It was, indeed, a pleasure."

I opened the windows of my room and looked out onto the square, busy enough in the early evening. The light was golden, reflecting on the art deco buildings around the square, the tiny figures strolling under the gigantic arch of the Monumento a la Revolución.

I left the window open, knowing that nothing, not even the sounds of voices rising up from the street below, could get in the way of blissful sleep.

I was startled awake by the phone. Totally disoriented, I groped for it and brought it to my ear, eyes still closed. The voice belonged to Ines and it felt like a long-distance caress. "Elena? It's Ines. It is gone seven o'clock. We have your table waiting."

I looked at my watch. I had been asleep for more than two hours. I sat upright.

"I'll be there. Five minutes, Ines."

It was more like fifteen minutes by the time I'd show-ered, changed, and found the book that I'd been reading on the plane. I was about to open the door, but something made me turn back and look at myself in the mirror. I wasn't too dissatisfied with what I saw, but the warmth of the evening made me pull out a scarf to wrap around my locks, lifting them away from my shoulders. I noticed that, already, a few hours in the sun had brought a healthy glow to my cheeks. I rummaged in my handbag for a gold-tinted lipstick and applied it to my full lips.

Ines's smile was warm with a hint of relief as I stepped out of the elevator. "Elena! You look lovely." For a mo-ment I wondered if she was speaking to someone behind me, and then realized that, yes, I was a beautiful African woman, skin as rich and dark as the Mexican soil.

Ines gestured in the direction of the dining room and I followed her glance. I walked through the double doors and was greeted by a smiling maître d'.

"Miss Maclaren? Your table is this way." He showed me to a table in the corner and, as I sat, spread the linen napkin across my lap. Bending low, he murmured, "We have instructions from Ines to take good care of you." He handed me a menu and his silent footsteps disappeared to the farthest reaches of the room.

I realized that I hadn't eaten since a desultory airline meal several hours before. I studied the menu eagerly, try-ing to recall what I'd tried in tapas restaurants back in London.

There was a shadow across the table and I looked up to find Emilio standing, waiting for me to acknowledge his presence.

"Emilio, hi!" I smiled up at him, actually strangely happy to see him. He took my smile as license to touch my hair gently, rolling a wiry lock between his fingers.

"I'm eating alone, too, Elena. May I join you?"

I moved my novel to the floor by my bag and gestured to the spare chair.

"Please do, it would be a pleasure." I meant it. "What would you recommend to eat?"

He studied the menu for a moment. "Do you want something typically Mexican?"

I nodded.

"Something hot and spicy?"

I nodded again, knowing that there was no *double entendre* behind the words. He gestured to the waiter and took the decisions out of my hands.

Soon our glasses were being filled with white wine and I sipped gratefully, knowing that I didn't really need the alcohol to relax me, the atmosphere and the company had already done that.

"So how long will you be in Mexico City?"

"Just four days, and I want to head out to Xochimilco and Teotihuacán."

He smiled at my inexpert struggle at pronunciation. "I won't have much use of my driver for the next two days. If you wish, he will be at your disposal."

My British reserve took over and my lips were just about to form "No, I couldn't possibly . . ." when I remembered that I was in Mexico, a continent and light-years of history away from London.

"Thank you, Emilio. That's kind."

I gorged my way through seviche and Pescado a la Veracruzana, red snapper reminiscent of how we stew it back home, spicy with chilli peppers. I finally leaned back and he was looking at me with that amused, slightly inquisitive look on his face.

"Tell me about Jamaica."

I was momentarily disconcerted, forgetting about my

slight manipulation of the truth of where I'd come from. I wasn't sure where to start. What did he want to know about the land of my ancestors?

Maybe it was the visit to the museum but I found myself telling him about my last trip to Jamaica, at Christmas. Jonkunnu. *Run! Run! Jonkunnu a come!* The parades, the bands winding their way through the streets, their members chasing screaming, fearful children who, moments before, had been taunting them.

Emilio talked about the Dia de los Muertos, "Day of the Dead" festival when Mexican families gathered to pay homage to their ancestors with offerings placed at gravesides. His eyes were lively, dark and bright as his fingers traced pictures in the air, animating the stories that he told. I found myself drawn into the scene that he evoked and as I leaned toward him, he reached out and stroked my hair, loosening the scarf, allowing the mass of dark, crinkly tendrils to fall around my face. I looked up at him and he ran his fingers through my hair, lifting it in wonder.

"Your hair . . . It feels so strong, so electric, like fine wool. Soft. I expected it to be different. You are a remarkable woman, Elena."

He stood then and took my hand in his once more.

"I have an early morning. I will send the car back for you. Good night, beautiful Elena."

I looked down at my watch. 10:30. I was surprised that it was so late. I smiled at Emilio. "Good night. And thank you once again, Emilio."

"*Hasta mañana.*"

And he was gone.

My first day in Mexico City and I had already made a friend. I thought it was possible that Emilio might become a friend; he'd been kind, thoughtful, and had made no demands. I smiled, feeling good about the country, the whole continent. I reached down to pick up my book and handbag when I felt a gentle touch on my shoulder. I looked up. It was Ines, no longer wearing her uniform, but in a simple orange cotton dress. Somehow, out of the dark uniform, she was like a different person, more vividly alive.

"Good evening, Elena. Were you about to leave?"

"No, I was just about to order coffee. Would you like to join me?"

"May I?"

She sat, but not opposite. She took the chair beside me and gestured to a waiter. He was soon at our table pouring coffee and placing a glass of a smooth, dark liquid by the side.

"Kahlua. I thought you might like to try it."

I took a sip. Sweet coffee flavor. Potent alcohol in an innocuous disguise. I knew I needed to take it slowly.

"You like?"

"Yes."

"How was your first day here in our city?"

"Fabulous!" I described my afternoon in the museum and the meeting with Emilio.

"Ah, Señor Duran!" Her voice was low, expressionless.

"He has been very kind."

Ines made no response for a while, just sipping at her coffee, staring into her cup with the tiniest crease of a frown between her brows. And then she looked up, pushing her hair behind her ears in that gesture that was becoming familiar. She gestured to my hair.

"How do you do it?"

I lifted one strand, rolling it around my fingers.

"It's simple. You just let it be free. I used to help it along by twisting it like this, but now, I just leave it to do what it wishes."

She was unconsciously mirroring my movement and I laughed.

"Ines, I'm afraid that it just won't work with your hair." She laughed, too, looking at her fingers as if they were beyond her control.

"I have such . . . disobedient hair!"

I reached over and stroked her hair. "When I was growing up, I would have given anything for hair like yours."

"But why? Yours is magical."

"I know that now."

The liqueur was making me drowsy and I knew that I would need to find myself in between those cool, crisp, white sheets very, very soon. It was as if Ines read my mind. She put an arm around my shoulder and kissed me lightly on the cheek.

"You are very tired, I see that." She stood up. "Until tomorrow, Elena."

A shaft of light spread out from a chink in the heavy stone door, the flickering that of a candle, or maybe many candles. I stretched, yawning, forcing myself awake, the heavy gold bracelets jangling along my wrists. The bright swathe widened as the door opened fully allowing in the midday sun. The figures were but dark silhouettes, black against the bleached whiteness, tall shadows gliding toward me, their sound the chattering of birds. I stood then, rising taller than all of them as they flittered around me. They seemed tiny, those women as they wound a white cloth around my body, covering the beaded girdle that fell from my waist to the top of my thighs.

Like a flock of silent geese they surrounded me and ushered me from the coolness of the cave out into the open where the burning sun beat down on the rock face. I looked down at the countless steps carved in the side of the stone leading down to the village. It had been many years since I'd been allowed down those steps, instead, they came to me. I had counted the notches that I'd etched into the wall, one for each rising and setting of the sun, so I knew that the day had come.

We climbed the steep path that rose farther up the hillside, twisting and winding through the trees. The women stopped beyond the line of trees where a patch of deep blue glinted through the leaves. Hidden from sight was the deep lake carved out of the hill, lined with stones and filled with water diverted from the stream.

They were silent now as they unwound the cloth and pushed me toward the edge of the water. She was waiting there: Ines. Ines of the dark eyes and hair soft as a bird's wing. She took my hand and led me along the slippery, treacherous path that circled the lake, branching off to a clearing in the trees. The space had been especially prepared, a rough seat carved from a fallen trunk, tiny pots of ointment clustered on a pile of burning pebbles.

Ines made me sit and, without a word, rested her warm hands on my neck, smoothing down my shoulders, pressing hard, massaging the muscles of my back, my arms. I leaned against her and she picked up a small amphora and poured a pool of oil into her hands, rubbing them together, and then holding them against my throat for a minute or so, allowing the warmth to seep through to my body. The heavy herbal scent rose, intoxicating me, and I closed my eyes as Ines's strong hands rubbed down my back, around the curve of my hips and down, past the beaded skirt, along my thighs, right down to my feet.

I was slipping into a trance as she repeated the movement, her hands slick against my silky skin. Round and round, in minute spirals, her fingers inched down my chest, around the outside curve of my breasts and down, into the triangle of my waist, along to my belly, drawing concentric circles around my navel. I felt the warmth from Ines's thighs against my back, the heat from the sun heavy on my breasts, the dew of sweat forming on my forehead. My body was warm, drowsy, drugged by her touch, and I raised my face to her. She gently, carefully, wiped the moisture from my face and then lifted my hair from my shoulders, twisting it, piling it high on my head. She knelt before me and, pouring more oil into her palms, applied it to my breasts, cupping the undersides, tracing the outline of my areola with one, sharp fingernail. I sighed, shifting on the wood, the cool, heavy beads rolling against my clitoris, the sensation like a flicker of lightning. I forced my thoughts away, knowing that the time had not come. I closed my eyes but Ines raised a finger to my face and traced the outline of my lips. I looked down at her and her expression was full of loving, caring, and a question. She needed to know that I trusted her implicitly. I knew what she was asking and nodded.

Ines stood then and walked behind me. I watched as she delved into a leather pouch and returned to me carrying a shard flint blade. She knelt between my parted knees and pushed aside the beads. I recalled the regular, monthly routine and looked away, concentrating on the ripples in the blue water as she placed the sharp edge against my skin and slowly, cautiously slid the blade across, shaving away any regrowth of hair. A prickle of heat rose across my hairline each time I felt the touch of the sharp stone. It wasn't until I felt the warmth of Ines's touch against my inner thigh that I looked down at the naked flesh, strangely vulnerable and acutely sensitive. I quickly clenched my thighs together and Ines smiled,

standing and taking me by the hand, leading me toward
the shimmering blue of the lake.

Together we walked into the cool water, a welcome release from the heat of the day. I stood, chest deep, allowing the water to gently buoy me. As Ines reached for me, I
looked toward the other women, a dark line, each holding
a spear, forming a guard, protecting me from unwelcome,
prying eyes. Ines's touch was practiced as her fingers
glided across my flesh, washing away any trace of the oils,
and I lay back in the water, allowing my body to drift, trying to use the discipline I'd learned to ignore the sweetness of her touch as her hands flickered over my skin,
burning here, ice cold there. As her hands curved over my
rear, I shuddered gently edging closer to her as her finger
slipped into the crevice between my buttocks, smoothing
along the crack, headed toward the dark, shielded opening. I turned then, kicking away, presenting my heavy
breasts to the sun, distancing myself from her fingers. I
rolled into a ball and dived down beneath the cool, clear
water, opening my eyes, looking down to the green
depths. For the briefest while I could be free of all obliga-
tions.

I rose to the surface, lifting my head out of the water,
my hair heavy, loose, dragging me back down. I lay back
and Ines was beside me, spreading my locks out into tiny
serpents clamoring around my face and shoulders.

"There's not much time." Ines's voice was low, steady,
as she looked up at the sun. We swam toward the bank
and I stood, silent, unmoving, waiting for Ines's ministra-
tions. She bunched together a pad of reeds and rubbed
them against my skin, along my back, down over my buttocks, around my breasts, the friction almost unbearable,
and then down, between my legs, the slightest touch

against my exposed pussy lips making my vagina contract and sending small shudders quivering through my
body. She dropped the reeds then, and I watched them
float away. And then the smooth, gentle caress of her fingers replaced the reeds, gently whispering against my exposed clitoris, dancing down to my opening and resting
there, playing softly there in a perfect, tight circle. I bit
down on my lip, feeling an intense, white heat between
my legs. I moaned and Ines covered my mouth with her
hand, looking around in alarm. She placed a finger to her
lips to silence me and led me out of the water, back to the
green clearing.

I stood as Ines placed a series of gold bands around my
neck, each one smaller than the last, the weight forcing
my shoulders down. I held my head higher. Again, as the
warm sun dried the moisture from my skin, Ines lifted my
hair, brading the locks into thick plaits, winding them into
a heavy coil secured by an ivory comb. She fitted belts of
heavy shells around my waist, leaving long tassels dangling down between my thighs. Finally, she anointed my
skin with a heady, musky perfume and I was ready. Ines
inspected me slowly, head to foot, back to front and, as if
some silent signal had been given, the women suddenly
returned. They formed themselves into a royal guard and
began a measured walk back to the cave mouth.

As we neared the edge of the trees, I heard the mourn-
ful wail of a flute, the drumlike pounding of feet, and the
regular chants that welcomed me back to the fold. There
was something eerie, forbidding beneath the ritual song.
My feet wanted to stop, but the convoy sped me ever forward. Ahead, lining the steps down to the cave were hundreds of men, women, and even children, their arms
reaching toward me. There could be no turning back.
When we reached the edge of the first step, the circle

around me dissipated and there was a communal gasp as my body was revealed in all its splendor. I looked around and only Ines was by my side. She moved in front of me and signaling to me with her eyes, took slow steps downward, toward the dark mouth of the cave. Myriad fluttering fingers like scurrying ants reached for me as I proceeded toward my fate. I wanted to reach out for Ines, but knew that protocol forbade that. I raised my head farther, stared straight ahead, stopping only when Ines did, a foot away from the cave. Ines nodded and I turned toward the crowd for a moment, using their chorused moan as my signal to disappear into the darkness.

In my absence, the space had been transformed. Hundreds of candles glimmered from crevices in the wall. Animal skins draped the floor. A fire burned, taking the edge from the chill. And there, kneeling, muttering a prayer to the gods was a dark figure, his identity hidden by the shadows cast by the fire. Ripples of reflected light glanced off the dark sheen of his skin. I stood, silent, waiting.

There was a sudden silence as he raised himself from his knees. He made one last bow toward the corner and turned to look at me. I lowered my eyes modestly, but not before I'd recognized the man before me: Emilio.

He turned to Ines then, and I heard her voice, clear as a bell: "She's ready." She retreated to a corner of the cave, and I knew that she would not leave.

He moved toward me and my body trembled. I could feel his intense energy reaching out to me. I was suddenly nervous knowing that the moment that, for so many years, I'd been preparing for had finally arrived. I tried to recall all the instructions, but my mind was a blank. All I could think was that I was a vessel. His vessel. But what that meant I couldn't remember. Something to do with the life of the tribe and that's why there was the sound of constant moaning and keening outside the cave.

Emilio reached out to me, took both my hands in his, and led me to the fire. I looked up at him, the light flickering across his face making him look stern, almost cruel, even though the corner of his lips turned upward in a slight smile. He placed his hands on my shoulders and pressed down. I knew that I was meant to sit cross-legged in front of the flames, and I obeyed his unspoken command. The reflected light from the gold ornaments on my body was almost blinding and I looked away to the corner, to where I knew Ines waited.

There was a flurry of movement at the corner of my vision and I turned my head as Emilio threw a handful of herbs onto the fire. Immediately, there was a sizzle, the flames turned blue and a sweet smell rose into the air. The smoke caught in my throat and my eyes began to tear. Another handful, but this time I was prepared, controlling my breathing but beginning to feel light-headed. Then Emilio handed me a cup of warm liquid. I sipped gratefully at the bitter fluid, breaking my three-day fast. For a moment, my vision shimmered and I closed my eyes.

When I looked up again Emilio was seated opposite, his bare skin gleaming, his eyes intent on mine. I finished the potion, unable to tear my eyes away and suddenly, as Emilio lifted his hand, I felt myself drawn to him, through the flames, as if I were air, invulnerable but powerless to resist his call. I surreptitiously touched my feet to assure myself that I was still in the same position, on this side of the fire. I hadn't levitated. But then, he looked down at my naked breast and I could feel his touch, dancing across my skin. He blinked and his fingers were no longer gentle, his nails scraping the tender, sensitive nipples. But he hadn't moved. I could see that. His hands were cupped around his genitals, as if protecting them from someone. From me.

I fought to tear my eyes away and I could feel his fingers grasping at me, the nails biting into my flesh. I heard myself groan in pain, but he didn't seem to hear and there was no motion from Ines. His fingers were cruel, pulling squeezing until I turned my eyes back to him and I felt his thoughts relax, the pressure ease, transforming into the gentlest, most tender of caresses. My body responded and, against my will, I could feel it reaching out to him. He smiled that vulnerable, shy smile, and I felt the shells quivering between my legs, resonating as if from the effect of an earthquake, and the sensation was so incredibly intense that I let my knees fall apart so that he could watch the effect of the shells, slithering like snakes along the naked lips of my pussy. I leaned back on my elbows, watching him through the dying haze from the burning herbs. The flames seemed to flicker along my body as if some fuel had been poured in a trail from my thighs to my breasts, but the caress didn't burn. Instead, it stopped to fondle, to squeeze, to mold, to kiss its way from my throbbing vagina right up, around my nipples, into my throat, and then into every pleasure zone in my brain.

His eyes swirled around my nipples, trickled down my stomach, centered on my clitoris, and then stabbed at the opening between my legs. I sensed danger. I felt a thrusting against my pussy lips. I longed to open up, release myself to his touch. I was on fire, needing to feel his touch inside me, but I knew that this was the battle that I'd been prepared for.

I sat up and broke off eye contact. I reached down between my legs with both hands and, holding my lips open with one hand, traced round the reddened circle with my finger. I stared hard at the hands that protected his penis.

I concentrated and let out a slow smile as his hands fell away, revealing a cock that was hard, pointing skyward, quivering as I glided one finger, then two inside my pussy, moving them slowly in and out. I stared at his penis as it grew harder and knew that, almost more than anything, I wanted the feel of him deep inside me. I was ready to surrender as my thumb edged toward my clitoris.

I stopped suddenly as I sensed a pressure from behind, a gentle whispering. I moved to one side and then stayed motionless. I watched in wonder as Emilio struggled as if against an invisible assailant. His hands moved toward his genitals, but I could see that he was trying to force them away. I knew what I had to do. I needed to join forces with Ines. I opened my legs wide, letting him see the opening that was glistening with hot moisture. I lay back and tilted my hips toward him, the firelight accentuating the deep red flowering of my sex. I stared at him, drawing him in. His knuckles were almost white, tense, fighting against the need to touch himself. I concentrated harder, my eyes narrowed until, finally, he gave up the fight and both hands grasped around his purple cock and he began to rub, gently at first, and then faster, faster, his hands moving in a blur until he collapsed to the floor, curling into a tight ball, jerking the circle of his fingers faster and faster. His body suddenly tensed, became rigid, and he spurted his cum, his frame convulsing as the orgasm wracked his body.

I turned to the corner and felt the glow of Ines's eyes. I knew she was proud of me. I'd passed the crucial test. We'd be able to face the tribe, triumphant. But before that, I lay back, letting her eyes wash over me. Her hands reached out across the darkened space and caressed my pussy, her fingers plunging down and then up inside me. I felt the soft touch of her lips against my pulsating clitoris, her gentle tongue lapping at my vagina. I'd held myself back for so long, fought the demons, and now I surrendered, gave in to the delicious touch of her tongue as it plunged between my thighs, up, back, licking up to my clit, flicking fast, faster, over and over until I shuddered with the blessed release.

We waited, gently holding each other, Ines eight feet away. And then we walked, together, out of the cool cave into the heat of the sun and the gratitude of the tribe. We'd slain the demons.

I awoke, refreshed, so over the jet lag. I leaped out of bed, searching for the robe that I knew I'd discarded somewhere near the bed. I headed toward the shower and stopped, looking at the door leading out into the hallway. I was almost certain that I hadn't left it ajar the night before.

*About the Author*

Saran Thornton is a twenty-year-old student currently majoring in History at a university. Born and bred in Bristol, she is of mixed Guinean-English parentage. "Hotel Room" is her first piece of creative writing and reflects her dream of being wealthy enough, student loans permitting, to travel the world one day.

Don't miss Cydney Rax's

*My Daughter's Boyfriend*

Available now from Dafina Books!

# 1
# Tracey

It was the second Thursday in November. It was also the day that my daughter, Lauren Hayes, turned seventeen. As soon as I thought she'd woken up, I burst into her bedroom with a card, a glass vase stuffed with pink spray roses, and a tiny rectangular birthday cake punctured with a single burning candle that spelled out the word CELEBRATE. We ate one thick slice of her favorite, German chocolate, and my daughter then informed me that the festivities would continue that night. She'd been invited out for a bite to eat.

Later Lauren was surging through the apartment looking for her sling-backs and fussing with her French twist. And because I like to cool down after putting in my eight hours of workplace labor, I started my weekday ritual. As soon as I get home, I close the blinds and disrobe—my way of enjoying my world in comfort and without distraction. This particular evening I had on some white lace panties and a matching bra.

I was passing through the dining room, which has a mirrored wall. Everything was fine until I noticed my reflection. For most people there's always one body part or another that they don't like, and I'm what some might consider "thick," but even so, I'm proud of my creamy-looking legs and voluptuous thighs.

I was captivated by my appearance, but felt annoyed when I caught my daughter staring.

"Don't you have to get ready, girl?" I asked her from the mirror.

My daughter, five-seven compared to my five-five, inherited her daddy's fair complexion and long skinny legs. Although several people accuse Lauren of tinting her hair, those reddish and blond roots come natural. She has a mole above her lip. And she is blessed with some Beyoncé-type eyes: wide, exotic, and sparkly. In spite of Lauren's cockeyed stare and her mouthing off that "Ugh! Nobody wants to see you half-dressed," I was too unnerved to admonish her for her ill manners. She shoved a red T-shirt and some black leggings in my hand, and stormed off to her bedroom. I slipped the T-shirt over my head, but thought it was too warm for the leggings, so I laid them on the brown leather sofa.

Once Lauren disappeared, I stole a look at my surroundings. Under normal circumstances our apartment was low-maintenance and free of excessive clutter. But tonight the place looked jacked. Piles of T-shirts and musty-smelling jeans made a trail from my bedroom to the living room. Dirty plates and crusty silverware littered the kitchen counter, and I wanted to start organizing the magazines that had multiplied all over the front area.

There's a wide column of built-in shelves that take up a wall in my living room. I was crouched in front of it, busy doing my domestic thing, back turned, when I heard this voice rush from behind.

"Well, hellooo, Mrs. Davenport."

I turned my head so sharp I heard a bone pop. A flush of heat penetrated my face from the inside out. I had on the T-shirt, but he could still see my panties, and my legs were uncovered. I didn't know if I should excuse myself, or skip the apologies and shove a huge throw pillow against my lower half. But, paralyzed as I felt, all I could do was stare.

Even though he'd been dating my daughter for quite a few months, it was always hard to catch him for long stretches of time; it seemed he and my daughter were always running in and out of the apartment to be with each other.

But tonight, Aaron Khristian Oliver hovered over me dressed in a wine-colored suit and a multicolored necktie. In some ways his looks reminded me of a tall version of the actor RonReaco Lee. His dark wavy hair, lightly trimmed mustache, and athletic body made it difficult to deny that Aaron Oliver put the "hot" in "hottie." His hands were shoved in his pockets and he tried to play things off, raising his eyes a little, but I knew he noticed my legs.

I turned from Aaron and my mind said, *What the—okay, don't say nothing, just leave the room, no, no, his staring feels kinda—but this ain't cool, Lauren's only a few steps away . . . what if she . . . oh God, Jesus God.*

Once those thoughts vanished, I felt a teensy bit tensed, but managed to sigh like his standing near was no biggie. I don't like letting any guy intimidate me, even if he does intimidate me. But just when I thought I was the one who controlled my world, I heard Aaron say real low yet audibly, "Mmm, mmm, wow."

At first his flirtation seemed silly. *Yeah, right, he's*

*gotta be kidding,* I thought. *Young fool, he's just messing with me. Ha ha ha, funny, funny funny.*

I started to go on about my business, but Aaron wouldn't stop staring. Usually when men stare, I get annoyed and want to look anywhere except at the man whose eyes won't let me go. But with Aaron, this was different. I felt myself blushing, wanting to smile almost. Yet something screamed, *He's crossed a line. Perform tongue-fu on him. Tell him his ass is grass and you're the lawn mower.* But then another instigating inner voice said, *Eat it up, Tracey Lorraine Davenport. It's okay for him to stare.*

It felt weird to admit that I liked the way he lifted me. And after what I'd been through on my lunch break that day, hearing a long whistle and assuming it was a man, just to find out it was a bird, this was definitely an upgrade.

I turned and smiled at Aaron as widely and sweetly as possible. His body was so close he could have reached out and caressed my arm. I felt frozen to the floor.

"Mmmm, you look . . . never mind," he said in a low voice. Then he made a what's-the-matter-with-me groan and looked at the ceiling, at the floor, then back at me. I waved my hand at him so he could keep on talking, but without warning, he gave me a hardened stare and backed away.

Can you believe I felt a tiny stab of loneliness, just that quick? From enjoying the highs of feeling like an "it" girl, to being so-last-year, just that fast?

I stood only a couple feet away from him, but it felt like he was on the other side of the earth. He was standing next to the door, mumbling what sounded like "damn," and he was clutching and turning the door-knob.

"Hey," I said, stepping close to Aaron and forcing him to look at me again.

Aaron lifted his head and opened his mouth, but instead of hearing his words, I heard, "Mom, what are you *doing*?"

Right then I felt like the child and not the mother. I jumped back from the guy far enough to create some innocent distance between us. I covered my thighs with my hands, then grabbed a few magazines and placed them in front of my crotch with an overdue "This is so embarrassing. Aaron, don't you know how to ring a doorbell instead of just walking in here?"

I glanced at Lauren, apologized with my eyes. Her terse expression softened a little, but not enough to make me feel totally at peace.

The entire atmosphere shifted, the tantalizing moment escaping with few promises of a return. I even retrieved the leggings from the couch and scurried to my room and slid my legs inside them. Once my hands stopped shaking, and when I felt calm enough to emerge, I rushed past Aaron and resumed stacking magazines.

Aaron hung around for a little bit longer, until Lauren was ready. She grabbed him by the hand, snatching him through the door and toward the safety of the outside world. Yet before they left, and all the time he was standing there, I never made eye contact with him again. But I'd bet a hundred bucks, even though all three of us were in the same room, that my daughter's boyfriend sneaked another peek at me.

She didn't have to worry, though. I liked his attention, loved how good his stare made me feel, but after thinking about things long and hard, I decided I wasn't going to be a fool. Once I knew they were gone, I said out loud to the mirror with a strong voice, "Aaron is just a kid. And I don't do kids."

If you enjoyed *Hot Chocolate*,

Don't miss Geneva Holliday's

## Groove

Available now from Dafina Books!

In my bed that April night, my mind everywhere but where it should have been, which was on my ex-husband's tongue as it slid across my stomach and down my side.

Instead, my mind was on how hard my life was. How hard it was in so many different ways. Hard like a stone when you're black, female, and a single mother holding a GED instead of a high school diploma.

I wasn't thinking about how good it felt when he pushed his fingers through my hair and moved his tongue in circles around my navel. No, my mind was on the fact that I had missed three weeks of Calorie Counters meetings and how in that time I had stopped counting points, calories, carbs, and everything else.

Now my size-sixteen skirts and pants were giving my size-eighteen hips hell! Every morning it was an out-and-out fight. And I was steadily losing. Not the weight, of course. And on top of it, my Calorie Counters sponsor, Nadine Crawford—a former soda-guzzling, pound cake–eating accountant and mother of three, who'd joined the program three years earlier, had shed half her body weight and was now a size six and Calorie Counters' biggest cheerleader—was now calling my house every other day like a goddamn bill collector, talking about "When are you coming back, Geneva?" and "I'm here for you" and "Let's get together for an eight-point lunch and talk about it." I know I should have followed my first mind and joined Weight Watchers!

My mind was everywhere but in that bedroom where it should have been.

It was on my two-decade-old secondhand Cold Spot refrigerator that was humming so loud, it sounded as if any moment it would hack up something green, cough, and drop dead.

If that was to happen, it would take Housing a whole month to get me another crappy refrigerator in this apartment, and then how would I keep the milk cold for my sixteen-year-old son's morning cereal?

And he was another problem—my son, Eric Jr., who we all lovingly refer to as "Little Eric."

Little Eric hasn't been little since he was ten years old, and now he's a sophomore in high school, towering over me at a staggering six feet, and that boy still has years of growth ahead of him. Just trying to keep him in sneakers is going to send me to the poorhouse.

He was a good kid, even though I knew he was sampling weed. I mean, do these kids think we weren't kids once too? Do they think we were all born big?

The other day he strolled into the house, smelling like he'd been rolling in a field of reefer. I snatched him by his collar and dragged him through the living room and into the kitchen where the light is better and looked him in his eyes and asked him if he'd been smoking. Of course he lied and blinked those big

brown eyes at me and said, "Look at my eyes, Ma—
they ain't even red or nothing. I was just hanging out
with these guys that was smoking it, but I didn't."

I said, "Fool, I know Visine gets the red out, but it
don't take the scent out of your clothes or off your
breath!" And with that I popped him upside his head
and sent him on his way. I told him that if he came back
in my house smelling like a pothead, I was going to call
the police on him my damn self!

*"Ohhhhhhhh,"* I moan, just so Eric can feel like he's
doing all of the right things even though my mind has
skipped over to my best friend, Crystal.

Not only is she my best friend, but she has been on
many occasions a godsend as well.

I've had some rough times, and Crystal has always
been there. Like the time when I was still on welfare
and I had just collected my money and food stamps for
the month and was on my way downtown to buy Eric,
who was just about four years old then, a new pair of
shoes. I hadn't even stepped off the bus good when two
young boys rushed toward me, ripped my pocketbook
from my hands, and then took off across Union Square.

I didn't even have a token to get home. It was Crystal that I called, and she left her job and came downtown and got me and then took me to the supermarket
and filled up my refrigerator and cupboards with food.
When I collected again the following month, she
wouldn't even let me pay her back.

Crystal is also the one who saved me from the cos-
metics counter at Macy's and got me a job as a receptionist at the Ain't I A Woman Foundation. Ten dollars

an hour is certainly better than seven-fifty and standing on your feet for eight to ten hours a day. Much better, and I will be forever grateful to her.

But lately Crystal just hasn't been herself. Something is bothering her; I see the sadness lurking behind that phony smile she walks around with all day.

I keep asking her what's wrong, but she just says, "Nothing."

I guess she'll tell me in her own good time.


"That feel good, baby?" "*Oooooooooooooooooh* yeah, baby, real good."


Okay, now where was I?

Oh yes, my mind being on everything outside of this here bedroom.

Well, I've also been thinking about Chevy. That's another friend of mine, who is just . . . just—I don't know—just crazy is the best way to describe her. Crazy and a chameleon. You can never tell what Chevy was going to look like the next time you met up with her. She could be sporting a long weave, short weave, hazel contacts, red weave, blue contacts, blond Afro puffs, green contacts. Who knows!

Dr. Phil said that a person who needs to change her appearance as many times as Chevy did is unhappy with herself.

I believe that. But what I want to know is, what does it say when that same person can always find money for a new pair of La Blanca stilettos or a slinky thong from La Perla but ain't never got enough money to pay her light bill or rent?

She's making at least twice my hourly rate, for chris-sakes! And don't have chick nor child to worry about. Not a dog, goldfish, or hamster, just her! As my mother says, "When she eats, her whole family has eaten."

Crazy is all I can think to call her. Oh yeah, and *selfish* is another word that fits too. It's all about Chevy, all of the time.

"You want it, baby, you want it?"

"*Ooooooooooh* yeah, baby, I want it *reaaaaaaaaaaal* bad."

Now finally, there's Noah.

A dead ringer for Howard Hewitt, except fairer-complexioned. A successful merchandising manager for the high-end casual clothing company QV, and a Cancerian, so he can be a moody something.

When we were younger, Noah was the best double Dutch jumper in our building and could corn braid better than any of us. The highlight of his year was the Miss America beauty pageant, which we had to watch with him. Afterward he'd reenact the last fifteen minutes of the pageant—the surprise on the winner's face, the tears, the halfhearted hugs she shared with the losers—then he'd plop a lampshade on his head and tie a bedsheet around his neck and prance back and forth across the living room, demonstrating the proper way the new Miss America should have strutted down the catwalk.

Do you see where I'm going with this?

We've known Noah was gay since forever and have always accepted him. His Jamaican mother, on the other hand, is still in denial and even to this day still tries to fix Noah up on blind dates with her friends' daughters.

Noah is about the only one that I'm not really worried about. He seems happy with his career and has met some new man who lives in England, so he's always flying back and forth to London to be with him.

Yeah, I think that Noah should be the least of my worries right about now.


Now me; besides the war with my weight and a pack-a-day cigarette habit, I guess I don't have any real pressing concerns. Well, not that living in the projects is a great joy, but at least I'm not on the streets.

I'm thinking about going back to school. College. To major in what, I have no clue, but I think a college degree is something I should have. Well, I know it's something I need if I don't want to be a receptionist forever. And besides, maybe it will motivate that son of mine to do the right thing with his life.

Okay, enough of that, Geneva—try to concentrate on all of the kisses Eric is covering your body with, I tell myself, and I try, but my mind won't stay put. It keeps straying to the load of clothes that needs to be washed, the pile of unopened bills sitting on the kitchen table, and that goddamn pervert with the chiseled good looks and expensive suit who flashed me on the C train this morning when I was on my way to work.

"Turn over," Eric says, and I do and so do my thoughts.

He enters me from behind and I grip the headboard, not because it feels good—it does, though—but to hold on tight to try to keep it from banging too hard against the wall. Little Eric should have been asleep hours ago, but I don't want to take any chances.

Eric stops, his body shudders, and he withdraws. This is his control method. It's been the same for years. Our sex life should have ended when I caught him cheating, moved out of our Queens apartment, and signed the divorce papers, but it didn't. It went on through all of it and still goes on.

Why? I don't know. Stupid, I guess. Or just plain horny.

"Where are you, Geneva?" Eric coos.

"I'm here baby, I'm here," I assure him and push my behind up into his chest.

He starts kissing my back while his hands massage my shoulders.

He begins to ease his penis back inside me. "You like it? You like it, baby?" he whispers in my ear.

"Uh-huh," I say, and in my mind I start to separate the white clothes from the dark, flip through the mountain of mail on my kitchen table, and clip coupons.

Eric's body trembles with excitement and then he whispers, "You want me to put it in your ass?"

My mind comes to a sudden and complete halt.

I've allowed him there only twice in my life, and both times we were still Mr. and Mrs. and I was really in love then. So in love that all I wanted to do was please him. But now I just wanted to be pleased and had no desire to have my asshole stretched out of shape. And besides, anal sex is notorious for leaving one unable to control the passing of air, if you know what I mean.

"Uh-uh," I say and start to turn back over and onto my back.

"Oh, c'mon, please?" he begs and gives me that puppy-dog look of his.

"Uh-uh," I sound again and shake my head from side to side.

After the day I had I thought some sexual healing was in order, but my mind won't let me concentrate on it, which means I'm dry as a bone down between my legs. Really and truly, all I want to do is just have a beer, maybe some chips, and a couple of spoonfuls of ice cream.

"Turn back over," Eric presses. "I won't put it in your ass."

Now Eric is one who cannot be trusted. He's a liar, cheater, and all-around crooked cop. Oh yeah, he's one of New York's finest. And I do mean *fine!* Six foot four and chocolate-colored. He'd been working out a lot lately and so was cut and as solid as a rock.

"You know, Eric, I don't think I want to do this," I say as I clamp my legs closed and reach for the sheet.

Eric looks surprised. His erect penis looks even more astonished than he does.

"What?" He half laughs.

"I said I don't think I want to do this," I say again as I catch hold of the sheet and try to pull it up and over my naked body.

"You're fucking kidding me, right, Geneva?" His rock-hard dick gives me an accusing look. "What the fuck am I suppose to do about this?" he says, indicating his stiff member with his index finger.

"Whatever you do when you're alone," I say and try not to smile. "I'm just not here. I'm sorry."

Eric looks down at his penis and then back at me.

I could tell he was having a conversation with it in

his mind. His dick was his best friend, and any woman who had ever been with him knew it.

Suddenly his features softened and a mischievous smile spread across his face.

"How about a little licky-licky, then?" he says, and sticks his long pink tongue out at me.

I think about it for a minute. If I let him eat me out, it would release some tension. No effort on my part. It seems like I win all the way around. But then I remember who I'm dealing with and say, "What do I have to do to you?"

"Suck my dick, of course," he says proudly and thrusts his hips toward my face.

"Nah," I say and pull the sheet up to my chin.

"You're so fucking selfish," he hisses and sticks his lips out like a two-year-old.

"Then leave."

"Aw, c'mon, Geneva." He laughs.

"Nope."

Eric lets out a long sigh and looks around the bedroom for a moment. "Okay. You win."

Wow, I think, this is a first.

He pulls the sheet away from my body and gently separates my legs before moving into "eating" position.

Eric loves to eat pussy; always has. It's like a delicacy for him.

He begins by teasing my clitoris, rolling his tongue across it and then darting it in and out of my hole, bringing me to the point of orgasm seven or eight times before I finally scream, "Please, please!" when I know I can't take much more.

"Okay, baby, okay," he pants and takes a deep breath before moving in for the kill.

"Motherfucker, motherfucker!"

The firecrackers go off behind my eyes and bells ring in my head, and how it is that my behind and the heels of my feet are able to levitate above the sheets for a moment is anyone's guess, but they do.

That's how Eric makes me come: cussing, screaming, and levitating, which is why even after all of the low-down shit he's done to me and the half-ass child support he pays I'm still fucking him.

I don't have any excuse and won't even try to make one up. All I know is, a good dick is hard to find and an orgasm that can shoot you to the moon and back is even more elusive.

After my body stops shaking and I begin to feel uncomfortable in the wet spot, he lifts his head off my thigh, looks up at me and asks, "You sure you don't want me to fuck you?"

"N-no." I can hardly speak, and I lock my hands around his head and guide his mouth as far away from my vagina as possible.

Even if I wanted to fuck, I wouldn't allow it—shit, my pussy might explode!

Eric looks up at me and smiles. "I am good, ain't I?" he gloats and moves up beside me.

All I can do is shake my head in agreement and turn over onto my side.

Eric kisses my shoulder and then tries to put his arms around me, but I don't want that part of it. That tenderness belonged to us a long, long time ago. What we do now is primitive and carnal and that's the way I want it to remain.

"What's up with you?" he says and sucks his teeth in disgust.

"Shouldn't you go home to your wife now?" I say before punching the pillow and readying myself for dreamland.